Seco

M000031814

Triple J Ranch
Book 1

Jenna Hendricks

Cover Design by Victoria Cooper

First Edition December 2019

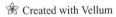 Created with Vellum

BOOKS BY JENNA HENDRICKS

Triple J Ranch –

Book 0 - Finding Love in Montana (Join my newsletter to get this book for free)

Book 1 - Second Chance Ranch

Book 2 – Cowboy Ranch

Book 3 – Runaway Cowgirl Bride

Book 4 – Faith of a Cowboy

See these titles and more: https://JennaHendricks.com

OTHER BOOKS BY J.L. HENDRICKS (MY 1ST PEN NAME)

The Voodoo Dolls

Book 0: The Voodoo That You Do (Join my Newsletter to get this exclusive freebie)

Book 0.5: Magic's Not Real

Book 1: New Orleans Magic

Book 2: Hurricane of Magic

Book 3: Council of Magic

Worlds Away Series

Book 0: Worlds Revealed (join my Newsletter to get this exclusive freebie)

Book 1: Worlds Away

Book 2: Worlds Collide

Book 2.5: Worlds Explode

Book 3: Worlds Entwined

A Shifter Christmas Romance Series

Book 0: Santa Meets Mrs. Claus

Book 1: Miss Claus and the Secret Santa

Book 2: Miss Claus under the Mistletoe

Book 3: Miss Claus and the Christmas Wedding

Book 4: Miss Claus and Her Polar Opposite

The FBI Dragon Chronicles

Book 1: A Ritual of Fire

Book 2: A Ritual of Death

Book 3: A Ritual of Conquest

TABLE OF CONTENTS

CHAPTER 1

"Woohoo! Faster, faster!" Elizabeth Manning pounded her hands on the dash of Max Reinhard's Jeep 4x4 as they sped through the rolling hills around Beacon Creek.

Max laughed. "Alright, alright. I'm going as fast as is safe. I don't want to crash with you in the Jeep."

Elizabeth put her hand on his arm and squeezed. She realized she had finally found a good man.

"Ahhh!" Elizabeth grabbed the padded roll bar above the Jeep's door with her right hand and wrenched her left hand from Max's arm as she grabbed the handlebar attached to the front of the dashboard. The Jeep had just jumped a bit off the ground when Max quickly crested the small hill in front of them. Her blood was pumping, and she couldn't keep the smile from her face. It was going to be a permanent look for her if this kept up.

"Oomph." Max winced when his head hit the soft top above him. "That landing was a bit hard." He was glad he'd used the soft top instead of the hard one. Otherwise, he would most likely have a bump on his head. He certainly didn't want Elizabeth hitting her head on the fiberglass top.

Both laughed and commented on how much fun they were having riding through the country. And they were both very glad that no one had sent their cattle to this part of the region today.

They were no longer on Triple J land, which was owned by Elizabeth's family. They had instead crossed over to the neighbor's property and were about to head into Mr. Johnson's land. He raised cattle and would be rotating them between various patches of grazing land this time of year. They were four-wheeling through one of his grazing fields. It wouldn't do to drive through a patch of land where the cattle were lazily munching away on grass. They could get in the way of the Jeep or possibly cause an accident.

At the very least, seeing a Jeep jump a hill could easily cause a stampede. The last thing Elizabeth needed was Mr. Johnson calling her parents and complaining—again. Not that Elizabeth had caused a stampede. At least, not recently. But there was that one time when she and her brothers were out riding their ATVs and just happened upon a group of calves and scared them, which in turn caused an issue with their mommas. Of course, she had no idea that they were all in that part of the Johnsons' pastures. She and her brothers had spent the next two Saturday nights helping Mr. Johnson with repairs to his barn as punishment.

"Are you ready for lunch? I packed us a picnic. Just over the next hill is a nice, shady spot perfect for lunch." Max slowed up on the gas and crested the small hill.

He stopped at the top, and the sight stole Elizabeth's breath. "I'll never tire of this view."

She was glad she had decided to come home to Beacon Creek and join Milton's veterinary practice. She was afraid all the old memories of He Who Shall Not Be Named would ruin it for her. Even though they'd broken up over ten years earlier, she knew she couldn't live in the same town as him ever again. Especially the one they grew up in and had planned to come back to once they were done with college and ready to take on their dream jobs, together.

She sighed and looked out to the hills covered in tall grass and dotted with large oak trees. It was August, and the grass had already turned brown. Some blades were the color of oatmeal, and others the blond shade of wheat so common in the neighboring farms and ranches. She picked up on scents of cedar and sandalwood and knew she was home. With all the beauty of big sky country surrounding her, she knew she would have never been happy anywhere else.

The sun was at its peak and bright enough to hurt her eyes with sunglasses on. The day was going to be a hot one, but that was only the norm for a Montana summer day. It was probably already eight-five degrees. The forecast called for low nineties, and she wanted to be inside with air conditioning once it got that hot.

Elizabeth Manning had been spoiled while she was away attending college and then veterinary school. All classes, except for the live animal labs, were held inside in nice, air-conditioned classrooms. Even some of the large barns had fans running through them to keep from getting too hot. She'd thought about having her family's farm install some of those large fans to help keep the horses cooler during the hottest time of the summer, but they couldn't afford it, yet. Maybe one day.

"Come on." Max held his hand out to help Elizabeth down from the Jeep. "Let's get the picnic set up and have some of the sweet tea your mom made for us. It's getting hot."

"I totally agree." Elizabeth took Max's hand and jumped down from her seat to the hard ground.

Even though she was tall—five feet, eight inches—it was still a jump from her seat. Max had put on huge tires and raised the jeep higher than normal. It helped when there were flash floods in the area, but it wasn't the easiest vehicle to get in and out of.

She ran a hand through her wind-blown, long auburn locks as she surveyed the land. Her blue jeans, button-up short-sleeved shirt, and boots were perfect for ranch life, and were also quite comfortable in the heat and dirt.

Elizabeth narrowed her green eyes that held flecks of golden brown here and there. Some would say her eyes were more hazel, but she always said they were green since there were only a few flecks the color of her boots in her eyes. "Max, how'd you know old Mr. Johnson had already moved his cattle from this pasture?"

It was obvious cattle had been through here recently by the lack of tall grasses. The land looked as though someone had come through with a dull blade and hacked away at the poor grass. What had once been high grass blowing in the breeze was now chopped and not the least bit natural looking.

Cattle had definitely been feeding here, and recently, as she could still see hoof prints and horseshoe imprints in the dirt where they stood.

"Three days ago, I was at his ranch helping him order some parts for his baler. Thankfully he had most of his hay in before it started acting up. He told me he'd just finished moving the herd to the north." Max smiled at Elizabeth, and his chocolate-brown eyes sparkled like they always did when he talked about John Deere equipment. He had definitely found his passion.

Max was a John Deere salesman. He also advised ranchers and farmers when they had issues with equipment.

He wasn't a repairman, per se, but he knew tractors and all the equipment any ranch could possibly need.

She chuckled and shook her head. "Boys and their toys."

He grinned. "Yes, ma'am. We love our toys big and green."

"With a bit of yellow." Elizabeth reached into the picnic basket and began pulling out the lunch her momma had packed for them once Max had smoothed out the blanket.

They enjoyed their lunch talking about everything and nothing. By the time they returned home, Elizabeth was ready to check on the mare about ready to give birth to twins. She and her boss, Milton, were taking turns checking on the poor little momma. It was her first time to foal, and she was blessed with twins.

Elizabeth was a twin, but back then her momma had already given birth to her older brother Matthew and had an idea of what to expect. *Would a young mare be ready to give birth to twins on her first pregnancy?* Elizabeth had tended to many foals, but this would be her first set of twins, and she was excited.

She grabbed a thermos full of coffee, a blanket, and the basket full of fruit and jerky her mother had prepared for her and took off for a long night of what she hoped would be helping a new momma bring her babies into the world.

When she arrived, Jewel was already lying down and breathing hard.

"Just in time. I think she's ready to deliver." Mr. Picket smiled up at Elizabeth as she entered the barn and set her basket and blanket down on the table just inside the door.

"Really? How's she doing? Any distress?" Elizabeth wore a backpack with her medical supplies packed in it. She never knew what she would need and always wanted to have her hands free, or as free as possible, so she wore a backpack instead of carrying the usual black bag the local vets preferred. Plus, with all the various pouches, she had her bag organized much better than anyone's black bag. She never needed to rummage around until she found what she wanted; she knew exactly where everything was located.

Mr. Picket took his cowboy hat off his head and swiped at the sweat across his brow. "She seems settled at the moment, but not thirty minutes ago her eyes were wide, and her head was jerking around. I was afraid she might hurt herself. If she kept it up, I was going to get one of the boys to hold her head."

Elizabeth nodded and took her backpack off. She pulled out her stethoscope and slowly walked to the horse. In a soothing voice, she let Jewel know exactly what was happening before she leaned down and rubbed the little momma's neck. "Shh, it's alright. Your babies are coming. Everything is just fine. I'm going to take a listen and make sure all heartbeats are what they should be."

She leaned down and placed the stethoscope on the mare's body and moved it around until she found the heart-beats she was looking for. Both of the foals' hearts sounded strong. Then she went searching for Jewel's heart rate. While she was listening, she noticed Jewel's water had broken.

"It's starting. If you want Becky to watch, you better get her quickly." Elizabeth knew that Mr. Picket wanted his four-teen-year-old daughter to see her horse give birth. Becky had been very excited to take part in this, and had even said she was thinking about becoming a veterinarian.

While waiting, Elizabeth collected samples from the ruptured chorioallantois in case anything went wrong with the birth so they could test it. Once she put it away, she pulled on her long gloves so she could check the placement of the foal before it began its quick journey into the world. With two foals inside this mare, it was even more important to make sure both were in the correct position.

She said a quick prayer and patted the horse's neck before reaching inside to ensure the correct placement of the little foal. All seemed fine, so she sat back and waited. There was nothing more for her to do.

"Coffee? I'm not sure how long this will take—it's my first set of twins—but coffee is always a good thing right about now. Would you care for some?" Elizabeth walked to where she'd set her thermos down and grabbed it.

"No, thanks. I already had my fair share today, ma'am." Mr. Picket tipped his hat her direction and went back to watching his little Jewel prepare to give birth.

His daughter came running in with her hair flowing behind her and eyes wide. "Is it time? What can I do to help?"

Elizabeth and Mr. Picket both chuckled. While Elizabeth poured her coffee, Mr. Picket spoke to his daughter. "Becky, for now just stand off to the side so you can watch. If the doc needs anything, you can fetch it."

The girl complied, but the excitement in her eyes dimmed as she slumped her shoulders and stood out of the way.

"Don't worry, this is only the first time. I'm sure once you've seen a few births, your papa will allow you to help." Elizabeth smiled at the girl, and Becky's eyes sparkled with hope.

While Elizabeth drank her coffee, Mr. Picket moved to the horse's head and began murmuring to her and patting her neck and stroked down the front of her head. Elizabeth realized he was worried about his mare and knew she had to do something to help him as well as his horse.

"Papa, can I come in and help calm Jewel?" Becky's small voice showed her reverence for the occasion, but there was also a hint of wistfulness as she kept her eyes glued to the horse's head.

"I'm sorry, Becky—we can't have any more people inside the birthing stall than necessary. If Jewel starts to move around too much she could hurt you, or any one of us. We need to keep the area clear so we can quickly move out of the way if need be." The vet tilted her head and wished she could allow the girl inside to help.

"Will this be your first set of twins?" Elizabeth's voice was calm, like she was asking a normal question and had no worries in the world, even though she was worried. Although, she remembered her training and knew there was nothing to worry about. The foal was in the correct position, and she only had to wait. Normally it would be less than twenty minutes once the water broke, but with twins, things were always different.

Becky stayed quiet, but her father nodded. "Yes."

"Do you have names picked out yet?" She hoped to get them both talking and relax a little bit.

"Yes," Mr. Picket responded, while Becky continued to look on in silence.

Couldn't he do more than answer in monosyllables? It was always frustrating to get men to talk when they didn't want to. And he didn't want to. She knew, because he wouldn't look at her. He kept his attention on his horse and kept murmuring encouragement to Jewel.

When Jewel's stomach quivered, Elizabeth knew it was time.

"Alright, Mr. Picket. Please stay right where you are and don't move. Keep a hold of her head and make sure she stays down. The first foal is coming." She turned to look at the teenage girl. "Becky, you can move around outside the stall, just don't get in the way of the door. But make sure you can see from wherever you stand." With a huge smile on her face, she headed to Jewel's other end and waited for the little hooves to come out.

Once she saw the tiny hooves, Elizabeth moved closer and took hold of them and helped to get the little horse partway into the world. Once the shoulders were out, she moved back and let the little momma finish the work for herself.

Normally she would have left the stall to let the mother and babe bond and find their way on their own, but with a second foal coming, it was important to move the babe to its mother's head and make room for the second one.

"It's a girl. Congratulations, Mr. Picket, you have a brand-new filly. What's her name?" Elizabeth took her stethoscope out and listened for the heart rate, then went to the lungs. Everything seemed normal, and she smiled as she put her stethoscope around her neck.

"A filly?" He sighed and smiled. "Yes, her name is Emerald." He watched with a tear in his eye as Elizabeth moved the little filly.

While Jewel was waiting for foal number two, she licked her first baby clean and began the bonding process.

Once the second one was born, Mr. Picket whooped and hollered his excitement. Several ranch hands came over and looked over the fence of the birthing stall.

"Alright gentlemen, it looks like little Emerald has a baby brother. What name do you have for the little colt?" Elizabeth looked from Mr. Picket to the two ranch hands smiling brightly over the top of the stall.

"Jasper," Becky called out before the men could get the word out. Then they all nodded their agreement.

The vet chuckled and shook her head. "I guess you all decided together what the names would be?"

"Yes, ma'am," one of the men standing outside the stall answered. "We held a contest to see who could come up with the best names. Not too many jewel names that work well for a colt, but everyone agreed on Jasper."

"Sounds like a great name. What do you say we leave momma and her babies alone to get acquainted?" As Elizabeth stood back up, little Emerald tried to stand as well. Her legs wobbled and her front hooves crumbled in on themselves, but her second try had her standing.

"Great job, Miss Elizabeth. Thank you so much for being here and helping Jewel get through this. Everyone here really appreciates you coming by the past few nights to check in on us." Mr. Picket put his hand out, and Elizabeth took it.

"My pleasure. I'm glad I was the one here and not Milton." She walked over to the tack room, where a small sink and faucet stood just waiting for her to clean up. She yelled over her shoulder, "Milton or I will be back tomorrow to check on the foals. Have a great night, Mr. Picket. Oh, and be sure to call me if there are any issues."

Mr. Picket raised a hand when she walked out of the tack room. "Thanks again. See you soon."

CHAPTER 2

The next night after a fun date with Max, Elizabeth pondered their evening together and her feelings for him. It was entertaining, like all their dates, but her friend, Harper, had said something earlier in the day that made her wonder.

They had met for lunch at their favorite diner, Rosie's, and she couldn't get the conversation out of her head.

"I must say, I think I'm a bit jealous of my sister and her new husband." Harper looked into her chocolate shake and shook her head. "I know, it's stupid, right?"

"Wait, back up a bit. I'm confused. Did you say you were jealous of your sister? The one who never had dates while you went out almost every weekend?" Elizabeth was shocked. Harper was one of her best friends in high school who just happened to be a blonde bombshell. She never needed to worry about dates or even *if* she would have a date to an important event.

But Harper's sister, Mimi, had needed to worry. Mimi suffered from a very severe case of shyness, and her complexion was nothing anyone would want. However, after college she'd changed. Somewhere along the line, Mimi learned how to take good care of her skin and even came out of her shell, if only just a bit.

Now Mimi was married to a very handsome man. One, if Elizabeth were honest with herself, she might be a tad bit jealous of as well. Said husband was also a successful rancher in Wyoming. Elizabeth had only met Mimi's new husband once, but he seemed to be in love with his wife, and they made a really cute couple.

"I know, I know! It's crazy, right? But Mimi keeps talking about her husband and how he treats her. The sweet things he does for her, the little love notes he leaves her sometimes." Harper turned to Elizabeth with wide eyes. "Last Sunday morning, his only day to sleep in, he got up early to make Mimi breakfast before church! Can you believe it?" She sighed.

"I thought you didn't want to get married, ever." Elizabeth raised a brow at her friend. For the past few years, when Elizabeth and Mimi discussed men, it was always to say they never wanted anything permanent. Or anyone to get close enough to hurt them.

While Harper had never been hurt by boyfriends, Elizabeth had. She wanted nothing to do with men who would make promises to her and then break them. She wasn't even sure she ever wanted to marry. She was happy with the way things were.

Elizabeth was also working on building her status as a top-notch vet in the area and had no time for men—well, at least that was what she'd always told herself until Max came along.

Now she was having fun with Max, but love?

"I didn't. At least, not until my last visit with my sister. Now I think I want what she has. My longest relationship, if you can even call it that, was two months. And that was back in senior year of high school." Harper shrugged and let out a long sigh. "I've had lots of men give me flowers, and even one who wrote me a poem, but I haven't connected with anyone the way Mimi and her husband do. They finish each other's sentences and work so well in the kitchen together. They don't even have to ask for what they need. When making dinner, they seem to have this silent form of communication. When one needs something, the other just gives it to them."

"Huh? I don't understand." Elizabeth shook her head.

"Well, my sister was making pasta one night and her hands were all dirty. I was about to ask if she needed help when Hank just walked in and went to a cupboard and pulled out a bottle of spice and handed it to her without a word. He kissed her cheek and she smiled up at him as though he was her everything." Harper dipped a fry into her shake before eating it.

"I felt like I was intruding on a private moment. It happened several times while I was there. Sometimes he just seemed to come from nowhere at the perfect moment, and others it happened while they were both working on the meal together. Whoever brought the missing ingredient always gave the other one a kiss. But they both looked at each other as though they were the world." Harper's nose twitched, and she blinked a few times before taking a long drink of her shake.

"Intimacy—*true* intimacy. That's what they have. My parents are the same. Well, not in the kitchen. Momma always shoos Pops away when he goes in there while she's cooking. But my dad also shoos my mom away when she gets near his BBQ grill." Elizabeth chuckled.

"They have their space and respect that space. But the

look they give each other when they do it is one of pure love." Elizabeth's nose crinkled. "I guess I see what you mean. They always seem to know what the other needs at times. It's like they're two parts of one whole."

Elizabeth had always wanted what her parents had. She knew when she was a kid that she would only marry someone if they were the perfect match for her. She'd thought she had that once, and knew she'd never have it again with anyone else. When *he* left her, he took part of her heart that she could never get back.

Harper bit her lip before whispering, "Do you think you and Max have that, or at least are on your way to getting it?"

Elizabeth sat back in her booth and thought about Max. He was a very good-looking man, and also successful. She would never have to worry about money once they had kids. She always knew she wanted to be a stay-at-home mom once kids came along. But love, with Max? He was a good man, to be sure. Max was very generous and thoughtful, but there was something holding her back from him. She couldn't put her finger on it, not yet.

She shook her head. "No. At least, not yet. It's only been a couple months since we started dating. I'm not in love with him, and we don't jive like my parents, or your sister and her husband. However, I think that takes time."

"Do you think it's possible with him?" Harper asked.

Elizabeth took a bite of her fries drenched with ketchup. Then she shrugged. "I don't know. I think it's too early to tell, and I'm not even thinking about love. I'm just enjoying my time with Max." She frowned.

"What? I know that look. Something's bothering you. Did Max do something?" The shake in front of Harper was almost gone, but she still had half a plate of fries to dunk and she'd been about to order another shake before Elizabeth's frown stopped her.

"No. Yes. I don't know." Elizabeth blew her bangs out of her eyes and realized it was time for a haircut. "Last week we were in Bozeman for dinner, and when we came out there was a homeless woman on the street begging. Something inside me said to give her my leftovers instead of money. So I did." She sighed.

Harper motioned her hand for Elizabeth to continue. "And?"

Elizabeth moved around on her seat, and the booth made a creaking noise as well as the normal bothersome squeaking of denim rubbing up against the cheap vinyl of the seat. "Max tried to stop me from giving her my leftover steak. He said if she was hungry she could work for her meal, or go to the soup kitchen." She winced.

"What did you do?"

"I gave her my bag and said a silent prayer for her. She's still on my heart, and I want to go back and find her. Find out if there's anything I can do to help her." The food in front of Elizabeth didn't look very appealing anymore, and she felt guilty for not doing more to help the elderly lady in need.

"I'll go with you, if you want company. We could bring her a gift bag of some basics, like socks and a gift card to one of the local fast-food joints. And then maybe we could even see what she needs and provide it for her." Harper had always had a huge heart. Whenever someone was in need, she would be there. No one had to ask her—she just showed up.

Elizabeth nodded and smiled. "Yes! That's exactly what we'll do. How about Friday? I'm off that day, and we could spend the entire day there seeing if there are others who need our help. Maybe we could even get a few more girls to come and join us?"

Both girls were bouncing back from their sour moods and ready to do something nice for someone else. Growing up, they both learned that it was always better to give than to receive. Whenever they helped someone, they always felt right. A peace enveloped their souls, and they knew they were doing what Jesus would have done.

Sometimes, it was the simple things in life that brought the most joy.

"Are you going to invite Max?" Harper asked between bites of her fries and stolen dips into Elizabeth's melting shake.

"No. I think this is something for us girls to do. Don't you?" She smiled at Harper and batted the girl's hand away from her shake. "Hey, that's mine. Get your own if you want more."

"I thought you liked to share? Mine's all gone." Harper's sad, puppy-dog eyes batted a few times, and Elizabeth shook her head.

"Alright, you can have the rest of those calories. I don't need them, anyway." Elizabeth smirked, knowing that would stop her friend from stealing her monthly treat.

Not that either girl worried too much about their weight. They regularly ate healthy, and their jobs kept them moving most of the day. Both girls always walked at least fifteen thousand steps a day, and that was on a slow day. But they knew that no matter how much work they did, having a chocolate shake more than once a month just wasn't healthy. Their concern was more about clean, healthy eating than gaining weight.

Harper was a nurse at the local health clinic and always stressed the importance of clean eating, and not eating a lot of dairy or carbs. Instead, it was important to eat fresh fruits and vegetables grown from your own garden, or that of a neighbor's. Fresh meat was easy, since just about everyone had their own cattle, or bought their meat from a local ranch. It wasn't about dieting, but about putting something healthy into your body instead of pre-packaged foods full of chemicals. Or fruits and vegetables covered in pesticides.

Harper frowned. "Thanks for ruining my one decadent treat this month." She sat back in her seat and kept frowning.

"How about we split what's left of my shake? I know you only come to Rosie's when we have our monthly treat." What Elizabeth forgot to share with her friend was that when she'd gone out to dinner with Max the week before, she had shared a chocolate crème brûlée with him. She didn't normally do desserts, but he was celebrating a large sale he had just completed, and she knew the crème brûlée there was the best in the state.

"Deal!" Harper's million-watt smile was back.

They chatted about nothing important the rest of their time in the diner. But when Elizabeth was walking back to her office after lunch, she thought again about her date last week with Max.

She knew she could spend a lot of time with Max and never run out of anything to talk about. He wasn't perfect— no man was—but he was her friend, and that was what mattered. Who said a kiss had to make your knees quake every time?

She had only experienced kisses from one man—or rather, one boy—who had always made her knees wobble, and he ended up being a louse.

No, it was better to have a relationship based on friendship and common interests. Max was a good-looking man. He treated her well, and in general was thought to be a nice person. But she couldn't get a niggling feeling out of her head.

When they'd met the homeless woman, Elizabeth had felt compassion and wanted to help. But Max seemed more perturbed by the interruption and didn't seem to care at all about the well-being of an older woman who obviously lived on the streets. Her clothes were dirty, and her hands looked as though they hadn't been washed in days, not to mention the stringy hair falling down around the poor woman's face.

No, Max wasn't always a nice guy. *But maybe he was just having a bad night?* Elizabeth didn't want to think he was a bad man. It was possible that something had happened to cause Max to react in such an un-Christian manner. She just didn't know what it was.

Content that it was just a one-off event, she walked through the entrance of the vet's office where she worked and prepared to finish off the paperwork from the previous day's visits.

As she readied for bed that night, she thought back to their date that evening and didn't see any red flags. Again, she decided the incident in Bozeman with the homeless woman had to be a one-off event. Maybe it was even supposed to happen that way. Had it not, she doubted she would be heading back there in a few days with her friends to find that woman and help her, along with other women living on the streets.

CHAPTER 3

With an SUV full of spunky girlfriends ready to lend a helping hand, Elizabeth and Harper took off for Bozeman Friday morning.

Mia, who was sitting in the back, leaned forward. "So, do you know where to start?"

Elizabeth smiled at her friend in the rearview mirror. "Yes, I was thinking we should start near the restaurant where I first met the woman last week. I don't think homeless stray too far from their own turf."

Another one of her friends, Sophia, pulled a little brown bag from the rear cargo hold and looked inside. "You've been busy." She pulled out two pairs of white cotton tube socks, a rolled-up dark-blue t-shirt, and two $10 gift cards to a local fast food joint.

"Yup, I went to the general store and asked them if they had any t-shirts they wanted to donate, and they did," Harper replied cheerily. "A few years back they ran a special event and there were over a hundred t-shirts left. They tried to sell them, but no one wanted to buy them, especially after half the town got one for free. So Mrs. Hayes donated them to the cause."

"And I ordered a case of tube socks online with overnight shipping. Then went yesterday after work to the grocery store and bought up a bunch of gift cards to two different fast food restaurants. Harper came over last night and we put the bags together." With her eyes on the road, Elizabeth tapped the steering wheel to the beat of the Toby Keith song on the radio.

She hoped she had enough bags to help all the homeless women they came upon. Last night, while they were putting together the bags, she realized she probably should have also bought some men's socks. She regretted only planning for homeless women. But Harper told her that if they gave the bags to men, they could always use them to trade with women who needed fresh socks.

Next time, she would have a selection for both men and women.

Did that mean she was already planning a next time? Elizabeth considered what her mind was doing and realized she did want to make this a regular event. Even if they only helped one or two people at a time, it was still worth it.

However, when she met one particular woman on the street—one who had bruises on her face and arms—she wondered if her heart could handle this. "Excuse me, but I have a gift for you." When Elizabeth extended the bag to the woman, who appeared to be in her thirties, the woman flinched and backed away.

The woman before her had stringy black hair, with dark eyes that had most likely seen way too much evil in the world. The woman looked at her with something besides fear. Trepidation? Or was it weariness? Either way, the homeless woman didn't trust her, and Elizabeth guessed she didn't trust anyone.

Knowing that the woman before her had at the very least been beaten, and most likely brutalized, she decided to treat her like an injured horse; she spoke softly and decided to give her some space. Elizabeth wanted the woman to know she wasn't a threat of any sort.

Taking two steps back, Elizabeth pulled the bag back closer to her own body. "I'm not going to hurt you. I'm here to help." She opened the bag and pulled out the socks, t-shirt, and two gift cards. "This is for you. No strings attached."

The other woman looked around her and quickly snatched the bag and the items from Elizabeth's hands. Then she turned and ran as quickly as she could to the Farmer Basket on the corner with her pushcart rumbling along behind her. Which just happened to be where one of the gift cards was for.

Harper walked up to her. "I take it she was glad for the gift card?"

"Hmm? Oh, yes. I think so. But there's something else going on with that woman." As Elizabeth tore her gaze from the homeless woman, an idea sparked in her mind when she laid eyes on her friend.

With large, sparkling eyes focused on her, Harper fidgeted and felt awkward. "What? Why are you looking at me like that?"

"I think you're hungry. Come with me, I know just the place to go." She pulled Harper by the hand and headed to the Farmer Basket.

"Wait, I'm not hungry. We just ate not that long ago." Following her friend, Harper was clueless as to what was going on.

Elizabeth turned to her friend. "Didn't you see the woman? I mean, really see her? She was covered in bruises. Someone had beat her up, badly. Then when I gave her the bag and she saw the gift card, she looked around before grabbing it. I think there might be a bully on the street hurting these women. Or at least this one. Her gift card was only for ten dollars. I want to make sure she gets enough to eat and maybe even give her another gift card with the hopes that she can keep it."

Harper looked around at the various people on the streets around them. "Do you think whoever hurt her is watching us?"

That caused Elizabeth to stop. She hadn't thought about that. It might be dangerous to them both, as well as to the other lady, if her attacker saw them giving out gift cards. Since the homeless woman had a roller bag she was pulling behind her, Elizabeth figured the woman wouldn't have trouble keeping the clothing items, but the food and gift card might be a problem.

Not wanting to cause more pain for the homeless woman, she thought about how she might help her.

"I didn't think about that. Come on, we can still check on her and make sure she's okay. Maybe we can even find a local homeless shelter to help her. Can you look that up on your phone while I try to talk to her?" Elizabeth started walking again, but with purpose and a desire to help the woman. Something inside her was drawing her to the lady. She wasn't sure if it was God leading her or just her own intuition, but the sad woman needed her help, and Elizabeth wasn't going to turn her back on her.

It only took ten minutes and another cheeseburger for the homeless woman to give them her name—Mary—and to finally speak to Elizabeth and Harper. "Thank you." The woman spoke so softly, they could barely hear her.

"I'm glad we could help." Elizabeth bit her lip and looked to Harper, who nodded encouragement. "I was wondering about your injuries." She took a deep breath before continuing. "Is this a regular occurrence? Does the same person, or people, do this to you regularly?"

She didn't want to assume anything or make the poor woman uncomfortable, but she had to know if Mary was in danger. There were several options for a woman in Mary's situation, and she knew Harper would help any way she could as well.

Mary didn't speak; she continued to eat the food set before her. She had already consumed two small cheeseburgers, a medium order of fries, and a large Coke. Now she was on her second Coke, third cheeseburger, and a large order of fries, compliments of Harper.

When the woman continued to eat in silence, Elizabeth thought of ways to coax her to speak again. "When was the last time you ate a meal?" It appeared as though she hadn't eaten in days and wasn't sure when she would eat again.

Mary shrugged and looked at the two women seated with her, then went back to her meal and shoving food into her mouth, as though this were normal.

Harper decided to try her hand at getting the woman to open up. "If we gave you a couple gift cards, would you be able to use them for yourself?"

This caused Mary to stop eating and just stare at the plastic tray containing what was left of her lunch. She gulped and took a long drink of her Coke. Just when the girls were about to give up, Mary said, "How do you know?"

It felt as though a ton of bricks had just dropped on Elizabeth's shoulders, and she slumped in her chair. Before saying anything, she looked around the restaurant to make sure no one was paying them any attention. When she was confident they weren't being watched, she asked, "Who's stealing your food and money? We want to help you, Mary."

"Big Bart. He owns the streets, and we have to pay him for protection." Mary looked back down at her food and pushed a fry around in the pool of ketchup on her cheeseburger wrapper.

"Then why are you all bruised? Did he hurt you? Or someone else?" Harper asked in a low voice.

Elizabeth knew that, as a nurse, Harper had seen a lot. But in their hometown, she doubted there were many cases of women being abused, at least not this bad. Had a woman been beaten this horribly, word would have spread like wildfire through Beacon Creek.

Mary shook her head and pulled her hands into her lap. "I couldn't pay. Someone had given me five dollars for food and Big Bart said it was his. I refused to give it to him, so he made me give it to him. He said I was an example of what happens when we don't obey him."

Elizabeth put a hand over her mouth and tried to stifle the cry that was aching to come out. She told herself she could cry later. Right now, Mary needed her to be strong. *She* needed to be strong. Even though she knew crying wasn't weakness, society said it was. So she tried very hard not to cry in public, especially in front of a woman who was battered and broken.

"That stops today. I found a shelter online that isn't too far from here. Will you let us take you there?" Harper moved to put her hand on Mary's back, but at the last second pulled it back. She knew someone in Mary's position wouldn't want a stranger touching her—not yet.

"But they don't let us stay very long. After a few days,

I'll be back out on the streets again and Big Bart will come looking for his money," Mary whispered.

"Don't worry about him. We'll deal with him. We want you to get a good night's sleep and maybe get your injuries looked at. I'll speak with the director of the shelter—maybe they can help you get a job and move to a safer place until Bart is gone." Elizabeth wasn't exactly sure what could be done about Bart, but if he had beaten up a woman in front of witnesses, maybe they could all work together and report him to the cops. Getting Bart off the streets, even for a little while, would be good for everyone.

Once Mary was finished, Elizabeth and Harper took her to the women's shelter a few blocks away. They were more than happy to help Mary, and promised to keep her there until all her injuries were healed. The director even offered to take her to a different area once she was ready to leave. They didn't have an employment program at that shelter, so Elizabeth was going to do her homework and find someone who could help the women on the street get back on their feet.

When they walked back to their SUV, they noticed a couple men watching them. At first Elizabeth thought they might be homeless men. "Do we have any more of those gift bags?" She nodded toward the group of men leaning against a wall with their arms crossed and eyes narrowed.

Sophia and Mia looked uncomfortable. Mia said, "I think we should go. Those men aren't happy about you taking that woman away."

Elizabeth's brows furrowed. "What do you mean? Mary? Why would they care about her?"

"Because the tall guy, Bart, owns the streets, and the homeless work for him, or so he says. He told us to leave and not come back, or next time he would drive home his words."

Sophia's jaw tightened, and she looked like she was ready to spit fire.

"Did they hurt you?" Harper asked incredulously.

Sophia was one of the women Elizabeth never had to worry about. But in this case, knowing what she did of Bart, she hoped that Sophia didn't have to use her skills learned in the army. No one was exactly sure what Sophia did, but she served her country well in Europe—not the Middle East, as most had assumed. Elizabeth had her suspicions, but had never asked Sophia about it. She knew that when her friend was ready she'd talk about it, if she could.

Harper and Elizabeth both stared at the four men across the street. The tall one, Big Bart, had on jeans and a button-up cowboy shirt. His black hair was long and mostly covered by his big cowboy hat, but it looked clean, as did his clothes. The other three men all wore basically the same thing as most cowboys in town. Looking at them, no one would think they lived on the streets. So why were they claiming to own the streets and shaking down the homeless for what little money and food they had?

Was this some sort of gang?

While Elizabeth continued to stare at the men, Bart pulled away from the wall he was leaning against and strode across the street without even looking for cars.

"What? Didn't your friends tell you to leave?" Bart looked her up and down and sneered. "This is my town. If I catch you interfering again, you won't walk away unharmed."

One of his friends scanned the rest of the girls. "You rich chicks are all the same. You think you can come into our town and help the homeless by giving them a few scraps and then leave feeling good about yourselves," he chortled.

The hairs on the back of Elizabeth's neck stood on end. "Why are you stealing from the homeless and beating them up? You look like you could work for your own money. Why don't you?"

All four men laughed, and Bart took a step closer and invaded Elizabeth's personal space. She wanted nothing more than to step back away from his bad breath and imposing figure, but she knew that would signal weakness, and he would only take advantage.

Instead, she put her hands on her hips and narrowed her eyes at him, daring him to touch her. She'd grown up with five brothers on a ranch and knew how to protect herself. Plus, she had Sophia backing her up. These men wouldn't know what hit them if Sophia lost her cool.

"We *do* work. We work the streets. We're the ones who keep the inhabitants safe here. This is our territory. If you want to help them, feel free to leave any donations with us next time, and we'll see to it that anyone who has need will get it." Bart snorted, and a bit of his spittle sprinkled her cheeks.

She wiped her face with her hands. "No. Leave them alone, or you won't be the ones walking away at all." Elizabeth was itching for a fight, but she knew that not all her friends were up to brawling in the streets with men bigger than they were. She wasn't sure she could best Bart, but she would give it her all if she had to.

Lord, I don't know what you want from us here, but please protect us and help us to do the right thing. Your Word says to turn the other cheek, but are we to let these bullies get away with hurting homeless women, or even ourselves? she prayed silently, hoping God would intercede on their behalf.

While she did want a fight, especially after hearing everything Mary had to say, she knew it would be wrong to goad a fight out of them. It would be easy, but not the Christian thing to do.

~~Big Bart brought his beefy hand up and grabbed her~~ shoulder. Before he could get a word out, Elizabeth grabbed the thumb, pushing in on her shoulder and twisting it back, causing the big man to cry out and fall to his knee. She couldn't be sure, but she thought she might have broken his thumb.

She stepped back and growled through clenched teeth, "Never touch a woman without her permission. If you ever try anything like that again in front of me, I'll make sure you're singing soprano for weeks to come. Got it?" She raised her eyebrows and looked at the men with Big Bart.

Sophia stood next to Elizabeth, flexing her arms and staring them down. Anyone who looked at Sophia would know she was strong, especially when she flexed her guns. Thank goodness the woman worked out practically every day. She did own the local gym, after all.

Bart stood up. "This time you're getting away with this. But if I catch you in my neighborhood again, no matter why you're here, I'll pay you back for this."

All four men turned around and headed away from the girls. A group of locals had formed a crowd and were watching. Some had their phones out taking video, but not one of the men in the crowd had come forward to help.

"Why is it that people are always anxious to run to a scene and take videos or photos and post on social media, but not one is willing to step in and help?" Elizabeth shook her head at the watchers and wondered why none of the men in the crowd had offered to help them.

Could Bart be so scary that even the local cowboys feared him? She had never seen so many men ignore women in need of help. Not that Elizabeth thought she and her friends needed rescuing, but someone should have stepped in and at least looked like they were going to help defend the ladies. It was part of the cowboy code, after all.

Before the girls could get in their car to leave, a police cruiser pulled up and called out to them.

"Great, just what we need." Elizabeth shook her head and sighed and realized they were going to be lucky if they made it home in time for supper.

CHAPTER 4

"Ma!" Logan Hayes called out as he entered his parents' kitchen. "Ma, I'm home."

"Upstairs, honey," his mother, Judith, called out. "I'm with your dad. I'll be right down."

Hank, Logan's dad, had recently suffered a heart attack and was home resting. The doctor said he would be alright, but no one was taking any chances. Hank was stuck in bed with a hovering wife who wouldn't let him do anything.

Logan had quit his job in LA to come home and help the family business. It was always the plan to come home and take over, but Logan had enjoyed his time away in LA, especially the beaches. A buddy of his had a family home in Venice, and they spent several weekends each summer at the house on the canal.

Now he was home, and would begin the task of managing the family's general store in Beacon Creek, Montana. While he wanted to jump right in and start making the changes he and his dad had spoken about over the past year, he knew he first had to get the books in order. And before that, he needed to see his dad and make sure he really was going to be alright.

The stress of the business problems had caused his father, who had always been healthy, to eat wrong and forgo exercise. Which in turn caused his heart to weaken from all the stress. Logan wished his father would have been upfront with him about how bad things had gotten. He would have come home much sooner if he knew what was really happening with the business.

Logan put his suitcase in his room and decided he'd unpack later. Instead, he went back downstairs and began dinner preparations so his mom wouldn't have to worry. He knew his sister, Leah, was watching the store, and she'd be home sometime after the store closed at seven o'clock.

While he was looking through the fridge, he realized that he would need to go grocery shopping the next day if he wanted to make sure everyone, including himself, ate healthy.

One of his friends back in LA was doing his cardiology internship, and he stressed the importance of healthy, fresh foods for the whole family. Especially Logan's father while he recovered from his heart attack. He said to go light on the beef, but heavy on fruits and vegetables, with seafood and poultry as much as possible.

Montana wasn't a hotbed for seafood, but they did have great trout streams, and his father also liked the local bass. He had heard there was a salmon farm, so he'd have to look into getting some salmon as well.

While he was thinking about all he needed to buy to get their stores up to par, his mother came down to help him.

"Logan, it's so good to see you again. Thank you for coming home, son." Judith walked to her son and gave him a kiss on the cheek.

"I wish you would have told me how bad it was sooner. I'd have come home," Logan chided.

His mother sighed. "I know, dear. I told your father we

should bring you home, but he insisted that you should get as much out of LA as possible. He's always been healthy, and we had no clue this would happen." Judith looked at what Logan had pulled out of the fridge and she scrunched her nose.

Logan chuckled. "I know, it's not much. I'll go do some shopping tomorrow morning and get the house stocked with healthy choices. No more greasy cheeseburgers or frozen meals, Ma. We have to cook fresh foods going forward."

He looked at the head of lettuce on the counter and the meager salad toppings he had discovered. There was a bag of sunflower seeds and a balsamic vinaigrette dressing, and that was all they had besides the chicken breast he had pulled out of the freezer.

Shaking her head, Judith went to the pantry and looked through it. "I guess we'll have to get rid of croutons and the packaged bacon bits?"

Logan nodded. "I can cook up some bacon and crumble it for future salad toppings, but we need to prepare as much fresh food as possible. The vitamins and nutrients are exactly what Dad needs right now. Not to mention, it will help to keep us from getting run down or sick as well."

He knew that changing their eating habits was going to be difficult. It was for him when he'd first moved to LA, but he'd never felt better once he got all the toxins out of his system. Even though he was twenty-eight years old, he felt more like he did when he was in high school, like he could play an entire basketball game and then get up the next day and work on the ranch without any cares. Which was something he had done many times.

"Is Pops up for a visit from his wayward son yet?" Logan grinned at his mom as he waited for the chicken to defrost in the microwave.

"I think he would really enjoy that. I'll finish the dinner if you want to go up and see him. He really has missed you, Logan." His mom's genuine smile sent warmth to his heart.

He had missed his family. It had been two years since they came out to visit him in LA. Logan hadn't wanted to come home since *she* moved back; it would have been too difficult to see her and not kiss her. Now that he was home, he'd have to find a way to deal with his emotions. There was no way in the small town of Beacon Creek they could stay away from each other. At some point, he'd see her and have to be polite and talk to her. He only hoped the first time he saw her she wasn't with a boyfriend.

Leah had told him his high school sweetheart was dating someone rich and handsome, but he didn't want to think about it. All he wanted to do was help his father recover and get the business back in the black.

Family was all that mattered.

Family was everything to Logan.

Later that night while he was readying for bed, Logan reflected back on what his father had looked like when he entered his bedroom. Logan knew the man would be pale and sickly, but he wasn't prepared for how gaunt his face was. His father wasn't obese or anything, but he had always been stalky and strong. Lifting bales of hay and carting around fifty-pound sacks of grain kept a body strong. But when he looked at his father, he could have sworn the man had been bedridden for ages.

Hank's face was pale, as expected, but his cheeks were sunken in, and his brown eyes had lost their shine. Logan could tell his father wasn't feeling well at all. He even wondered if the man shouldn't still be in the hospital. Logan hated that insurance companies kicked patients out way too soon, but couldn't he have gone to a nursing home or something?

Thankfully, they had purchased a higher level of insurance, the kind not available through universal healthcare—a.k.a. a Cadillac Plan. A nurse would come into the house every day for a few hours until she wasn't needed anymore. Logan was very grateful his parents hadn't cut back on their insurance plan when money was tight. So many other Americans had done just that and regretted it.

Guilt riddled his mind and his heart. He knew he should have come home sooner. His father kept saying it was all under control, but deep down, Logan knew it wasn't. If only he wasn't so selfish.

Had he come home a year ago like he'd originally thought he would, his pops may not have had a heart attack. He could still be working the store and teasing him mercilessly about his bad haircut, or some such nonsense. But nooo, he had to be selfish and stay in LA with all those models—whom he never had the guts to ask out—and his easy lifestyle. If only he would have listened to his heart instead of his head. That was his problem: he always listened to his head and ignored his heart.

He'd be married to the most wonderful woman in the world right now if he had only listened to his heart.

Sleep was a long time in coming, and he couldn't stop his mind from going back to high school and all the great times he had with Lizzie. If only he could turn back time and change the one decision he'd regretted for the past ten years.

If only…

CHAPTER 5

"Alright Pops, I'm heading into the store. Leah's going to train me today. Not that I need training. I helped you run the store most of my life, but she says you've made a lot of changes since I went away." Logan shrugged and decided he wouldn't let his father know how much it bugged him that Leah had to show him the ropes in his family store.

It was his own fault for not being more involved over the years. Even when he did come home for Christmas or another holiday, he'd stayed away from the store. Logan had no desire to let his parents think he had wanted to come home before now. Another mistake on his part. If only he had been a better son.

"Leah, I don't see much has changed since I left for college. You have a few new lines of product, but everything else seems to be the same." He scratched his head and looked at his little sister as they toured the family's general store.

The feed section moved to a different spot, but it looked like it was just to make more room for the farm and ranch equipment they sold in the store. He was surprised to see so much of what could easily be purchased online sitting in the store. If he had been running the place, he would have had samples on hand and then drop-shipped the larger tools and equipment to ranches and farms instead of carrying so much in inventory. Especially since they seemed to be very tight on funds as of late.

The clothing section looked better, more up to date. That had to be Leah's influence. He was glad his sister had updated the fashions for the local cowboys and cowgirls. His mother and father had always kept such outdated choices in stock. Which they rarely sold. Only the basics, like work jeans and shirts, ever sold much. Certainly with some updated fashion choices, the local men and woman would choose to shop here more often than travel to Bozeman for their needs, or go online.

But what did he know? He purchased most of his clothes online. He did buy his suits from a local men's shop, but only because the owner was someone he knew from church. Otherwise, he probably would have continued to buy his suits from Penny's, like he had done growing up.

After taking another stroll through the large store, he realized there wasn't anything that necessitated his sister *showing him the ropes*, as she'd put it earlier.

Was this some sort of ploy for her to be his boss? He thought they had outgrown such nonsense long ago, but maybe Leah was trying to get back at him for all the times he'd lorded his position as big brother over her? He wasn't sure, but he wanted to give her the benefit of the doubt.

"Actually, big brother, I wanted to make sure I had the entire day with you. There are a few things, like the cash register and accounting system, that have changed, but for the most part it's all the same. However, I think we need to talk about a few things, and I didn't want anyone getting in the way." Leah bit her lip, and her nervousness was evident in the way she fidgeted and wouldn't look him in the eyes.

He crossed his arms over his chest and took a deep breath, waiting for the shoe to drop. "Alright, give it to me straight. What's going on?"

At his tone of voice, Leah looked up with wide eyes and stammered, "Ah, um, well, I think it's good you're home." She winced and twirled a lock of hair around her finger. "But a few things are different. Like Dad. He won't be able to work for a while. And when he does come back to the store, it'll only be part time. His doctor said his heart was too weak to deal with much stress." She gulped and waited for his response.

Logan ran a hand over his chin. "This required us both in the store all day? Of course Pops isn't ever coming back to running the store. That's why I quit my job and moved home instead of taking a leave of absence." He wasn't sure what

Leah thought about his move back home, but surely she realized he was home for good, right?

"There's more." Taking a deep breath, Leah prepared herself to tell her big brother the other things going on, but was interrupted by the high-pitched and annoying chime of the door.

Logan chuckled. "Yeah, I don't think a serious conversation is going to happen in the store. We should go for a walk after dinner tonight."

Without waiting for a response from his sister, Logan made his way to the front of the store to greet the customer.

"Logan? Is that you, son?" A burly man at least eighty years old greeted him with a toothy smile when he stepped past the counter displaying large and shiny belt buckles.

"Mr. Macon. So good to see you still alive and kicking. How long's it been—what, eight or nine years since the last time I saw you?" Logan chuckled and looked around conspiratorially. "I hear you're dating Ms. Barton, you old coot! I knew you were a ladies' man, but a woman ten years your junior? Good for you." He put his hand out to shake the older rancher's hand.

Mr. Macon smiled. "Please, you're an adult now. Call me Charlie."

They shook hands, and Logan asked, "How can I help you today, Charlie?" He realized then that the old man had ignored his teasing about the widowed school teacher.

Even before Logan left for college, everyone knew that Charlie had a crush on Ms. Barton, but she wasn't ready to take off her widow's clothes. It seemed she finally had, and had been seen in Charlie's company for the past few months. Logan hoped they could find happiness together. Not that he was a romantic or anything, but he did think that it would be nice to grow old with someone, someday. And he thought all nice people deserved happiness.

"Oh, I don't really need much. Just checking on my regular order of grain and hay. Plus"—Charlie looked around to make sure no one was listening, then lowered his voice—"I heard you were back, and I wanted to see if you had met the new John Deere rep."

Logan's brows furrowed. "No, not yet. Is it someone I know?" He couldn't figure out why meeting the new rep would be important. Well, okay, maybe it was important since they were the local John Deere distributors, but still, why did Charlie care? Unless it was one of his old buddies from high school? That might make for interesting gossip.

Nothing was more important to the elderly around town than gossip. He remembered as a boy working in the store that Charlie and a few of his buddies would sit in the corner by the window, playing chess or checkers and talking about everyone who walked by the store or came inside. Most of it was harmless chatter, but once in a while they would end up with something salacious. Almost as crazy as the women who sat at the front booth in the diner across the street doing basically the same thing.

Charlie's deep chuckle and grin had Logan curious. "No, I don't think you do. But he's someone you should probably get to know."

"Well, I suppose I'll meet him next time he comes to the store." Before Logan could ask anything else, the bell chimed again and he looked to see who was coming in.

"Go on, help your customers. I'm just going to get a drink and head to the game table and wait for the boys. We have a checkers tournament going this week." Charlie waggled his bushy brows. "And the stakes are high this time. We're betting on BBQ."

"Uh oh, you better pay attention. You don't want old Mr. Cannon winning." Logan smiled and walked away, remembering the last time he'd had BBQ from Mr. Cannon. It was black, and so dry he had to drink a whole glass of lemonade just to get a few bites down. No one wanted anything that old man cooked.

The customer who came through the door wasn't anyone he remembered, but he still needed to keep a friendly smile on and greet them. Hopefully he could get a few good sales in today and end up in the black for the week.

He'd also need to speak with his mother about some of the high-end merchandise they held. In this day and age there shouldn't be a need to keep that much in stock, unless it was just something they did for the harvest season. He hoped they would sell the equipment soon and get the expenses off their books before the Christmas shopping season.

They'd need the capital to help stock the shelves with Christmas decorations and supplies. Even though online shopping was picking up, they still had plenty of foot traffic from late fall through the Christmas season, or so Leah had said. Even for them it was one of their best times of the year.

"Hello, welcome to Hayes General Store. How can I help you?" Logan gave his best welcoming smile and hoped the man walking into his store was there to buy equipment. Maybe even something large.

The customer turned to him and smiled in response. The man looked to be a rancher or a farmer, with dirty jeans, a half-untucked button-up shirt with smudges on the front, and a large-rimmed cowboy hat. He appeared to have spent most of the morning outside working.

"Hi, you must be Logan. I heard you were returning to help your father. I was very sorry to hear about his heart attack. My wife, Suzy, is sending over a roast with fresh vegetables and a fruit salad. Her father suffered a heart attack a few years back, and his doctor said he needed to stop eating sweets and get in more fresh veggies." The man shook his head.

"Thank you, Mister...?" Logan raised his brows and waited for the man to introduce himself.

"Oh, where are my manners. Sorry about that—I'm George Lincoln. We bought the old Hernandez ranch a few years back. I guess we're sort of neighbors." The man put his hand out, and Logan shook it.

"Yes, my dad told me about your family. We were very happy to hear that someone was able to buy the land and bring it back to its former glory. I was very sorry that none of Mr. Hernandez's children wanted to run the ranch once he passed away. And thank you for thinking about my family. A change in diet is going to be very important, and I'm sure Ma will appreciate any help your wife can give her in regards to recipes and ideas for healthy meals." He was very grateful for any help his parents could get.

Maybe if more locals can share their recipes and experiences, my family will have an easier time making the changes needed to help Pops. Logan knew it was going to be an uphill battle to get his parents to eat right. They had a nightly ritual that always included ice cream, even in the cold of winter. That was one more thing he'd have to add to his list of items to look up online. There had to be healthy ways of making ice cream without too much dairy or any of those harsh chemicals.

Logan looked expectantly at his customer and neighbor. He wasn't sure what the protocol was in this situation, but he was raised to be a gentleman, so he wouldn't push the man into buying anything. "Are you raising cattle as well as farming? I think my pops said something about you having a very rambunctious bull?"

Mr. Lincoln chuckled and rubbed the stubble on his chin. "Ah, yes. Duke. It seems he doesn't take too kindly to being penned in. He keeps breaking the gate and getting out. He's even made his way to your pastures. I think he has a thing for one or two of your heifers. He continues to search them out." He wiggled his brows and laughed.

Logan shook his head and smiled. "I see. Well, I guess you're here to find something to keep your gates locked tighter?" This wasn't the first time a rancher came in needing help to keep a rambunctious bull in check. And he was sure it wouldn't be the last, either.

"Follow me. I'll show you a few items we have to help keep the gate locked." Logan led Mr. Lincoln to their shelf full of locks and chains. That crazy bull probably needed a chain on his gate. He was also going to need a metal gate, if he didn't already have one, just to make sure that the bull didn't break it with his eagerness for the girls.

CHAPTER 6

While Logan was in the back checking a phone order, he heard the ring of the bell and his sister called out that she would help the new customer. He went back to his work without paying any attention to the front of the store.

When he was done filling the order, Logan went out front to see if he was needed for anything, and he stopped in his tracks. His heart began beating so fast he thought he was going to have a heart attack. His hand went to his chest, and he rubbed at the pain he hadn't felt in several years. In fact, he hadn't felt this pain since the last time he had seen her.

For the past ten years, he'd regretted his decision every single day. Logan had tried to talk to her last time, but she'd refused. She had just walked away from him without a word. When he tried to get her to stop, she waved a hand and took off running. Still without a word. She hated him so much, she couldn't even stand to look at him or at the very least say hi.

She hadn't noticed him yet, and he questioned his sanity when he took another step closer to her. He wanted nothing more than to say hi and see how she was doing. Leah had told him when she'd come home from college, and that she was dating again. But he still wanted to hear all the details of her job. Did she like it as much as she always thought she would?

As his steps brought him closer and closer to the only woman he would ever love, his mouth went dry, and he had to put his thumbs in his back pockets to keep himself from reaching out to her.

Her back was still to him, but he knew it was her. He would never forget the way her hair shone and the beautiful auburn color that always made him smile when the red in her hair caught sun's rays. It was also tinged with a few strands of very light brown. Most likely from her mother's side of the family.

Leah looked up at him with a frown just before the woman of his dreams turned around.

"Logan? What are you doing here?" Lizzie blurted.

He couldn't speak. His heart leapt with the sound of her voice. Those six little words, while not quite welcoming, were an improvement over the last time he saw her.

She'd spoken to him.

It had been nearly ten years since she'd railed at him for leaving her, and every time he had seen her since, she ignored him. Finally! Words directed at him, and they weren't harsh or loud. The beginnings of a smile formed on his lips, and he was about to answer her when his sister did.

"He's back home for good. Didn't you hear?" Leah furrowed her brow in confusion, certain she had told her friend that Logan was moving home.

Elizabeth shook her head. "Yes. Sorry, you did tell me he was moving back. I guess I had thought he would only be here for a few days to help your dad during his recovery. I never expected he would be in the store." She turned her back on him again as though he wasn't even there.

But Logan wasn't going to let this chance get past him.

"Hi, Lizzie. It's good to see you again. You haven't changed a bit." *Stupid. What a stupid thing to say the first time speaking to her in almost a decade.*

Without turning around, she responded, "I don't go by Lizzie anymore. It's Elizabeth now."

Logan's stomach churned at the cold, dismissive tone of her voice. "Sorry, Elizabeth. How's your practice? I heard you were working with old Mr. Owens."

"Fine." She took two steps away, and Leah followed Liz... Elizabeth, the two of them speaking about an order she had placed.

It was progress. He had to believe that what had just happened was progress. She'd spoken to him. If he was going to have a chance with her ever again, he had to remember to take it slow. He would see her a lot more now. With such a small town, and theirs the only general store in town, he knew their paths would cross. Plus, they went to the same church.

Well, unless she had changed churches in the past few years, but he doubted it. Leah had told him all about the church picnic and softball game last year. Li ... *Elizabeth.* He was going to have to remember to call her by her full name until she gave him permission to use the nickname he had given her as kids. Anyway, Elizabeth had helped his family's church win the tournament against the Catholic church in town.

There were only four churches in Beacon Creek. One Catholic—St. Marks. Then there was St. John's Presbyterian, and two independent churches—Grace Christian and Beacon Creek Baptist. They all went to the Baptist church. He wondered if she would change churches because of him, but shook away the idea as preposterous. Elizabeth had grown up at Beacon Creek Baptist, just like he had. She wouldn't leave the only church she had ever been a member of. Well, in the area, anyway. He didn't doubt she had found a good church close to her college, but that was a long way from Beacon Creek.

When Elizabeth left the store with her order in hand, she didn't even look his way. He made sure she would see him when he walked to the counter and stayed behind it until after she left, but she gave him the cold shoulder.

His sister came over and sighed. "She's never going to forgive you. You know that, right?"

He hung his head. "I know. I was so stupid. I wish she would give me a chance to at least talk to her and apologize."

Leah screwed up her lips and considered a moment before speaking. "I probably shouldn't tell you this, but everyone in town already knows, so it's not like it's a secret, but Max is the first guy she's dated since you dumped her. She hasn't been able to trust any guy. I don't think she even dated in college. You did a number on her."

Logan hung his head even lower. "I know, and I feel awful about it. I haven't had more than a handful of dates myself since making the biggest mistake of my life. Instead, I focused on school and work. I had to learn to be the best at what I did so I could come back here one day and help the business move to the next level."

His sister patted his shoulder. "I know. But you ripped her heart into shreds and she's never recovered. I think"—she tapped her chin—"no, I *know* that if you give her time and don't try to have an actual conversation with her, you will get her attention. Give her time to warm up to the idea of being around you again. I doubt she'll ever go out with you. Max is pretty hot. All the girls around town want him. A few have even tried to steal him from Elizabeth." She chuckled and walked away when another customer entered the front door.

Elizabeth had never been so happy for church to end. She sat in the back pew, away from her family, who typically sat close to Logan's family. They had done so most of her life. However, Elizabeth couldn't handle Logan watching her like he did in the store the other day. So instead, she arrived late and sat in the back. The second the preacher was done with the invitation, she ran out. In fact, she didn't speak to more than two people the entire time she was there. And they only received her attention during the welcome and shaking hands part of the service. She stood stock still in her pew and refused to look at Logan.

Now it was Monday, and Max would be back soon from his latest trip. She knew once he arrived she'd feel better. Logan had to know she was dating, but she doubted he had met Max yet. Once he saw her with Max, she hoped he would leave her alone.

Too many memories were popping up in her mind whenever she saw Logan or thought of him. It made her heart hurt even more. The only really bad memory she had of her time with Logan was when he broke up with her. They had spent their lives together. First as childhood friends, and then as they grew up, it morphed into a romantic relationship that everyone spoke about. Their love was the talk of the town.

She would bet big money that the town was talking about them again, probably taking bets on when they would get back together again. And she wanted nothing to do with it. Why couldn't people leave her and Logan alone? She was with Max.

Max, the man the entire town had googly-eyes over, was a much better match for her than Logan ever was.

Max was very respectful; he even called her every night he was out of town. Or at least he texted, if nothing else. While they weren't in love or headed down the aisle any time soon, he was a good boyfriend.

Later that day, Elizabeth met Max for dinner at the local diner. They tried not to eat at each other's homes unless there was a chaperone, or another couple. So they ate out a lot when they wanted to share a meal.

Elizabeth wanted to wait for marriage before sharing a bed with a man. Max wasn't too happy, but he respected her and said he wouldn't push. She very much appreciated his support and understanding. But she knew he hadn't waited, and therefore she didn't want to put herself in a situation where he might push things further than what she wanted. Her ideas about marriage and sex might have been a little bit antiquated, but she believed what the Bible said about sex being something reserved only for a man and his wife.

Even if she never married, she would follow the Bible. When it was just the two of them, staying clear of his apartment or her house helped keep them both in line.

Monday night was a standing date night at the local diner, when Max was in town.

"Max, I missed you." Elizabeth kissed Max's cheek and hugged him.

He smiled at her, but said nothing.

Once they were seated and had their menus, he said, "I

heard you went to Bozeman and got into some trouble the other day." His tone was calm and neutral, but his eyes were blazing with fire.

Was that anger? Or was he just happy to see her?

She wasn't exactly sure how he felt, but she could tell he was holding in strong feelings—probably anger. What she did was a bit crazy. But she'd had to defend herself and her friends. You never backed down from bullies or they just kept coming after you. Everyone knew that. Maybe the physical altercation was a bit much, but again, she had to defend herself and her friends.

Wait, why was she feeling so defensive? All he'd asked was a simple question. He wasn't accusing her or saying she was stupid to do it. He just wanted to know what went down, that was all. Right?

She nodded her head as she scanned the menu. "Yup, a group of us went to help the homeless. We brought them a bag of essentials. Some socks, a t-shirt, and a couple gift cards to the local fast food joint. It wasn't much, but we were also able to help a woman who had been beaten by a local thug get into a shelter."

His nostrils flared, and he glared daggers at her when she looked up from her menu.

Not wanting to let him think he could make her feel bad, she sat up straight and put her menu on the table and waited for him to respond.

He looked around, making sure no one was watching them. "What do you think you were doing? I thought you knew better than to slum it like that. You could have been hurt."

"But I wasn't. God was with us. He protected us. I believe He led us there at the right time to help that woman." Elizabeth sighed and slouched a bit in her squeaky pleather diner booth seat. "What upsets you more? That me and a few other girls gave out gift bags to homeless women in the middle of the day, or that I spent time talking with one of them and helped her get into a shelter?"

He raised his hand and snorted. "Both. But that's not all. I heard you got into a fight with men, not women. Were you going to tell me about that?"

She blinked, and her mouth opened and closed. "How'd you hear about that?"

"When I came home earlier today, I stopped in here for a coffee. The Diner Divas were more than happy to tell me about your little excursion. Did you really fight with a street thug? Really?" He shook his head in disgust.

Instead of asking if she was alright, he was angry with her, and she was shocked that he was so upset.

"Wait, how did they hear about it? I haven't even told my parents or my brothers." She shivered at the thought of her brothers hearing about the street fight. They would not take too kindly to any man putting a hand on their sisters. Even though they had fought their entire childhood, it was different. No one touched their sisters and got away with it.

"Well, it looks like some of the other girls in your party weren't so careful with keeping their mouths shut. Word is probably all over town by now. Why would you do it?"

"Because they attacked us. I had to fight back. Did you expect me to just take their assault lying down? Really?" She looked at him incredulously.

"No, that I totally expected. I could never expect you *not* to defend yourself. What were you thinking, going to the homeless and interacting with them? It's dangerous, even in the middle of the day. As evidenced by your experience on Friday." He raised an eyebrow, and his lips formed a tight, thin line as he waited for her to apologize for being so stupid.

She put her hand up in front of her. "Wait, you're mad at me for helping others? Really? That's what has you so fired up?"

"Yes. I told you that night we went out to dinner in Bozeman and the woman came up begging for money that you shouldn't help them. It never benefits you to help the homeless. They're on the streets for a reason. They could get jobs if they wanted, and then an apartment, but they're too lazy to work. People giving them handouts just keeps them from doing anything with their lives." His whispered words struck her heart, and Elizabeth was sure she had no clue who the man in front of her was.

He had always been one of the first to volunteer to help the church when they had church cleaning days, or to help the school when they set up for the carnival. His generous spirit was one of the things that had attracted her to him in the first place. Well, that and his Hollywood good looks. Who was this man in front of her? Surely he was just upset because she almost got hurt. That had to be what had caused him to react this way. She couldn't believe he had such a cold heart.

"You mean to tell me you've never helped the homeless? And you truly believe they're just lazy? Really?" She shook her head, not able to bring the words out that she really wanted to say. How could he believe those things?

He narrowed his eyes and leaned closer to her. "Homeless people are…"

Before he could finish his sentence, Judy the waitress came up to their table. "Hi sweeties. Will it be your usual? Or are you finally going to try the special of the day?"

She looked between the two of them and took a step back. "Maybe you need some more time? I'll bring you both a glass of water." Judy walked away as quickly as she could.

Elizabeth watched her walk straight to the Diner Divas

sitting at the counter and begin to speak to them. She knew that before they were even done, the entire town would know that she and Max had had an argument. By tomorrow, the rumor would probably be that they broke up. It was always that way. The divas would gossip, and it would get twisted around to be as salacious as possible.

And with Logan in town, it would most likely include him. That was the last thing she needed.

"The divas are already leaving to spread their gossip. We should eat dinner and talk about this later. Put a smile on your face. Don't let anyone know anything is wrong." Elizabeth plastered a fake smile on her face and sat back in a more relaxed pose. She wasn't going to make it easy for the town gossip mill to make this out to be more than it was.

After a quiet dinner with fake smiles and nods to people as they entered, Max and Elizabeth finally left the diner and headed to her place so they could talk.

"I think you should come in so no one sees us arguing outside." Elizabeth let herself out of Max's truck without waiting for him to open her door. She went up on her porch and waited for him to join her.

"Are you sure? We made a deal—no being alone in a house." He smirked, knowing there was no way she would be tempted into anything romantic, but still wanting to get in a jab. He hated that she wouldn't be alone with him in either of their homes, as though he was nothing more than a hormonal teenage boy who couldn't control himself.

Just as he closed the door to her house, her phone rang. She glanced at the caller ID and put up a finger. "Hi, Milton. What's up?"

She sighed when she hung up. "You aren't going to believe it, but Milton is sick and can't go out on a call. He needs me to head out to the Miller ranch. They have several heads of cattle that might need to be put down. I have to examine them and see if it's contagious or just bad luck." Elizabeth grabbed her bag and walked them outside. "I guess it's a good thing I rarely wear dresses outside of church." The sardonic smile on her face was anything but happy.

"I want to continue this conversation tomorrow night," Max said as they walked down the steps. "Maybe we could just meet up for coffee and go for a walk along the creek?"

She nodded. "Yeah, sure. Call me tomorrow afternoon."

CHAPTER 7

T he cattle at the Miller ranch needed her and Milton's full attention for the next few days. They had to sort through all the cattle that showed signs of illness and separate them from the rest of the herd. Elizabeth wasn't sure if it would infect the entire herd or if just a few were infected. Mr. Miller had recently purchased one hundred head of calves, and it seemed the majority of those sick were the new ones.

She suspected it was shipping fever, but couldn't be certain until she had quarantined them for the week. If no others came down with the respiratory symptoms, then she knew she at least had it contained. She immediately focused on testing the animals for the most common illnesses and treating them.

She and Max weren't able to finish their conversation from Monday night because he had to take another short trip later that week. They had only seen each other twice, and Elizabeth was too tired to argue. They discussed their schedules and agreed that they would continue their discussion when he returned home the following week.

All week, the town was agog about the argument between

Max and Elizabeth. Some speculated Max left town because of their fight, while others realized he did travel for work a lot. Elizabeth rolled her eyes at most of the garbage going around.

That is, until Logan's name entered the gossip mill.

On Wednesday, Elizabeth entered the diner to get a cup of coffee to go. She had to head back out to the Miller ranch and check on the cattle again. But when she entered, she overheard the Diner Divas discussing her and Max. She was going to ignore them until she heard *his* name.

"You know they only fought because Logan's back," Lou Ann Dobbs exclaimed in her southern drawl. "Everyone knows this, Cindy."

"Well, of course, Lou Ann. But do you know exactly what the issue was?" Cindy paused for effect. "Max is jealous! I saw Elizabeth chatting with Logan in his store the other day as though they were old friends." Cindy Macon's large pink pouf of hair bounced as she bobbed her head with her storytelling.

"No, you're telling it all wrong, Cindy. They were flirting! You know those two should be together." Martha Stanhope shook her head and sat up tall in her seat at the diner counter.

All four of the divas were sitting in their usual seats at the counter, where they held court each day and discussed everyone's lives in town as though they were the queens of Beacon Creek and everyone else their subjects to gossip and prattle on about.

"Well of course they were flirting. They are violently in love. I always told you they would get back together. Poor Max. Do you think my Lola Belle would help him get over his broken heart?" Goldie Walters had been trying to get Max and her granddaughter together since the day Max stepped into town. Not that Max had even noticed Lola Belle, but that didn't stop Goldie.

The grandmother wanted her twenty-three-year-old granddaughter settled already. Lola Belle was pretty, but not gorgeous. She was sweet and quiet, the complete opposite of her grandmother, but she was a bookworm. Lola was going to start her second year of a master's in library science in the fall. She wanted nothing more than to be a librarian. Most men in town hadn't given more than a passing thought when it came to the quiet and bookish girl.

Too bad Goldie never asked her granddaughter what she thought about Max. Then maybe, just maybe, she would have stopped dropping hints as giant as boulders on Max's step. Lola Belle was probably the only woman in town who didn't care for Max.

"Hi ladies. What's today's gossip?" Elizabeth asked. "Did you hear about old man Tom Addison? How did his surgery go?" She wanted them to stop talking about her.

Walking in on them discussing her love life wouldn't get them to stop—she knew that from experience. The only way to get the divas to move on was to introduce a new topic. Not that Elizabeth wanted to gossip, but maybe if the old biddies spoke about someone who'd just had surgery, they would inspire someone to go and check on him, maybe even get a group of people to make some meals to take over for his recovery period.

"Has anyone started the prayer chain for him? Or what about meals? Who's scheduling those? I'd like to sign up and bring him dinner one night." Elizabeth really did want to help the old postman. He always had a smile on his face whenever he delivered a letter or package to her at the ranch while she was growing up. He had retired a couple years ago, and the new mail person wasn't as nice. She missed seeing his crooked smile.

Cindy raised her hands and whooped. "Oh yes, dear me. That's my job. Thank you for the reminder. I have a list here somewhere." The woman had gone all gray years ago, but now she had pink-tinted hair.

She must have gone to the Blow-n-Style down the street that day, as not a single strand of hair was out of place, even after all her head bobbing. *The new stylist liked her hairspray a bit too much*, Elizabeth thought.

"Yes, Cindy. I need to sign up as well." Goldie, who had been sitting on the end, stood up and walked behind her friend and took the sheet out of her hand. "I'll sign up for tomorrow." She began to write her name down and stopped. "Does he have any dietary restrictions?"

While the ladies discussed what they thought Tom Addison should and should not eat, Elizabeth smiled and went to get her cup of coffee to go. She'd sign up later. Right now, she needed the Diner Divas to forget about her and focus on someone else for the rest of the day.

While Max was gone, Elizabeth took the time to think about their relationship and what he had said. She was convinced he was only stressed about what might have happened to her, and he really didn't believe what he'd said. How could he? Only a heartless moron would believe the garbage he'd spewed Monday night. No, it had to be fear that drove him to speak that way. Taking this week apart would do him good.

Sunday came much faster than Elizabeth was prepared for. While she loved her church and everyone who attended, she was leery about seeing Logan.

She had decided to sit in the back of the church again, but her twin sister grabbed her arm before she could sit down.

"Elizabeth, what are you doing? Come up front with the rest of the family."

Panic rose, and Elizabeth pulled her arm back. "Chloe, maybe you haven't heard? Logan's back. You know he's going to be sitting with his family. I can't do this." She shook her head and began to think of excuses to leave.

"Stop it," Chloe hissed. "Everyone is watching us."

Elizabeth scanned the crowd and realized she was going to be the talk of the town again if she didn't get control of her emotions. She plastered another fake smile on her face, like she had been doing all week, and hugged her sister. "I've missed you. How did your interviews go?"

"Really good. I think I'll be getting a few offers over the next week or so." Chloe's excitement was evident in the way she bounced on the balls of her feet. "We have to head to the ranch for supper today, so I can tell you all about it."

Elizabeth's twin had been out of town for ten days, with job interviews covering four different towns. She was glad her sister was back. She needed to talk to her about everything that had happened, and supper at the ranch would be the perfect time.

Fearing she would see Logan, Elizabeth sat at the far edge of the pew her family always commandeered at church. They took up almost two pews since the family was so large. The men in her family all were built for ranching, and with their broad shoulders they needed more space than the women did. So she had no problem hiding behind two of her larger brothers, Matthew and Mark.

Matthew smirked when he realized she was using his bulk to hide. He watched as she leaned forward and peered at the Hayes family, who sat across the aisle from the Manning family. When she had done it a third time, he decided to relieve her tension. "He's not going to be here today."

She frowned and looked up at her big brother. "What?"

"Logan. He had to stay home and watch his father this morning. The doctor still doesn't want Mr. Hayes to get out of bed or be alone. So, until further notice, they'll all take turns staying home to watch him." Matthew mussed her ponytail and chuckled.

"I... I wasn't looking for him." Elizabeth winced when she realized she had just lied in church. She said a quick prayer, asking God to forgive her, and then opened up the bulletin and pretended to be interested in the latest church news and schedule for summer. Their annual fall festival was coming soon, and she wanted to see what she could do to help with the planning. Other than Christmas, it was the biggest celebration in town, and she loved to be part of it all.

Besides, she had zero desire to discuss Logan with anyone, especially her big brother. He and Logan had been friends during their childhood, and she feared Matthew would try to get her to speak with Logan. Never again did she wish to speak to the man who had torn her heart out and made it impossible for her to trust anyone outside of her family.

Once the service started, she put the bulletin away and gave her full attention to the pastor. Today's message really hit home...hard.

It was about forgiveness.

The verse the pastor was reading enveloped her and caused her heart to stutter and then stop for a moment before picking up speed. She knew this was from God, and she needed to pay attention. She could almost hear her Lord telling her to listen to what he had for her today.

Mark 11:25 – *And when ye stand praying, forgive, if ye have ought against any: that your Father also which is in heaven may forgive you your trespasses.*

Elizabeth thought about her argument with Max, and her

fight with Bart and his gang, and realized she hadn't forgiven any of them. But she also hadn't spoken to Bart since their *incident*, as she preferred to call it. And she hoped never to see any of them again. However, she still needed to forgive Bart.

That was something she could do in her heart, even if Bart never knew.

While the pastor continued to share verses about forgiveness, she prayed. Elizabeth asked God to help her forgive those who had wronged her, like Bart and his gang, as well as Max. She was certain Max didn't mean what he'd said, but no matter what, she forgave him.

She also forgave Big Bart.

Elizabeth knew there was nothing she could do to combat Bart; she wasn't a law enforcement officer. All she could do was give the situation over to God and do her best to help the women on the street get the food and clothing they needed. She had even decided to begin witnessing to those she met.

No way was that one trip going to be it. Even her friends had expressed interest in going back. Harper had suggested they make up lunch sacks and hand out healthy meals to everyone they came into contact with.

Mia had suggested they find a church in the area to partner with so they could send the women somewhere for follow-up witnessing and help, where possible.

The woman Elizabeth met at the shelter that day seemed very nice and helpful. She would have to go back and talk to her and see if there was something that could be done to help more women get off the streets. Maybe her family's ranch could even do something. She had no idea what a group of homeless women could do on the ranch, but she felt led to ask her father and brother what, if anything, they could do on the ranch to help.

She realized she'd missed a lot of the service and decided to get a copy of the sermon so she could hear the rest of what the pastor had said. With all the decisions she had come to just from the first few minutes of the service, she knew the rest had to be really good. She would also share it with Max.

When she walked out of the church, she felt like several bales of hay had been taken off her shoulders. Most of her stress seemed to dissipate as she continued to make plans in her mind.

She was so in her head that she didn't see the person walking toward her, and instead of stopping, she walked right into her twin. "Oh, Chloe." She chuckled. "Sorry about that. I guess my head was in the clouds."

Chloe smirked. "Thinking about Logan?"

Small crinkle lines formed between Elizabeth's eyes and along the center of her forehead. "Why would I be thinking of him?"

Now it was Chloe's turn to be confused. "Well, duh. That sermon." Her hand flew up, pointing to the church building. "It seemed to really hit you. I saw you praying during the service a few times. Did you finally decide to forgive Logan?"

Elizabeth shook her head. "I'm not sure what you heard, but I heard that I needed to forgive Max and some bully in Bozeman." She never even considered needing to forgive Logan. Why would she?

She didn't even want to think about him. Every time she did, her heart ached and then her anger rose. That sorry excuse for a man did not deserve to be forgiven. Not once did he even try to ask her for forgiveness. It had been ten years, and all she wanted to do was forget the man ever existed.

"Um, I know you, sis. You haven't forgiven him for what he did to you. And it's eating you alive. Even after all these years, you're still torn up over it. Maybe if you forgive him, you'll be able to move on and get rid of the pain you've gripped so tightly over the years." Chloe knew her sister better than anyone. Even though they hadn't spoken about Logan in years, she knew her sister still hurt and needed to release that pain.

To change the topic, Elizabeth asked what her sister was doing for lunch that day, forgetting that she had already discussed it before church started.

Chloe blinked a few times. "I'm going to the ranch. We have family supper every Sunday."

Biting her lip, Elizabeth responded, "Oh, that's right." She shook her head. "I have to stop by the Miller farm really quick. I'll meet you at the ranch." She didn't normally work on Sundays. She and Milton took turns being on call during the Sabbath, and it was Milton's turn this week, but she needed to escape the knowing eyes of her sister, even if only for a few minutes.

Besides, the cattle needed checking in on at the Miller's ranch. She and Milton were confident they had quarantined all affected cattle, but you couldn't be too safe when it came to contagious respiratory diseases. There was only one day left of the quarantine, and she wanted to see how the calves were progressing as well.

CHAPTER 8

Logan stopped short right before he ran smack dab into a very familiar face. "Chloe. I see you still have your head in your phone? How many people do you run into each day?" He chuckled.

"Well I'll be. Elizabeth said you were back in town. Good to see you again." Her smile was warm and just as sweet as he remembered, which surprised him. His meeting with Lizzie—or Elizabeth, as she now preferred to be called— didn't go nearly so well. He thought for sure her twin would hate him.

"Nice to you see you." Standing at least a head above the auburn-haired girl who looked so much like the love of his life, he had to do something to get his mind off the woman he couldn't have. Even though the two girls were as different as night and day personality-wise, they still looked identical. Most people would have a difficult time telling them apart. But not Logan; he had always known the difference.

The woman in front of him didn't stir his heart like her sister did. But she did act as a conduit for the memories he was currently trying to block out.

"What's up? I thought you wanted out of this two-horse town, as you so fondly called it when we were all in high school." He patted the top of her head like he had always done. Growing up he'd planned to make her his sister-in-law, so as far back as he could remember he had always treated her that way.

Chloe slapped his hand away from her head. "Stop that. We're not kids anymore. And I am planning on leaving, just waiting for my new position to start."

"Really? When?" He was surprised. Even though Chloe always talked about leaving Beacon Creek, he never thought she'd leave her large, loving family behind.

"End of summer. But don't say anything—it's not been announced yet." She shrugged. Chloe never was very good at keeping secrets. Not that she went around blabbing, but if asked a direct question, she usually answered truthfully. Only when she was sworn to secrecy did she keep quiet.

Later that night when Logan sat down to dinner with his family, he had both Chloe and Elizabeth on his mind. He worried about Lizzie losing her sister. Well, maybe *losing* was a harsh term. But if Chloe did move away, he wondered how Liz… Elizabeth would handle it.

It was going to be tough remembering to call her Elizabeth. She'd been Lizzie to him for as long as he could remember.

"Logan, Earth to Logan. Are you here?" His sister, Leah, waved her hands in front of his face.

"Hm? Oh, sorry. I was woolgathering, I suppose. What did you ask?" Logan looked across the table at his kid sister, who wasn't actually a kid anymore. When did she grow up so much? He really should have come home more often.

Leah was tall for a woman. She had to be pushing five feet nine inches, or very close to it. Her long brown hair had a silky shine to it he didn't remember from when she was a kid. Her chocolate-brown eyes made her face appear soft and kind. Or maybe that was just all Leah herself. She was rather beautiful.

His eyes narrowed and his brows furrowed. "Are you dating anyone?" Completely ignoring his sister's question, he turned the tables on her. It was high time he took up his big brother responsibilities and made sure his sister wasn't seeing any scoundrel.

Her cheeks flushed, and she stammered out, "Uh, not really." She took a bite of her chicken breast and tried to keep her mouth full so she wouldn't have to answer her brother's embarrassing questions.

Their mother laughed. It was the first time since Logan had returned home that he'd heard her laugh—*really* laugh.

Both brother and sister turned their gazes to their mother and waited for her to finish. Even though Logan was happy his mother was showing some signs of joy, he really wasn't too keen on being the brunt of a joke he had no clue about.

Out of the corner of his eye, he noticed that his sister looked just as clueless as he did.

"What's so funny?" Logan asked.

His mother wiped the laugh tears from her eyes and looked at her only son. "You two. It's as though you never left. You're both acting just like you did ten years ago." She smiled lovingly at her two children, sighed, and began eating her dinner again.

Leah looked at her brother with a question in her eyes.

He shrugged, and they both went back to eating dinner.

"Have you heard anything from Elizabeth since you saw her the other day?" Leah asked between bites of broccoli and chicken.

He shook his head. "I saw her down the street and was

going to talk to her, but she crossed the road to get away from me. I didn't want to chase her."

"Well, I dare say after the last sermon she's been thinking long and hard about forgiving you." Leah smiled before going back to her favorite meal.

"What do you mean? What was the sermon about?" Logan's brow furrowed, and he put his fork down on his plate and sat up straight.

"Well, you need to get the CD. It was about forgiveness. I looked over at Elizabeth during the sermon and noticed she was doing a lot of praying. I think God was speaking to her about the need to forgive you." His sister beamed with a knowing smile. She had always wanted her brother to marry Elizabeth, and was almost as heartbroken as Lizzie was when Logan broke up with her.

In fact, the entire town was upset with Logan when he broke Elizabeth's heart. Everyone had been planning on the two of them marrying since they first began dating.

"I doubt she'll ever forgive me. If she hasn't done so yet, she never will." He hung his head and lost his appetite. Every time he thought about how much he'd hurt the only woman he would ever love, he wanted to strangle himself.

He had resigned himself to her pack of brothers coming and beating him up any time he came to town. Instead, they either gave him the cold shoulder or told him how stupid he was to let the best woman he'd ever meet get away. Logan knew they were right. He was stupid. Grade AA stupid.

His momma had stayed quiet during the conversation between her two children, but when she saw the despondence in Logan's bearing, she knew she had to speak up. "Logan, I think you should get the CD. It might help you as well."

"I don't need to forgive her. Lizzie did nothing wrong. It was all me."

"Exactly. You need to forgive yourself. You can't keep wallowing in your guilt like a pig in the mud. You have to forgive yourself and move on. If that means without Elizabeth, then so be it. You need to leave your cares at God's feet and let Him decide what's best for the two of you." The loving smile on Judith's face warmed Logan's heart.

She was right, of course. His mother always knew exactly what to say to her kids. And most of the time it included something wise from the Bible.

"You're right, Momma. I think I'll spend some time in prayer tonight. See what the Lord has to show me. And tomorrow I'll stop by the church office and get a copy of the sermon."

"That's my boy." His momma had never quite gotten the hint that her son was no longer a boy, but a man. However, Logan had learned not to correct his mother when she called him her boy. It was her way of displaying her love for her son, and it would upset her if he didn't accept her display of affection. Even if it did rankle him.

Once the dishes were cleaned and put away, Logan went to check on his pops and then headed to his room for some quiet time with the Lord. After their discussion at dinner, Logan knew his family wouldn't bother him that night. They were right: he needed to lay his cares at the feet of his Savior and let the Lord guide his actions.

"Dear Heavenly Father, I know you understand all. You know what I'm going through right now. I need to give my cares over to you. I still love Lizzie, and I think I always will. But she won't forgive me. Not that I deserve her forgiveness, but I would like it. My heart aches for her friendship and love. If nothing else, can we be friends again? Can you help her to forgive me?" He wasn't really sure what else to ask for, so he began reading his Bible. He looked up verses on forgiveness and spent the next hour reading and praying.

By the time he went to bed, he was exhausted from pouring out his emotions and cares to the Lord, but felt much lighter. Logan came to understand what it meant when pastors extolled the virtues of sharing one's burdens with the Lord. Over the next few days, he was happier and lighter than he had been in years.

Even his mother and sister noticed the change in his countenance.

One day at the store, Leah came up to him during a lull in customers. "Hey, what's gotten into you?"

Logan stopped restocking the shelf of dog food and turned around to look at his sister. "What do you mean?"

Leah's hand flourished in the air. "I don't know. You seem so different this week. Have you spoken with Elizabeth?"

The smile on Logan's face dissipated, and longing filled his eyes. "No, she's still ignoring me. But I've given my cares over to the Lord. Since there's nothing I can do to make Lizzie forgive me, I had to lay this issue at the feet of my Lord and Savior. And you know what?"

"What?"

"I feel so much better. Better than I have since that fateful day over ten years ago. I made a huge mistake and never knew how to fix it. Well, that's not true. All I had to do was talk to her before the summer started and we could have fixed things, but I didn't do it. Even though I felt it was what I needed to do." Logan picked up a can of Pedigree dog food and began restocking the shelf again.

"I prayed after we spoke earlier this week and I read a lot about forgiveness in the Bible. I even asked Dottie for a copy of the CD. This week I've learned that I can't make Lizzie forgive me, but God can work on her heart if it's His will for us to get back together, or even to be friends again."

"Is that what you want? To get back together?" Leah practically whispered her question. She didn't want to scare off Elizabeth, but she'd do anything to help her sister get back with the love of her life.

Even his parents wanted him to marry his high school sweetheart. They were both so disappointed when he told them what he had done. He knew they loved him, but their disappointment hurt him and was also what helped him to realize what a huge mistake he had made.

His mother told him that had he broken up with her because he wasn't in love with her, they would have understood and supported the decision. But they knew Logan was head over heels in love with the girl, and they couldn't understand why he did it. His father assumed it was because he wanted to sow some wild oats in college and expected Lizzie to wait for him, which was just plain stupid in Hank's mind.

"Never let a woman like Elizabeth Manning sit around waiting. Someone else will come and win her heart. She's too good of a catch." Hank had already loved Elizabeth like a daughter, and had it not been his only son who'd broken her heart, he would have planted a fist in the man's face who hurt the lovely Lizzie.

Originally, that was part of what kept him away—the look he'd received from his parents, and even his sister. He couldn't stand the displeasure in their eyes. His original plan had been to go to college and then work for a couple years in marketing before coming home and helping out with the family store. He had stayed away so long because it was easier.

Even the townsfolk had been upset with him for breaking Lizzie's heart.

Now that he was back and had seen Lizzie—Elizabeth—he knew he had to do whatever it took to win her back, or at least her friendship. Logan had had many friends over the years, but none were as good as Elizabeth. While yes, he did miss her lips on his, what he missed more was her friendship. The way she always supported him and helped him make good decisions. He never should have made that decision without her input. He knew what she would have said, but it was too late to lament over what might have been.

Now it was time to repent for his mistakes and be a friend to Liz… Elizabeth, and maybe in time she would forgive him.

Logan moved one section over and picked up the bags of dry dog food and stacked them on the shelf. "Yes, Leah. I want my Lizzie back. But I know I can't make it happen. God has to intervene in this situation. I bungled it so badly ten years ago that I need His heavenly help."

Leah patted his back. "Good. I know just what we need to do to get her away from Max and back in your loving arms."

He turned around quickly and held up his hands. "Whoa, wait a minute. I don't know about any of your plans. They usually blow up in my face. I think we should wait on God to work this out."

His sister shook her head. "Don't you understand anything? Sometimes God uses others to help you out. It's not like he's going to come down in human form again and work to get Elizabeth back to you. He uses others to do His work. Like me." She beamed, and Logan couldn't help but laugh.

"That may be, but what do you think He's going to have you do? I was thinking it was a heart issue for Lizzie. She needs to forgive me. You can't make someone forgive another person—only God can do that." Logan knew forgiveness had to come from the inside of a person's heart or soul. Not even his meddling sister could get Lizzie to change her heart.

She put a finger to her chin and looked up. "Hmm, that may be, but first you need to show her that you care. Right now she only sees the Logan Hayes from ten years ago who yanked her heart out and stomped on it before he walked away. You need to show her that you're here to stay, and you want her forgiveness. That you still love her."

He chuckled. "And how do I do that?"

With a saucy smile, she walked away and glanced back over her shoulder. "Leave it all in my hands, big brother. It will all work out."

Logan wasn't sure if he should be happy or afraid of what Leah was up to. All he knew was that he needed help. If God did choose to use Leah to help him, he wasn't going to look a gift horse in the mouth.

CHAPTER 9

All week long, Elizabeth and Max had been playing phone tag. They only had a couple of very brief calls. No conversation had been long enough to discuss the issue of Elizabeth going to Bozeman to help the homeless. Not to mention the fact that Elizabeth wanted the conversation to be face to face and not over the phone.

By the time Max had come back to town, a week had passed. On Friday night they were to attend a church BBQ fundraiser for the harvest festival. That would be the first time she had seen him in person since their argument. She did not want to discuss the topic in front of the entire town.

"Max, when this is over, what do you say we find a quiet spot in the town park to continue our discussion from earlier?" Elizabeth whispered when no one was close enough to hear.

"What discussion?" He furrowed his brow and acted like there was nothing to discuss.

"The one about Bozeman and helping the homeless. Surely you didn't mean those horrible things you said." She looked around to make sure no one could overhear what they were talking about and plastered on another fake smile. She was getting very tired of having to do so.

"I thought I made my feelings very clear. Didn't you understand?" Max smiled and nodded at one of his clients who was coming near.

"This isn't over. We have to discuss this further." She turned around and walked away before Mr. Jones got close enough to hear her. She had no desire to begin the argument anew in public. They were going to discuss this issue that night.

Chloe had been sitting far enough away that Elizabeth didn't notice her, but her twin sister saw the exchange between the two and knew exactly what that particular smile meant. Leah was also sitting next to her.

"Chloe, I think it's time we stepped in and got our siblings to talk things over." Leah took a bite of her very tender and juicy strip steak. Today's beef had come from the Triple J Ranch, and she knew their meat was the best in town, maybe even the state. She hoped there would some left over to take home for her pops as well as for lunch the next day. Nothing was better than a cold steak sandwich.

Her mouth watered with the smoky flavors of the grill and steak. The meat practically melted in her mouth before it went down.

"Mmm, this is good. Your ranch always provides the best steaks for the BBQs. Thank you." Leah shrugged when she noticed the sauce dripping from her fingers and licked them clean. Then she wiped her hands on her napkin and chuckled at her lack of manners.

"Thanks, and I completely agree. Let's hurry and finish up, then take a walk. We have to do something before those two lose their chance to be together." Chloe finished her steak and downed the last of the sweet tea in her cup before standing to throw her trash away.

"Here, let me get that plate for you, Mrs. Merkle. Do you need anything else?"

The elderly lady smiled, and with a shaking hand gave her empty plate to Chloe. "No, I'm good, young lady. Thank you for your help." Mrs. Merkle took a napkin and dabbed her mouth like a proper lady would have a hundred years ago. For all Chloe knew, Mrs. Merkle might have been one hundred, or pretty close to it.

"Those Manning girls have always been so polite and helpful." Mrs. Merkle smiled at Cindy Macon, who sat next to her.

Mrs. Macon, the founding member of the Diner Divas, nodded, and the pink pouf of hair on her head wiggled but stayed in place due to all the Aqua Net she had sprayed on her hairdo before leaving the house. "Yes, yes they are." She watched as Leah and Chloe walked away and knew those two young ladies were up to something. Something she wanted in on.

"Alright, with the tensions between Max and Elizabeth, now might be the best time to step in." Chloe stopped next to the small river flowing on the outskirts of the park and looked back at the main picnic area.

Leah narrowed her eyes and watched as Elizabeth walked away from Max with her fake smile on, but she turned directions when she was about to approach the spot where her brother, Logan, was standing and chatting with a few of the elderly men who enjoyed playing checkers and chess inside the store. "How are we going to get them to talk? She can't even stand to walk near my brother, let alone talk to him."

Elizabeth's twin twirled a lock of hair around her finger and nodded. "I think we need to find a way to get them locked in a room or something. I don't think Elizabeth will agree to be in the same room as your brother again. At least not any time soon."

Nodding, Leah agreed. "Do you think we could lock them in the overstock room at the store?"

"Do you have a lock on the outside of the room?"

"We do."

Chloe thought about it for a minute, then asked, "How will we get both of them inside together at the same time?"

"Well, I could easily get my brother in there. All I have to do is ask him to get something from inside the room. But getting Elizabeth inside while Logan is still there might be an issue." Leah bit her lower lip and considered ways to trick Elizabeth.

Chloe tapped a finger to her chin and stood up straighter when a light went off in her head. "I got it! You tell Logan you need something heavy from the room. Then text me the moment he leaves your side. I'll be close by with Elizabeth. I'll tell her I need to show her something at your store."

Leah held up a hand. "Wait, how are you going to get Elizabeth to willingly come into the store? She knows that Logan's working there now."

"Don't worry, I got it covered. Just text me when he heads into the storeroom and I'll be right there with my sister." The gleam in Chloe's eyes told Leah she had something fun planned.

Leah wasn't the least bit worried about getting her brother to do what she wanted. She probably could have told him her plan and he would have agreed. From what she had seen the past week, Logan would do just about anything to get a few minutes alone with Elizabeth.

What she worried about was whether Chloe could deliver Elizabeth to the store. If they couldn't get her into the room, then their plan would fail for sure. She wasn't even sure if getting the two of them into a room would help matters or make them worse.

All she could do was hope and pray that if they were forced together, then maybe Elizabeth would forgive Logan and they could get back together again.

"Let's try this for Tuesday afternoon. What do you think?" Leah looked out and noticed her brother heading her way. "Shh, Logan's coming."

"Sounds good," Chloe agreed, and began thinking how she could wrangle Elizabeth into the overstock room at the general store before Logan stopped next to his sister.

"Ladies, how are you both doing this fine afternoon?" Logan had been watching them out of the corner of his eye and knew they were up to something. But he wasn't sure if it was going to be bad or good.

His sister was great at manipulating situations, and he wondered if she was going to cause a scene or if her machinations were about something outside of the BBQ. He narrowed his eyes when his sister smiled at him. When Chloe's smiled matched hers, he knew they had something in the works.

Logan weighed his options and decided to let the cards fall where they may. "I hope you two aren't up to no good."

Leah put a hand to her chest. "Who, me? You know me, I'm always as sweet as an angel." She batted her eyelashes, making herself look even guiltier.

When Logan chuckled, both girls giggled and left him standing alone by the water.

Elizabeth had kept her eyes on Max as she walked around and greeted the townsfolk. When she saw that Max had finished his conversation with his client, she made her way to him as he walked toward her.

"I think we need to talk." She looked around and took his hand in hers before heading to a storage shed behind the picnic grounds. Elizabeth led Max behind the shed.

He looked around for prying eyes or ears, then let go of her hand. "What didn't you understand? I don't want you anywhere near the homeless people—it's too dangerous. Especially now that that guy has threatened you and your friends."

"Are you upset because you think I was in danger? Or do you really believe that nonsense you spewed about the homeless not being worthy of my help?" She tilted her head as she waited for his response.

He took a deep breath in through his nose and slowly let it out of his mouth to calm himself down. It would do no good to get into an argument while half the town was only a few hundred yards away. "I do believe that the homeless are where they want to be. If they wanted to work and make a living, they could. They just choose *not* to work."

Elizabeth held up a hand. "Wait, you think all homeless could work but that they choose not to? Really?" She put both hands on her hips and stared at the man in front of her.

Who is this man? He seemed so nice and helpful with the

church and with others in town. Why does he hate the home-less so much? Elizabeth couldn't understand what Max had been saying; it was so incongruous with his actions.

"Yes, I do. There could be a handful of people on the streets who really couldn't do anything else, but for the most part, all who are homeless are in that situation because they're lazy and choose *not* to work." He emphasized the *not* to drive home the point of it being their choice, not a situation they had no control over. Max really did believe what he said.

"Look, I've seen homeless people turn down day jobs and keep sitting on a street corner begging for money. Then they take that money and spend it on drugs. If they really wanted to get their act together, they would stop using drugs and get themselves cleaned up and search for a job. There are a lot of agencies around to help those who truly want help."

"But Max, not all homeless are on drugs. I agree, some do drugs and don't care to get themselves cleaned up. But I think that if they had someone to care about them and help them, they could get cleaned up and get off the streets. I don't believe any of those living on the streets really want to be there. Some have mental issues that make it difficult for them to fit in with society, so they take to the streets where they can be anonymous. However, if given the chance I think a good portion of them would straighten up and get a job to support themselves." Elizabeth hadn't met many homeless people, but she had watched them. Sure, some of them were more into drugs than actually getting a job, but most did want to get off the streets and become active members of society. The problem was that they didn't always have the skillset they needed to get a job.

With the advancement in computers and technology, so many unskilled workers had lost their jobs, and there wasn't anything else they could do. More and more automation or outsourcing had caused large groups of people to become unemployed. Those who had lost their jobs to technology didn't always know how to combat the issues and find employment.

Elizabeth screwed up her lips and huffed. "Most of the people living on the streets just need a little hand to help them get back on their feet. Some could use job training, others could just use help with writing a resume, or a computer to use for applying for a job. I think we could help get a lot of people off the streets with just a little bit of love and some help with job placements."

Max shook his head. "No, I've seen others try to help homeless get real jobs and they weren't interested. They think it's easier to live on the streets and do what you want than it is to actually work."

She shook her head. "No, that's not true of all the people who are stuck on the street. How can you think like this? I don't understand you. When it comes to the church and others around town, you're always one of the first to step up and help. But when it comes to people who could really use your help—help that just might change their lives for the better—you turn your back on them. How is this?" She threw her hands in the air in frustration.

He heaved a heavy sigh and looked her in the eyes. "Elizabeth, you're just too gullible. The homeless are selfish and lazy. They only want others to do the work for them. It's easier to live in a tent in some back alley and beg for handouts than it is to get an actual job and take care of responsibilities like an adult. You're too nice to understand them. If you give them money, food, or clothes, they'll never get off the streets."

"You're wrong, Max. I agree that some are like that. Probably Big Bart is just like what you described, but most of those living on the streets are there because something happened to them and they couldn't get out of a hole. It may have been something they did on their own, but without anyone to help them, they won't be able to get out of it. All they need is a little love and understanding. Then maybe, just maybe, they can get a job and an apartment and begin contributing to society once again. The more homeless who get off the street, the fewer men there'll be like Big Bart. He could be forced to get a real job and pay taxes like the rest of us if he loses too many of the homeless he threatens to do his bidding."

Max interrupted. "I'm sorry, but you're wrong. If you help those people, they won't try to get a real job. They'll keep draining you and never take responsibility for themselves. Then men like Bart will continue to make money off the backs of those who beg for him."

She shook her head and sighed. "I don't understand you. I thought you were a nice guy who wanted to help others. But you only seem to want to help those who can help you in return. That's not generosity, that's selfishness."

Max's nostrils flared, and he took two steps closer to Elizabeth. With clenched teeth he whispered, "That's not true, and you know it. I just don't think it's helping the homeless when you keep giving them handouts. Even Jesus said we should teach people to fish for themselves, and not to just give them fish."

"He meant that we should help our brothers and sisters to get jobs so they can take care of themselves, yes. But He also said we should help the poor. If we can help the poor to eat and clothe themselves while we're teaching them to fish, then all the better. But we can't look away from the homeless and treat them like trash. That will only reinforce the way they look at themselves and keep them down. We have to build them up so they can learn to fish for themselves." She sucked her lower lip into her mouth and began to wonder if Max was right for her or not.

Until that day, she'd honestly thought Max was a good guy, someone who might help her get over Logan. Then she would be able to give her heart to him. But as she took off her blinders and saw the real man standing before her, she doubted they were a good match.

Great, another man who hid who he really was and only wanted what served him best. She was beginning to think that maybe the reason Max was so helpful to everyone was just a ploy to get them to trust him so he could sell them more tractors or services. Only a truly selfish person would act in such a way.

She didn't want anything to do with selfish people, but she wasn't sure she was ready yet to give up the only man since Logan who had attracted her. The only man she'd enjoyed being with over the past ten years.

"I know you just got back from a business trip, but I think I need time alone to think about all of this. You may not be the man I thought you were." She couldn't look him in the eyes. Elizabeth knew if she did, she'd be trapped in his kind eyes and forgive him. She wasn't ready to forgive his selfishness. He didn't deserve it.

Two days later, Chloe had come up with a plan to get her sister into the general store while Leah worked to get Logan into the storeroom.

"Logan, can you help me with a few of the fifty-pound bags of dog food? They're a little bit heavy for me." Leah smiled innocently up at her brother.

"What? Now that I'm here, you're too weak to carry bags?" He smirked at her, knowing she was being lazy. His sister had been hauling the large bags of feed since she started high school. There was no way she needed help.

When he came into the store on Monday, he half expected her to pull some sort of prank on him after the way she'd been scheming with Chloe at the church picnic. When nothing out of the ordinary happened all day, he thought he might have been overreacting. Now, though, he knew she was up to something. It was smart of her to wait until Tuesday. He might have forgotten what he'd overheard if he hadn't been so caught up in trying to figure out her game.

"No, I just know that you need to get back into shape. I'm not sure what you did in LA for exercise, but whatever it was, it didn't help you." She squeezed his biceps and shook her head.

Logan swatted her hand away and exclaimed, "Hey, my

guns are bigger now than they've ever been. I'll have you know I worked out regularly in a gym while I was away." He puffed his chest out and felt a small amount of pride at the way his body had developed.

His sister shook her head and pursed her lips. "Sorry bro, but a gym just doesn't do the same for a body as actual hard labor in the store or on a ranch." She shrugged and headed toward the storeroom with her phone in her back pocket.

Chloe and her sister were walking down the main road in town, heading toward the diner. "Oh, I need to head into the general store for an order I placed. Let's go there before lunch just to see if it's in yet."

Elizabeth shook her head and stopped on the sidewalk two stores away from Logan's family store. "How about I head over to the diner and get us a booth and order you a tea?" She had zero desire to see Logan again, and was planning on never entering the general store unless she knew he wasn't there.

Sighing, Chloe took her sister's arm and pulled her forward. "Come on, He Who Shall Not Be Named isn't in the store this morning. You're safe."

"How do you know he isn't?" Elizabeth hesitantly followed behind her sister. She could have yanked her arm away, but decided to move forward and see if the store really was safe.

"I heard him talking yesterday about having to deliver an order and being gone most of today. Don't worry—you'll be fine."

Not really sure what to do, she followed her sister into the town's only general store.

CHAPTER 10

The bell above the door jingled, and Leah told her brother she'd help the customer.

When she left the storeroom, he was sorting through the mess she had purposely made with the bags of dog food mixed with feed for the horses. She knew he'd be busy for at least ten more minutes before he wondered what his sister was up to.

With a devious smile and the thought that they might actually succeed at their mission, Leah walked toward the front of the store with some pep in her step.

"Chloe, Elizabeth, how can I help you today?" Leah's smile brightened her face as she stepped closer to her partner in crime.

"Hi Leah, I came in to see if my special order had arrived yet." The glint in Chloe's eyes would have tipped Elizabeth off to something if she had been facing her sister. Instead, her back was toward her twin as she looked at her partner in crime and waited for the sign to get things going.

"Yes, as a matter of fact, it came in with this morning's delivery. If you'll come with me, you can pick it up now." Leah waved for the girls to follow her as she headed toward the back room where her brother unknowingly awaited their trap.

"Why don't I just wait out here for you?" Elizabeth asked as she looked around the store, hesitant to head to the back where Logan could come in if he finished his delivery early.

Leah and Chloe stiffened and looked at each other. Chloe stuttered, "Ahh," and her eyes opened wide as she tried to come up with a reason to get her sister into the back.

"Actually, you might need to help your sister carry it out. The box is kinda big." Leah's quick thinking saved the day, and Elizabeth shrugged before following the scheming girls to the back.

When they arrived at the storeroom door, Leah opened it. "Please." She held the door open and motioned for Elizabeth to enter first. Chloe was right behind her.

But before Chloe could enter, Leah slammed the door and engaged the bolt and put the lock on it. She swiped her hands —"There, that's how it's done"—and put them on her hips. "Come on, let's get up front and leave them alone for a while. Something tells me they're going to be a bit loud at first."

Both girls giggled and headed to the front of the store with thoughts of late fall or early winter wedding bells ringing in their ears.

Elizabeth turned around when she heard the door slam and tried the handle. The door wouldn't budge. She pounded a hand against it and yelled. Nothing. "Come on, open up. Ha ha ha. Really funny, Leah."

She turned around when she heard the sound of boots slapping on the concrete floor. When she saw who it was, she put a hand to her chest. "Geez, you scared me. What are you doing in here?"

"I think the better question is, what are *you* doing in

here?" Logan looked at the closed door behind Elizabeth and scowled.

"I think our sisters locked us up in here. Together." She matched his scowl and vowed to get her sister back for this prank.

Logan walked to the door and pulled on the handle.

"Don't bother—they locked us in." Elizabeth sighed and stepped away.

He continued to pull on the door and yelled out, "Hey, this isn't cool. It's also a fire hazard. Leah, I'm going to kill you if you don't open this door right away!" He knew it was futile, but he had to try anyway. Even though he wanted time with Elizabeth, he didn't want it this way.

Forcing Elizabeth into a corner wasn't the way to get her to open up to him.

"I'm sorry. My sister means well, but her idea of helping is waaaaaayyyyy off." He sliced his hand through the air, huffed, and walked to the back of the room and pulled his cell phone out of his pocket. "I'll text her."

"It wasn't just your sister—it was mine as well." She pulled her phone out of her purse and texted her sister. She didn't move her eyes from the screen as she waited for a response. After five minutes of waiting, she sighed and put her phone in her back pocket after turning the ringer back on. "Looks like we're stuck here."

Logan ran his fingers through his hair. "Again, I'm sorry. But since we are alone, can we talk?"

The fear that shone in her eyes was enough to tell him she wasn't ready yet.

"I don't think so." Elizabeth walked to the other side of the room and sat down against the far wall.

At the front of the store, Leah turned to Chloe. "Let's go

back and check on them. I wonder if they're talking, or something else?" Leah giggled.

"Um, I doubt they'll be doing anything other than glaring at each other right now. My sister is still really mad at your brother for what he did."

Leah quirked her lips and thought for a minute. "I was really mad at him, too. I have no clue why he refused to call her up and apologize when he realized he made a big mistake."

"Men."

"Yeah, men," Leah grumbled.

After a few moments of awkward silence, Chloe decided to change the subject.

"Soooo, I hear you're dating that new guy who runs the Banner ranch. What's his name?" Chloe wiggled her brows and waited for Leah to answer.

A dreamy sigh escaped her lips, and she stared out into space. "Yeah, Westin is really nice. He's such a gentleman, and those blue-gray eyes of his mesmerize me every time I look into them."

Chloe giggled. "I guess you've found your man?"

She shook her head and felt the heat from a blush creep up her neck and into her cheeks. "I don't know. It's too soon to tell. What about you? You dating anyone?"

Chloe shook her head. "Nope, I'm too busy to think about men right now."

All Chloe could think about was getting a job away from this two-horse town and meeting new people. She hadn't met anyone interesting in town in years. In fact, she couldn't remember her last date. It had to be at least two years since someone asked her out.

Logan was tired of waiting for Elizabeth to be ready to speak with him. They had been in the room for close to thirty minutes without speaking since they were first locked in. He took a deep breath and made his way to the back, where Elizabeth had retreated.

"I'm sorry to bug you, but since we're in here, I thought maybe we could talk this out. Just so we can at least be in the same room moving forward. What do you think?" He stood a few feet away, not wanting to put any pressure on her, but close enough that they didn't have to yell across the room.

She sighed and looked down at her hands in her lap. Then she shrugged. She couldn't get her voice to work, but she knew he was right. Now that he was back for good, and ran the general store, she'd have to talk to him some time.

Maybe it was time to find out why he'd done what he did. She had always wondered what had made him break up with her. She'd told her mom she thought he had met someone in college, but Leah told her that wasn't the case. No one really knew why he'd broken her heart.

If Leah was to be believed, Logan regretted it. But he'd never called her up or written her a letter to apologize and ask her to get back together. She was confused and hurt, and he ignored her...for ten years.

He sat on the ground, oddly enough, next to the shelf of dog food he had been rearranging earlier. "First, I want to apologize and ask you for your forgiveness. I was a stupid kid when I broke up with you, and I know I did it all wrong."

While he looked at her, she kept her face tilted down and nervously counted on her fingers.

He waited a beat for her to say something—anything. But when she kept quiet, he continued, "I never should have broken up with you. I regretted it the moment I did it, but thought it was what was best for you."

Still she sat in silence.

"Ah." he rubbed his chin. "I know I hurt you, and it was a

stupid reason. I wish you wouldn't hate me. We started out as friends, and I hope one day we can be friends again."

She wiped a tear from her cheek. "You still haven't told me why."

Finally, he thought. At least she'd spoken to him. However, the *why* of the breakup was rather embarrassing, especially now, ten years later. "Well, you're going to think it's stupid. I know I did then, and I still do now."

She looked up, and her red-rimmed eyes stabbed him through to his heart.

He slouched and knew he had to tell her, but at the same time he wanted to pull her into his arms and hold her and never let go. His heartbeat picked up, and he felt sweat build up on his brow. It was now or never. He finally had the chance to talk to her and tell her everything.

Just as he was about to open his mouth and tell her the idiotic reason why he'd done what he did, the door opened.

No one walked in, but it swung open and fresh air made its way inside the room. Elizabeth jumped up and ran out of the room before Logan could ask her to stay.

He stood up and ran a hand through his unruly hair for the umpteenth time that day and wished he had ten more minutes in hell with her. Telling her his story was important, not only for him, but for her as well. They both needed to heal and get past this bump in the road. Well, it was more like a sinkhole, but they needed to get around it and find their way back to each other.

His heart couldn't take seeing her anymore without the right to hold her in his arms. He doubted she'd even let him talk to her again. Maybe his sister had done the right thing. While Elizabeth would most likely be mad at her sister for a while, Logan had decided not to get Leah back for the prank.

When he walked out of the room and into the store, only Leah remained.

"Well?" She looked at him expectantly.

He shook his head. "I needed about ten more minutes. I think it's time to start praying for another chance to talk to her. Who knows, maybe this time we won't waste it with silence."

Leah held up her hand. "Wait. You two were silent the entire time? But... But she ran out of here with tears streaming down her cheeks. What happened?"

Logan furrowed his brow and stepped toward the exit to chase after her, but Leah stopped him with a hand on his shoulder. She shook her head. "She'll be fine. Just tell me what happened."

A sardonic smile crossed his face, and he looked out the window.

When Elizabeth and Chloe made it outside, Chloe headed toward the diner, but Elizabeth made off for her car. She was done. Done with men, done with her sister, just plain done. She wanted nothing more than to lay down and never get up again.

When Chloe noticed her sister wasn't with her, she turned around and ran to catch up to her. "Wait, the diner is the other way."

Elizabeth held up her hand. "No. Leave me alone." After two more steps, she stopped and turned on her sister. "How could you?"

"I'm sorry. We thought that if you two were forced together, you'd make up." She wasn't about to say *kiss* and make up, but that was what she had hoped for.

Elizabeth felt betrayed, and worse than she had in many years. She still didn't have the answers she needed, but she wasn't about to turn around and head back to Logan. Not while she was crying. The last thing she wanted was for him to see her crying.

"You had no right to lock us in that room. I feel worse now than I did before." She turned and headed back to her car, ignoring her sister's protestations.

Chloe stopped about five paces away from her sister's car. "I'm sorry. I really am. Please forgive me, but I thought you two needed the push to talk. Did he at least tell you why he did it?"

She shook her head, and without another word got into her car, locked the doors, and drove away.

Rats! What were we thinking? Chloe hoped she and Leah hadn't made things worse, but she still believed they'd done the right thing. Maybe they had just let them out too soon.

Three days later, Elizabeth still wasn't speaking to her sister. She was, however, feeling guilty over how she'd reacted. With that feeling in mind, she set out to see Chloe and talk about possibly joining them on another expedition to Bozeman to help the homeless. Harper had called last night and wanted to get another trip set up for the following weekend.

"Elizabeth! I'm so happy to see you. Come on in." Chloe

opened the door to her small rented house that was within walking distance of the local clinic where she worked. She managed the billing.

Elizabeth smiled and entered.

"Do you forgive me?" Chloe asked.

Elizabeth pulled her twin in for a tight hug. "Of course I do. Can you forgive me for freezing you out the past three days?"

"You know it. Now come in and have a seat. Would you like a soda, or water?"

"Water, please." She walked into the open-space kitchen and dining area and sat at the table while her sister grabbed a bottle of cold water from the refrigerator.

The twins rarely fought, but when they did, they made up quickly and easily. Nothing ever kept them mad at each other for very long. Usually within a day all was well between the two cowgirls. If an argument lasted more than a week, their mother would step in and help them clear the air. That had only happened twice. Both times were in high school, when their hormones were churning like mad. Since they'd graduated high school, three days was the longest they'd ever gone without talking.

"What brings you here?" Chloe set the bottle down on the table and took her seat.

"I wanted to see if you'd be up for a trip to Bozeman a week from tomorrow to help with the homeless. Harper's called a few of the girls and wants us all to pass out more essentials. She also called the local church, and they're going to help." Elizabeth took a drink of the water and waited for her sister to respond.

"I like it. I don't have any plans that day. Should we all get together the night before and bag the supplies up, like you did last time?"

Elizabeth nodded. "I'm also thinking we should bring some guys along this time—you know, just in case that Big Bart guy gets any ideas. I don't want some punk to stop us from helping others, but we should be smart about this. Sophia is coming, and she's tough as nails, but we still should have some guys to help scare off the Darwinian misfires."

"Agreed. Will Max be able to join us?"

Elizabeth scowled and set her bottle back on the table before taking another drink. "No, he wants nothing to do with helping the homeless. He's even ordered me to stop helping."

"What?" Chloe shook her head. "Are we talking about the same guy who's always the first to sign up and help the church or the town with something? That can't be right."

Her sister nodded and bit her lip. "Don't you think it's strange that he's so willing to help the residents in this town, but not those in Bozeman?"

"Well, it is different. We don't have any homeless here in Beacon Creek. But did he say why he hates the homeless? I don't get it. He seems like the type of guy who'd be happy to help. Or at the very least come along as our muscle." Chloe worried her bottom lip.

"I know, right? But he says the homeless are there because they want to be. He thinks they're all lazy drug users. We haven't exactly spoken much since then. Plus, he's getting ready for the big race in three weeks, so he's been a bit distracted."

"I can't believe someone so level-headed loves to compete in demolition derby races." Chloe chuckled and took a sip of her sweet tea.

"It's actually a lot of fun. I enjoy watching the races and rooting for him. It's kinda like watching hockey fights, just one big mess. But instead of being on ice, it's usually on a muddy dirt track." Elizabeth took a short sip of her water and set the bottle back down on the table.

"Well, count me in for the trip to Bozeman. I'd actually like to meet this Big Bart guy and give him a piece of my mind. How can anyone take advantage of those living on the streets and then beat them up when they can't pay a few measly dollars? The guy sounds like a real piece of work." Chloe had never heard of anyone so cruel, and she really did want to give the bully a piece of her mind...maybe even a piece of her fist.

Elizabeth tilted her head and looked at her sister. "You would have loved how Sophia and I told him off." She chuckled and added, "And how I almost broke his thumb. Well, at least I think I came close to breaking it. Those self-defense techniques we learned from the boys really helped."

Chloe clapped her hands in front of her. "I know! We got free wrestling and self-defense classes growing up with five rough brothers. I bet Bart had no clue what you were about."

Elizabeth laughed.

"Right, so you're in. Who can we ask to come along as our muscle? Do you have any ideas?" Elizabeth walked around the kitchen table and sat down where she could see out the kitchen window above the sink.

Chloe tapped a finger to her chin and thought. The first name that came to her mind was one that she knew Elizabeth wouldn't want along. However, he would be good at helping them out. "Maybe we should ask a few of our brothers to come along?"

"Yeah, I thought of them, too." Elizabeth nodded and continued to stare out her sister's window. "But don't you think they're a bit hot-headed for something like this?"

While the Manning brothers were known to be gentlemen, once they grew out of their boyish ways they were also known to jump at a chance to fight. All of them had been on the high school wrestling team and never backed down from one single fight, whether on the mat or off.

"We'll need to explain to them that they aren't there to fight, but to make sure we *don't* get into any fights." Chloe shook her head and chuckled when she thought about how difficult it might be to keep her brothers on their best behavior.

Elizabeth turned back to Chloe and joined her sister in laughter. "I think we might have more problems with our brothers than with Big Bart."

"Hmm, maybe we should only bring two of them and maybe two more guys from town?" Chloe bit the inside of her cheek and decided she knew exactly who to invite. "You take care of getting two of our unruly brothers, and make sure they know to behave themselves, and I'll get two more level-headed cowboys from town to join us."

She wasn't about to let on who those cowboys were, seeing as how she only knew one to invite so far. She was confident he'd know who else to bring along; all she had to do was tell him what they were doing and that she needed two men to help, and he'd take care of it.

CHAPTER 11

F riday came way too fast for Elizabeth's liking. Max hadn't spoken but a few words to her all week, and she was worried about what was going to happen to their relationship if she went through with this trip to Bozeman the next weekend.

No man was going to dictate who she could and couldn't help. When she'd asked him why he was so dead set against helping the homeless, he clammed up. Something inside her spirit told her that he had been hurt by a homeless person, or maybe he had been homeless at one point himself. Either way, it was personal to him. But she wasn't about to write him off—not when the signs pointed to there being a reason for his behavior.

Whatever happened was no excuse to treat the homeless poorly, but she believed Max had some unforgiven hurt in his past. He needed to work on it and give it over to God to handle. All she could do was pray for him and be there once he decided he was ready to talk about it.

Before she even hopped in the shower, she was down on her knees next to her bed and praying. *God, you know what is in Max's heart. All I ask is that you bring forgiveness to his soul. I don't need to know what happened, but Max does need to let it go, whatever it is. Please comfort him and let him know You love him and are here for him. Help him to get through whatever it is that's causing him to hate the homeless so much. I truly believe he has a good heart, but he needs Your loving hand to move past this. Please help him. In Jesus' name I pray, amen.*

Praying had always helped Elizabeth feel closer to God, but also helped her to work through anything that was bothering her. She would continue to pray for Max and healing. Eventually it would happen; she was convinced God would help Max to forgive whatever happened in his past. Then they would be able to move forward. But until that time, she would have to be careful what she said around Max.

The Lord had given her peace regarding the homeless project, and she believed her course of action was exactly what God wanted her to do. She wasn't going to turn her back on anyone who needed her help, especially when she had it in her power to help.

Later that day, after she finished her shift with the clinic, Chloe went to the general store to see if a certain cowboy was up for a trip to Bozeman the following weekend.

"Hiya, cowboy." Chloe sauntered into the general store as though she owned the place. She wore a saucy smile to go with her red cowgirl hat, black snap-up shirt with a red tank top, paired with her favorite jeans and matching red cowboy boots. No one was going to miss Chloe when she entered the store.

Logan eyed her warily. He knew she had something up her sleeve, but couldn't quite figure out her angle yet. "What can I do for you, Miss Chloe?"

When she sauntered to the counter, swaying her hips, all

the men in the store stopped what they were doing and watched her.

"Well Mister Hayes, I see you're hard at work. Are you still planning on hanging around town?" She made sure to accent her words enough to sound like a real cowgirl, instead of the boring billing manager she really was. She knew the local men loved to hear the twang in a gal's voice more than anything.

He narrowed his eyes and lowered his voice. "What are you up to?" Logan knew she had no plans on any man in town; she was leaving this hick town, as she'd called it on more than one occasion. He had heard all the men were warned away from her. She had refused all dates for the past six months because she said she wanted no one to try to hold her back. So he knew she wasn't dressed to kill to catch a man's eye. At least, not to get one to ask her out on a date.

With a lock of hair wrapped around her finger, she twirled it and affected an air of bewilderment. "Who, me? I'm just here to ask an old friend for a favor."

Logan stood tall and crossed his arms over his chest. "Uh-huh. And would that old friend be me?"

Chloe released the hair in her fingers and put a hand to his bicep and gave it a light squeeze. "Actually, I'm here for your muscle." She batted her eyelashes and waited for his response.

When Logan chuckled, three men behind Chloe joined in.

"Well, little lady, if it's muscle you need, then I'm your man." Jonathan Chance stood right behind her and flexed his muscles, which were probably some of the largest in town.

She turned around with a huge smile across her face and reached out and squeezed his bicep. "My, I do believe you might be right." She continued to flirt with him and ignored Logan, who watched with amusement in his eyes.

He wasn't going to let anything happen to the girl he'd always thought of as his little sister, but he was curious about her game. He'd let it play out a little longer and see what she was up to. If he had to guess, she needed help packing and moving for this secret job she had mentioned to him.

Chloe was like a spider luring her prey to her web, and Jonathan was thoroughly caught in her eyes. The poor cowboy had asked her out before and been turned down. Logan wasn't sure why he was falling for Chloe's game, but he decided he'd better help his old friend out before she went too far.

Logan knew Chloe's heart was in the right place, but there were times she just didn't know when to stop. When she wanted something, she went full force for it.

The shopkeeper cleared his throat. "Chloe, what exactly do you need muscle for?" Logan looked between Jonathan and Chloe and waited for a response.

She rolled her eyes. "Nothing too difficult. Next weekend a few of us ladies are heading over to Bozeman, and we need some big, strong men to come with us. That's all."

He knew exactly what was up. He had heard all the gossip about the last time the group of girls went to Bozeman, and he would bet his share in the family business that the ladies were going back and wanted some men to accompany them, just in case that Bart fellow showed up again.

Nodding, Logan said, "Count me in."

Not to be outdone, Jonathan spoke up. "Me too."

The other men behind Jonathan nodded, and all of them wanted to be included as well.

Logan chuckled a deep, throaty laugh. "Fellas, you might want to hear exactly what the ladies are up to before you agree so easily." He raised his eyebrows at Chloe and waited for her to expound on her idea.

She batted her eyelashes at the cowboys surrounding her and began. Without going into too much detail, she explained how there was a group of women who were being abused by a really bad guy, and she and her friends wanted to help these women by passing out some essentials and making sure they knew of a good local church that was willing to help them.

"So you see, we just need a couple of strong fellas to help keep us safe as we try to help the poor ladies get a halfway decent meal and maybe some clean socks." When she turned around to look at Logan, she noticed he wasn't buying it.

"Chloe, the bad guy isn't by chance a big guy named Bart, is he?" He quirked an eyebrow, and she almost lost her composure.

"So what if he is? No man should be hurting women. Especially poor women who just need a bite to eat."

"I'm still in if you need my muscles, Chloe." Jonathan flexed his bicep, and Chloe smiled demurely at him.

The rest of the guys in the group agreed and began to flex their muscles.

"Oh boys, y'all are so sweet to want to help. Thank you so much. If y'all meet us here outside the general store on Saturday morning at eight, I'll bring coffee and donuts." She smiled at the cowboys in front of her, then turned around again to look at Logan. "And I know *all* of my girlfriends will be very grateful for your assistance." She gave him a conspiratorial wink and walked away. Before she exited the store, she looked back at the cowboys watching her walk away. She waved her fingers and smiled one last time before leaving them alone.

Logan chuckled and knew exactly what Chloe was about. He doubted Elizabeth knew he was going with them, and he'd let her stay in the dark.

CHAPTER 12

Three days later, Elizabeth cornered Max and demanded what was going on with him.

"Why are you ignoring me? I don't get it, Max." She put her hands on her hips and stared him down right outside the diner.

Max looked around and smiled and waved at the mayor and his wife as they entered the diner for breakfast. "What are you doing?" he hissed under his breath as soon as the door closed behind the mayor.

He took her arm and walked around the corner so they weren't on the busy main street anymore. Nothing would hurt his career more than the entire town hearing them argue. He knew he would be booted out on his keister should he do anything to hurt the town darling.

When they'd first started dating, several of the ranch owners cornered him in the general store to ask his intentions as well as to warn him not to hurt their beautiful and sweet veterinarian. No one ever said it, but he knew that if he ever broke up with Elizabeth and word got 'round that he'd hurt her, he would lose all of his business.

That was the problem with these small towns: they weren't very accepting of outsiders. They stuck close to those who grew up there. Sure, they were always nice and polite to him. He was even welcomed by several groups in the area, but if he stepped out of line, he was toast. The company would have to move him to another district and someone else would come in and take over his accounts.

"I'm not ignoring you." He took his Stetson off his head and ran a hand through his thick, dark hair. "Geez, Elizabeth. I've got a lot going on right now, and not everything is about you, alright?" He shook his head and pursed his lips.

She blinked a few times and opened her mouth, but closed it before she could go off on him. She took a few deep breaths and said, "Alright, but I do think we should talk. I'm going back to Bozeman with the girls to help the homeless…"

Max raised his hand to stop her. "I told you not to do that. Why can't you just listen for a change? It's too dangerous. I asked a few people I know in Bozeman about Bart, and he's bad news. I mean, really bad. His rap sheet is a mile long. I'm surprised he's still out on the streets and not in prison."

Elizabeth sighed. "If you would have let me finish, I could have told you that Chloe and I decided to take four men with us. I'm going to ask two of my brothers, and Chloe is going to get two local cowboys with muscle. She insisted on them having muscle." Elizabeth chuckled. "Anyway, we're going to have four strong and capable cowboys going with us. None of us will be alone…we'll be protected."

She put her hands on her hips and narrowed her eyes at Max. "Besides, all of us girls can take care of ourselves. You may not have grown up on a ranch, but all of us did. Ranch girls are tough; most of us are even tougher than townies. So get off your high horse and recognize that we aren't fainting misses who need your protection from the big bad wolf." She huffed and considered walking off and letting him stew in his own juices, but reconsidered; it wasn't very ladylike, and she was most definitely a lady. A lady who could kick some serious butt, but still a lady.

The face of the man in front of her changed from angry to condescending. "Alright, Elizabeth, I know you can take care of yourself. I've seen you stare down a bull and walk away the victor. But can you blame me for worrying for your safety? Especially after learning about Big Bart? He's worse than a bull with a thorn in his hoof. But I get it, at least y'all will have some backup if you need it." He ran both hands down his face and knew he would worry about her the entire time she was gone, but he also knew when he was beat. And this little filly definitely had him beat.

"If you promise to stick to one of your brothers' sides, then I won't complain. This time. But you really need to consider who those people are and why they're on the streets." He knew he wasn't going to change her mind, at least not yet. Once she'd spent some time with the homeless, she would learn.

"Max, that's just it—I do know. These women have been abused and thrown out. No one wants to help them. All they need is a little lift up, and I know in my heart"—she put a hand over her heart—"they will succeed in cleaning their lives up and become productive members of society again. They just need a little help."

Max shook his head, knowing that any further arguing would only drive more of a wedge between them. "I'm not going to argue with you. When you realize who they really are, I'll be here. Until then, I need to spend more time on my car. The derby finals are coming up very soon, and I have to get it in tip-top shape for the race. You're still coming to the semi-finals, aren't you?"

She nodded and smiled. "Yes, I wouldn't miss it."

He smiled and leaned down and kissed her cheek. "Good. I'll see you soon."

They walked back onto Main Street together and went their separate ways.

Elizabeth wondered if maybe Max would come around if she told him some of the stories from the women she had met and might still meet later that week. He couldn't be completely hard-hearted. She knew he had a soft side...she just needed to find it and direct it toward those who needed it most.

Later that night before bed, she got down on her knees and prayed for Max again. He needed healing. Whatever his past held, it was time for him to let it go.

Thursday night came quickly. Elizabeth had been very busy with the ranches she supported. She had seen three fillies born, as well as almost a dozen late-season calves. Not to mention all the inoculations she had to deliver to the surrounding ranches. Her days were long, and her nights not nearly long enough.

When the girls arrived at her house, she was thankful Chloe had thought to bring pizza.

"You are a lifesaver! Thank you, thank you, thank you!" Elizabeth hugged her twin when she let her in the door. "I've been so busy this week, I completely forgot to get something to make for dinner. You got the gluten-free crust, right?"

"Of course...I haven't forgotten Mia's sensitive to gluten. I also made some gluten-free brownies for dessert. I found a recipe online using almond flour. I tried one before leaving, and they're really good. Can't tell the difference." Chloe walked to the kitchen with the pizza box and then turned around to head back out to her car.

"Oh, what else did you bring?" Elizabeth followed her outside and helped to carry in a couple bags.

"Found some small first-aid kits in the back of the clinic from one of the fairs they did, and asked if I could take a couple bags of them to hand out. The clinic administrator thought it was a great idea. So we can hand these out to the women, and hopefully they can at least have a few bandages and first-aid salve should they get any scrapes." Chloe grabbed a couple bags and began to walk into her sister's house.

Without missing a beat, Elizabeth continued on, "This makes me think we might want to get a collection going from all the businesses in town." She picked up the rest of the bags.

"I wonder if we could even ask some of the ranch owners to make up sandwiches and treats to hand out? You know, get a circle going? Maybe once a month we do this, and each month a different ranch or business can sponsor the effort? We might even be able to get more people to join us." Elizabeth was getting very excited about her ideas to help those in need.

God had blessed her and her family so much, and she wanted to give back and help others. Something in her very being was waking up and speaking to her about this endeavor, and she knew it was from God himself.

Her twin bit her lower lip. "I have a little bit of bad news, though."

Elizabeth narrowed her eyes. "What's up? Did anyone cancel on us?"

Chloe nodded. "Yup, our brothers did. But don't worry." She moved all the bags into her right hand and held up her left hand, almost dropping the bags she was holding. "I have five cowboys who confirmed today that they're ready and willing to go with us tomorrow. We'll have more than enough muscle with us." She chuckled.

Elizabeth shook her head and knew that Chloe had no trouble getting men to join in on her crazy schemes. She only worried about what her sister had told them they were getting into. Sometimes she wasn't totally upfront with her requests. "Do they know what they're in for?"

Aghast, Chloe took a step back. "Of course they do. I wouldn't wrangle cowboys for something like this without telling them." She wasn't about to explain that it was really Logan who had told them. As long as they knew what was coming, it didn't really matter who did the explaining, did it?

By the time all the girls were at her place, Elizabeth was feeling relaxed and ready to enjoy a night with the girls, chatting about men and what they might experience the next day.

Harper was also excited. "I heard Jonathan is coming tomorrow. Is it true?" The dreamy look in her eyes told Elizabeth all she needed to know.

Her friend Harper wasn't quite ready to settle down yet. She enjoyed dating a guy a few times and then moving on before either one of them could get too attached. One of these days, Elizabeth hoped, a good man would come along and earn her trust. Then Harper would settle down and start having the babies she'd always wanted.

Chloe's eyes brightened, and she gushed her news to Harper. "Yes, and he's very excited to join us." She winked conspiratorially at her friends. "I think all the men are excited to join us tomorrow. Something tells me they're more interested in us then they are the actual work we'll be doing, but I'm hoping they'll get into it once we're there."

All the women in the room laughed, and they began chatting about who was going and who was cute, and who had the biggest muscles. Elizabeth sighed and chuckled at her friends' antics. "Sometimes it's nice having a steady boyfriend."

Chloe smirked. She hadn't given up hope of having Logan as her brother-in-law. Not yet, anyway. Under her breath, she whispered, "We'll see about that steady boyfriend after tomorrow."

CHAPTER 13

A bright, sunny day dawned, and Elizabeth excitedly got ready for the big day. While she was a bit nervous, she also knew God was on their side, and he would deliver them from any harm that day.

When she arrived at the front of the general store to meet up with everyone, she knew she might see Logan, but she wasn't expecting him to be outside with the rest of the cowboys who were going with them to Bozeman. Although, most of them were friends with Logan, so she shouldn't have been surprised that he would step out of his store to chat with them, something she was so not ready to do. Not after that forced confinement with him the previous week.

Since that horrible day, Elizabeth had successfully avoided the general store and the entire family who owned and operated it. When Chloe said that they would be meeting up with the guys there, she should have suggested a different place. The only problem with meeting somewhere else was that most places didn't have enough parking to hold everyone's trucks. The church would have worked, but it was on the opposite side of town from where they needed to be. The general store was the most central location, with Main Street leading to the highway that would take them to Bozeman. So she'd kept quiet. This morning she was regretting it.

Seeing him there in his cowboy boots, hat, and jeans that fit him like a glove, she was brought back to a moment in high school when he'd declared his love for her for the first time. She had known he loved her by all the wonderful things he had done for her and the flowers and gifts he had given her for years, but to have him say it out loud for the first time made everything real for her.

Now, those memories which had been locked away for so long came rushing back and caused her heart to ache for the love she'd once had. She had never doubted his love for her until that summer she graduated high school. The idiot had never even told her why he was breaking up with her. He just gave her some sort of stupid reply when she asked. *"You'll be much happier as a single girl when you get to college. These will be your years to date and experience all sorts of things you wouldn't get to if we stay together."*

She could feel the sting of tears in her eyes as she recalled that day. When she turned back to her truck, pretending as though she were looking for something, she wiped a few stray tears from her cheeks and sniffed.

When she felt a presence next to her, she stiffened and hoped it wasn't who she thought it was. His scent enveloped her—sandalwood, pine, and man. Logan's scent was all his. She had never met a man whose scent caused her skin to prickle like it did when he was near.

While she didn't miss him, she did miss his scent. It had always been home to her. One time while in college, she went to the local department store and tried to find his scent among all the cologne bottles, but nothing came even close to Logan. She hadn't sniffed another sample of men's cologne since then. When she got back to her dorm room, she'd felt foolish and chided herself for looking for him.

"Here." Logan handed her a handkerchief—one of those she had embroidered herself and given to him as a Christmas present in her sophomore year of high school.

"You still use these?" She took it and blotted at her eyes before blowing her nose. She hoped he thought it was anything at all besides tears from crying. She wasn't going to lie, but she would be mortified if he even suspected she was crying over him.

"Of course. I only have two left—the others have been washed so much they began to fall apart. But I still carry real handkerchiefs, and these are my favorite."

A tiny smile formed on her lips, and she pocketed the small piece of white cloth. "I'll wash it and return it to you later." It was the least she could do, since she had soiled it.

"No worries. I always keep a spare on me." He nudged her shoulder. "You never know when you might come upon a damsel who needs it." He had actually begun carrying a second one when he had a rotten bout of allergies and went through two handkerchiefs a day.

Elizabeth remembered the testing he went through that year and almost cringed at the memory of all the needles that went into his back. Turned out he was allergic to her perfume. She changed it out for something else, and his allergies went away.

"Thanks. Well, we'd better get going, and I'm sure you need to get back into your store. Have a nice day, Logan." She closed the door on her truck and moved back toward the group. "Alright, we have two SUVs. Who's riding with whom?"

A tall man stood at her back. He leaned over and said, "I'm riding with you."

Elizabeth jumped and turned around, shocked to see Logan standing there. "But... I thought... What are you doing?"

"I'm Team Muscle." He flexed his biceps, and Elizabeth couldn't help but look.

"Oh look, Martha. It's Elizabeth and Logan. Don't they just make the cutest couple?" Cindy Macon and her pink pouf were right in front of Elizabeth and Logan on the sidewalk.

Goldie Walters clapped her hands and smiled warmly at them both. "It's so good to see you two together again after all these years. It just warms my heart." She put a hand over her chest.

Elizabeth's heart stopped beating, and her face felt warm. She really hoped she wasn't blushing. She looked between the two Diner Divas and tried to stop their gossip in its tracks. "No, we aren't together."

Logan chuckled and put his hand around her shoulders. "We are still great friends." And he winked at them.

Elizabeth dug her elbow into his side. She knew she couldn't make a big display, but she had to drive home her point. "I'm dating Max, remember?" Her brows lifted, and she began to feel anger boiling up. Not at Max, but at the entire situation she'd found herself in.

Cindy swiped a hand in front of her face. "Phooey, you're standing here with Logan. The two of you look perfect together."

Elizabeth sighed. She knew where this was heading, and there was nothing she could do about it. "Cindy, one of these days God is going to call you to account for your gossiping ways. Just keep that mind." She turned and walked away from the two gossipmongers.

The older ladies giggled and walked away, already

discussing how great Elizabeth and Logan looked together and how cute their babies would be.

Elizabeth ran a hand over her forehead. "Who's going to watch the store today?"

Logan chuckled. "Leah has it well in hand. Saturdays aren't very busy right now, and Buck will be coming in shortly to help."

"Oh," was all she could think to say. With her heart beating so fast, she wasn't sure if she could even talk, let alone come up with something smart to say.

Not only was Logan going to spend the entire day with her, but by the time they came back, the whole town would think she and Max had broken up because she wanted to get back with Logan. While she knew she needed to do damage control, she also knew she didn't have the time to do it. She and Max would have to go out on a date that night to prove the Diner Divas' gossip wrong.

Chloe called out, "Alright ladies and gentlemen, pick an SUV and get yourselves loaded. We have a lot of work to do today, and it's going to be hot and humid, so the sooner we get started the better it will be for us all."

The forecast had called for seventy-six percent humidity with a high of eighty-seven for Bozeman. None of them would want to be out in the city past noon if they could help it. At least, not in the direct sunshine. Although, even in the shade it would be sweltering with that level of humidity. Summer was making its final notes felt, and fall couldn't come soon enough for anyone.

Elizabeth had no desire to ride with Logan; she didn't even want him on this trip, no matter how much he could help. So she watched to see which vehicle Logan chose, and then she chose the other one. It was the only way she could focus on the task at hand. Today was supposed to be about helping the homeless women of Bozeman, not trying to hide from Logan.

Logan knew Elizabeth was uncomfortable with his decision to join them. But he wasn't expecting her to be so upset with his decision to come and help. He only wanted to protect her and maybe do a little good while he was at it. When he heard about what had happened to Elizabeth and her friends on her last trip to Bozeman, he was angry at Max for not going along with them. He was also proud of Elizabeth and the girls for wanting to help those women and not backing down from a bully. While Bart was definitely more dangerous than your average bully, Logan wasn't going to back down from the sorry excuse for a man if he bothered them.

When Logan noticed Elizabeth waiting to choose a vehicle, he decided to pick one so she could feel comfortable in choosing to ride in a different car. He noticed that Chloe chose to ride with Harper, and that was when he chose the other vehicle. It wasn't that he didn't want to ride with Chloe and Harper; he just knew that Elizabeth would want to ride with her twin and her best friend.

His conscience was niggling at him for going along.

Once he realized that Chloe had plenty of male volunteers, he should have backed out. He knew that Elizabeth wouldn't be happy with him coming along, but he also still felt very protective of the only woman he'd ever loved. Even if she never forgave him for breaking her heart, he wasn't going to let her get hurt. He would take a bullet for the cute cowgirl who wore her heart on her sleeve.

And he wanted nothing more than to get her friendship back... Well, maybe a little bit more. But he would be very content if he could have his oldest friend in the world back in his life.

For some strange reason, it ended up being boys vs. girls.

All the girls rode in one SUV, and the guys all piled into the other one. He didn't care as long as they didn't lose the girls.

Logan sat in the front passenger seat and turned around to look at his fellow *muscles*. "Does anyone know exactly where we're going? What if we lose them on the highway?"

Drake smiled and nodded. "Yup, we're meeting them in the parking lot of First Baptist Church of Bozeman. They're going to give us some tracks with their phone number and address on it to add to the goody bags."

Logan nodded and turned back around to face front as they headed out.

It wasn't a long ride, and the guys chatted the entire way. Logan learned more than he wanted about this group of cowboys, most of whom were old high school buddies of his. It seemed Jonathan had gotten over his feelings for Chloe, but still found her attractive, or *hot,* as he called her. But it seemed he might also have a thing for Harper.

The man couldn't stop talking about the sweet-as-pie nurse. Logan would have to keep an eye out and see if Harper returned his friend's feelings. He hoped so; they would make a good couple. And if she didn't, well…he'd just have to make sure Jonathan didn't fall too hard for Harper.

He hadn't been to Bozeman in years, and as they approached the city, he noticed it had grown, but it still held the look and feel of the small Montana country town he remembered from his childhood. While it wasn't more than a one-horse town compared to Los Angeles, it was a big city to him when he was growing up.

As he exited the SUV in the parking lot, the smile on his face felt good. He hadn't had much to smile about since coming home, and he knew he'd made the right decision to join Chloe today.

He took a deep breath and was very grateful for the clean

air of Montana. While living in LA he'd tried hard not to breathe too deeply. When he first arrived he'd tried taking a deep breath, only to start coughing from all the exhaust fumes around him. Until that day, he'd never understood why the Asians always wore masks, even years after SARS went away. Now he understood.

SOMETHING in his heart stirred and told him to pay attention. *Yes, Lord.*

Even in LA he had known when the Lord spoke to him. So when he felt the stirring in his heart, he was glad he hadn't declined to join the group, even though he saw the distress in Elizabeth's eyes before they left.

There may not be any problems at all today, but he was going to stay vigilant and do whatever he could to help keep his friends safe, as well as the homeless women they were about to meet.

A tall, lanky man with a brown Stetson, blue jeans, and tan boots approached them. "Hi, I'm Pastor Langdon. I'm so glad your group reached out to us."

"Thank you," Harper said. "We're really excited to be here and hope that we can do something to help the women who need it most." She reached out and shook the pastor's hand.

"What can you tell us about Big Bart?" If the pastor had been working with the local homeless, he'd be the best person to speak with about the Bart issue. Elizabeth was anxious to learn as much as she possibly could about this current situation. He might even know how to avoid him, or better yet, why the local sheriff hadn't stopped the criminal.

"We've been working with a few of the local homeless women, but Big Bart always seems to stop the women from joining us on Sundays." Langdon shook his head. "He seems to own our homeless population. Just this past week I spoke with the sheriff about it, and he's looking into the issue."

"Why has it taken so long for the sheriff to do anything about this criminal?" Elizabeth stood next to her sister with her arms crossed over her chest.

The pastor took his hat off and scratched his head. "Well, Miss…?"

"Sorry, I'm Elizabeth Manning. Nice to meet you, Pastor." Elizabeth took three steps and shook the pastor's hand.

"It seems Big Bart is new to our fair city. As far as I can gather, he's only been here a few months. In fact, our local homeless population wasn't very large until Bart showed up. Which has me thinking he might be bringing some of them here from other parts." Langdon put his thumbs through the front belt loops on his jeans.

Jonathan interjected, "Do you think your crime rate has increased since Bart moved to town?"

Logan had wondered the exact same thing. If Big Bart was importing homeless people, there had to be a reason for it. Why would he want a collection of homeless here in Bozeman that he controlled? He had to be up to something.

The pastor grabbed the back of his neck and considered Jonathan's question. "I can't be sure…they've only been here since spring…but it does seem like local crime has increased. Although, it usually does when the weather is better. I'd say that's a question for the sheriff. But I do know that two ranchers who regularly attend my church have complained about missing tack, and another rancher said one of his prize stallions has been stolen."

"Is that normal?" Liam asked.

Logan couldn't be sure, but he didn't remember any of

their local ranches having horses stolen. Tack went missing once in a while and it usually showed back up, but horses didn't go missing. However, Bozeman was a much larger area than Beacon Creek; horse thieving might be a regular occurrence here.

"No, it isn't," another voice said from behind Logan. A middle-aged woman wearing boots and a long skirt with a white, short-sleeved blouse walked up to the pastor and stood next to him.

"Everyone, this is my wife, Bethany." The pastor put his arm around his wife's shoulders and drew her in for a side hug.

Everyone in the group waved, or said, "Hi" or, "Ma'am."

She nodded and smiled at the group. "A few of the ladies in my weekly Bible study have said they've seen an increase in items going missing. One even had her purse stolen by a homeless man she hadn't seen before. The situation is escalating, and the sheriff's wife told me yesterday that her husband does suspect something nefarious is going on with Big Bart and his gang."

Bethany stood tall next to her husband. She had to be around five feet eight inches tall. She had brown hair and sharp hazel eyes. Mrs. Langdon appeared to be a woman with confidence and presence.

Harper walked toward the pastor's wife and smiled. "It's so nice to meet you. I'm Harper. We've spoken on the phone."

Bethany clapped her hands together. "Yes, I'm so happy to see you. The women in my Bible study wanted to come out today to help, but one of our women is in the hospital, and they're all taking turns right now making meals and watching her children. She has eight kids all still at home, and her husband runs their ranch with only a few hands to help."

Harper shook her head. "Oh, don't worry about us. We'll be just fine. How is the lady doing? Will she be alright? What happened?"

Of course the nurse inside Harper would be interested in the medical situation of someone she had never met.

"Thank you for asking, but Marjorie will be fine. She had surgery yesterday and won't be released from the hospital for a few days yet." Bethany smiled at Harper, but didn't seem inclined to say anything more about the patient.

"Forgive me, I'm a nurse. Whenever I hear anyone is sick or injured, I kick into medical mode and try to find out all I can so that I can help. Occupational hazard, I think." Harper shrugged.

"Or just you being nosy." Chloe laughed.

The other girls in the group laughed along with Harper and the pastor's wife.

The pastor clapped his hands together. "Alright, where did you plan to start today?"

Elizabeth spoke up. "We were here a few weeks ago, and I thought we should go back to the same area…the Farmer Basket just off Bleaker Street."

Bethany nodded. "Yes, I know that area. It's smack dab in the middle of where Bart has set up shop." She chuckled. "You're sure to find plenty of women living on the street there. Wait here, I have a bag of tracks for you to pass out as well as some gift cards we had donated this past week." The pastor's wife left the group and headed back into the church.

"We've just begun our own homeless ministry," the pastor explained. "Several members have started a food and clothing ministry to take in donations that will go to those in need, including the homeless. One of the families in our church had an uncle who had been homeless until they took him in, and now they're all going out on a regular basis to witness to the homeless in our city." The pastor smiled, and a little bit of pride shone in his eyes and the way he held himself taller.

"Have any of your church members had issues with Bart?" Logan asked.

The pastor nodded. "A few have been run off by Bart and his gang of ruffians, but now when we go out, we go in larger groups."

"I'm saddened to hear that your church members have had issues with Bart, but I'm also excited to hear that they haven't given up," Elizabeth said. "So many people would have given up after being harassed by bullies. In fact, some of my own friends have said it's too dangerous to come back. But I don't believe in giving in to fear tactics. I think we should stand up to bullies and let them know they can't scare us."

The determination in Elizabeth's voice was evident, as was the strength in her convictions. She was not going to let one bad apple stop her from helping those in need.

CHAPTER 14

After Elizabeth and Harper thanked the Langdons for their help, the group got back into their SUVs and headed off to the Farmer Basket. It was as good a place as any to park and get started with their mission.

It really was a mission in the sense that they all wanted to give those living on the street some of the most basic necessities of life, as well as point them toward God. The goal was to eventually get them off the street, but more importantly, it was to help them find their Lord and Savior.

"Alright, does everyone know what they're supposed to do and who they're partnering with?" Elizabeth asked.

Logan stepped forward. "I think we should stay in larger groups like the Langdons do." The serious expression on his face stopped Elizabeth from disagreeing with him.

She tilted her head and thought about what he'd said. She herself had seen firsthand how Bart and his crew had no compunctions about cornering or assaulting women who were in a group. "Alright, what size and composition of group did you have in mind?"

While she had no desire to be partnered with Logan, he

would be helpful in a small group. Maybe he could go with three of the girls to help keep them safe.

As she was considering who else to have in her group, Logan answered her. "I think we should split up into two groups. Half the men go with half the women. There really is strength in numbers."

"Only two groups? But we won't be able to get to as many people today if we only have two group. I was hoping we could do at least four groups." Elizabeth worried that they wouldn't be able to help all those who needed it. And she hoped that she would be able to find the woman from last time, or at least find out if she'd gotten off the streets and joined the program Elizabeth had told her about.

Logan stepped closer to Elizabeth and put a hand on her shoulder. "Hey, we'll all stay here all day, if that's what it takes. We won't leave until we've given away all the bags, alright?" He tilted his head down closer to Elizabeth, and a jolt went straight to his heart when their eyes met.

Elizabeth's eyes widened when she looked right into Logan's eyes. At first when he touched her, a warmth radiated from his hand and calmed her. But when she looked into his baby blues, her world tumbled and shook, and she could only hear the rushing of her blood in her ears. It sounded as though she was about to go over Niagara Falls in nothing but a barrel. She licked her lips and tried to clear her throat. She had to get her emotions in check before anyone noticed anything.

Logan blinked and dropped his hand before he could do anything stupid. At that moment, all he wanted to do was grab his Lizzie and hold her tight…and never let go.

"Ah…well. That is…if you agree to my plan." He stumbled past his words and worried that all the men with him would know exactly what he was thinking and feeling. If they did, he'd never hear the end of their ribbing.

When Elizabeth couldn't take the intensity of the emotion flowing between the two of them, she turned her head and noticed that they were alone. She frowned and looked around her and found all their friends were back at Harper's SUV. They looked to be putting something inside the bags. How did she not hear them walk away? She shook her head and decided that she needed to be in a different group from Logan.

He confused her, but also distracted her. Today was not a time to be distracted. Distraction could be dangerous. She had to keep her wits about her and be on guard all day long, and not because of the homeless. While some of them could be dangerous, it was Bart and his friends she needed to keep an eye out for.

Without another word between then, they both began to head over to their friends.

"What's up?" Elizabeth tried to sound casual, but even she could hear the strain in her voice. She was embarrassed all her friends had seen the emotionally charged exchange between her and Logan. She didn't want to think about what it could mean—not now. So she turned her attention to the rest of her group and tried to paste on a smile, knowing it wasn't very realistic.

Chloe bounced over to her twin and smiled between Logan and Elizabeth. "While the two of you were staring into each other's eyes, we all decided to break up into two groups. Logan was right, it is safer this way." She handed her sister a tote bag full of smaller gift bags containing the items they had packed the night before.

Elizabeth looked inside one of the bags and smiled. "I see

you're putting the tracks the Langdons gave us inside each bag. Smart."

They had planned on filling up the tote bags with the small gift bags and taking them out to give away. Once they ran out, they would go back to the SUV to refill so that they didn't have to carry very many bags all at once.

Harper walked over with her tote bag full to the brim. "Since there are ten of us, it'll be easy to split up into groups of five. We have already picked the groups."

Jonathan handed Logan a black tote bag with a picture of a bull and rider on one side. He shrugged. "At least we don't have flower-covered bags like the girls."

Logan chuckled and took his tote bag. "Works for me. What group am I in?"

Chloe grabbed his arm and said, "Mine. Come on, let's get moving." She turned toward her twin. "Come on. You too."

Elizabeth sighed and resigned herself to having a difficult day. She knew she would be safe, but wasn't too happy about having to spend it all with Logan by her side. She was going to have a long talk with her sister once they were home. Chloe had to stop trying to force them together.

Behind her, Jonathan and Harper followed along with shy smiles, and Elizabeth couldn't help but stifle a laugh. She knew her friend had a thing for Jonathan, but she hadn't realized he might be interested in her. But then again, why wouldn't he? Harper was beautiful, smart, and a lot of fun. What guy wouldn't want to be with her?

She ran to catch up to her sister and called back over her shoulder, "Come on, you two, let's catch up to Chloe. I know where we should start." Elizabeth took the lead of their little group and led them to where she had seen Mary the first time.

"I want to see if Mary has come back, or if the assistance

group helped her get a job and maybe even a home of her own." Elizabeth looked down the street and stopped in her tracks. "What? I don't understand."

The rest of her group stopped right behind her and looked down the street.

Logan looked both ways and whistled. "You never said there were so many. How many streets look like this?"

Elizabeth and Harper looked at each other and shook their heads.

"It wasn't like this last time. There must be at least four times as many living on the streets." Elizabeth took two steps and stopped, her heart pounding in her chest.

Harper's face fell and she looked back at Jonathan. "I wonder, does the pastor know how many are out here these days?"

"Could it be that all of the homeless have congregated in one spot?" Logan ran a hand down his face and began to count. There were at least fifty people laying on broken cardboard boxes along the sidewalk, while another fifteen where walking down the street pulling pushcarts behind them, or pushing shopping carts in front of them. Some had both.

"Didn't the pastor say that he thought Bart might be bringing in the homeless?" Jonathan took his hat off and ran a hand through his dark hair.

Elizabeth's heart broke thinking about all these poor people and how Bart and his gang must be treating them. "There's so many. Do we have enough bags to help them all?"

Harper shook her head. "We have one hundred bags total. I'm going to call Mia and ask her to come over to this street. I think we should focus our efforts here."

Logan nodded. "Good idea."

When the other five joined them, the excitement had faded from their faces.

Mia bit her lip and looked down the street. "There are more here, but one block over must have had at least forty homeless hanging out on the sidewalks."

"This doesn't even account for the other streets, the park, or any alleyways." A tear trickled down Sophia's cheek. "How did this happen?"

"I don't know, but we need to find out." Elizabeth took a step toward the closest person in rags and took a deep breath. She coughed when she caught a whiff of the street odor. The acrid scent pierced her nostrils, and she tried hard to keep a straight face.

"We need to get them cleaned up and find out where they're all from." Harper's voice was right on Elizabeth's back.

"And how are we going to feed them all?" Chloe stood on her sister's other side. "Alright, come on. Let's stop feeling sorry for them and give them some goody bags with first-aid kits, t-shirts, and Farmer Basket gift cards."

The three women made their way to three different women and began to hand out their bags.

Logan and Jonathan looked at each other with grim faces.

"It's a good thing we all came today," Jonathan said.

"I wish the Manning brothers were here." Logan took a gift bag out of his tote and made his way to a guy leaning against a storefront.

The man gave him a weary look and had a toothpick in his mouth. "Who are you and what are you doing here?" he demanded.

"Hi, I'm here with my friends and we have some basic necessities for you all." Logan handed the man who reeked of stale alcohol one of the gift bags. He hoped it had a man-sized shirt in it. Since he hadn't taken the time to look inside, he really didn't know what was in it, other than what Elizabeth had just mentioned.

The man, who looked to be in his thirties but could be younger, spit his toothpick out on the ground and opened the bag. When he smiled, his crooked, yellow teeth caused Jonathan to turn back to the old man in front of him. "Perfect."

Logan narrowed his eyes and looked around. He noticed several men intently watching what they were doing. A red flag went up, and he immediately walked toward Elizabeth.

"Jonathan, come here." Logan waved his friend over before getting the girls all together as well. "Look." Logan pointed to several men making their way to the people they had already given bags to.

The yellow teeth guy ripped the bag out of the old man's hands. "That belongs to Bart. He'll give you what you need, when you need it." Then he pushed the old man down on the ground.

"Hey!" Logan yelled, and ran to the old man who was lying in a ball on the ground. "Why did you do that? He didn't even fight back."

Yellow Tooth laughed. "Because he opened the bag and was trying to keep it for himself. Everything belongs to Big Bart, and they know it."

"No, these bags belong to those we give them to. Not to Bart. And not to you." Jonathan stood next to Logan and had his phone up to his ear. "Yes, there's an old man who is injured. We need an ambulance on Sycamore and Pine."

Yellow Tooth laughed again. "He's not worth anyone's time or energy. Look at him—he's about to meet his maker anyway." The crook walked over to the next person, who handed her bag to the man without any question.

"It's only been three weeks since the last time we were here. How has it gotten so bad in such a short time?" Elizabeth asked a woman cowering next to her.

The woman, wearing battered jeans and a t-shirt that had seen better days, and who was in need of a long bath, looked around before whispering, "Bart brought in his gang from another state, and they brought a large amount of street people with them. It's been like this for a week."

Elizabeth looked around to make sure she wasn't being watched. She slipped a gift card she had kept in her pocket to the woman. "Thank you. I'm sorry you have to go through this. We're going to do what we can to help."

The homeless woman shook her head. "There is no help for us." She turned and walked away from the group, heading in the opposite direction of Bart's guys.

Elizabeth prayed that the woman would be safe, and that she would be able to use the gift card for some food without getting caught by Bart or his henchmen.

"Logan, we have to do something for these people." Elizabeth's heart was breaking for the way the men and women on the street were being treated. Granted, they had only been there for a few days, but she couldn't believe that the sheriff wasn't all over this. He had to know about all these people living on the street, and what Bart was doing. He had to.

He took in a deep breath and let it out slowly. If he wasn't careful, his anger would get the best of him and he'd do something stupid. What Elizabeth—and all of these people—needed was a level-headed person to come up with a plan to help, not a hot-headed idiot who used his fists instead of his mind.

"We will help them. Somehow, we will find a way." Logan prayed for wisdom and guidance in what to do next. His initial thought was that they should leave—this could become a very dangerous situation—but he couldn't leave the injured man at his feet. At least, not until the ambulance arrived.

Harper was down on her knees checking out the man, and she opened up one of the first-aid kits in the gift bags. "Sir, where does it hurt?"

The man said nothing. He lay there looking at the concrete beneath him.

"Sir, I'm a nurse. If you tell me where it hurts, I might be able to help you." Harper's heart had to be breaking for this man. She didn't even know his name, but Elizabeth knew she was going to keep him in her prayers. "Please, let me help you."

"He was right. I'm not worth it." The gravelly voice of the octogenarian on the ground caught the attention of Elizabeth and Logan.

Elizabeth reached out instinctively and grabbed Logan's arm. Her quick intake of breath only added to the worry Logan already felt.

"Lizzie, we aren't going to give up." Logan's ears pricked when he heard the sirens. "Listen, the ambulance is on its way now."

Elizabeth was so full of emotion; she knew if she spoke, she'd start to cry. She could only nod in response to Logan's words. She clutched Logan harder, and he pulled her into a warm embrace.

He whispered, "Shh, don't worry. He's going to be fine. He'll probably be much safer at the hospital. At least there he'll get a bath and some decent food. Maybe they can even find him a home to live in."

Elizabeth knew she needed to step back, away from Logan. He made her feel safe and warm, but it wasn't real. She wasn't safe in his arms. If she let her guard down, he'd only hurt her again. But he felt so good she couldn't move. Instead, she stayed in his arms until the ambulance arrived. Then she stepped back to watch Harper work.

When the EMT came over to check out the old man, Harper stood and introduced herself. As she listed off the issues with the man, the other EMT pulled out a gurney from the back of the ambulance and brought it over. The two medical professionals lifted the man and strapped him onto the gurney after doing a cursory exam of this body.

Once the ambulance left, Harper came over to Logan and Elizabeth with Chloe and Jonathan on her tail. "He's going to be fine. No broken bones, and from what I can tell, he doesn't have a concussion. But he did seem pretty out of it. I'm guessing malnourishment and dehydration. He'll most likely have some bruises from his fall as well. I hope the hospital keeps him overnight, since he's so old. I'll make a few calls and see if the hospital admin can get him moved to a home. There are a few places that will take elderly patients, even homeless ones. He looks like he qualifies for Medicare and Social Security, so I don't know why he's out on the streets, but I will find out. Don't worry." She put her hand on Elizabeth's shoulder.

"Thank you, Harper. I really appreciate your help. And I know he will as well." Elizabeth gave a tremulous smile and took a deep, cleansing breath. "Alright, we have more bags to hand out, and with the commotion of the ambulance, it looks as though everyone has left. Let's find people in small groups, but keep an eye out for Bart's crew." She told them what the homeless lady had told her about Bart and bringing in his crew.

Jonathan looked from Harper to Elizabeth and over to Chloe. "I don't know, I think it might be best if we all went to see the sheriff. He has to know what's going on here."

"Let's go see him after we give out a few bags. I don't want to bring these back home with us. These people need some help. Did you see the rags they were wearing? They all need new clothes." Elizabeth was convinced she would be protected by God and that He wanted her to stay there and do His work.

"And most of them looked like they hadn't eaten in a while. They need sustenance. We have to find a way to give them the gift cards without Bart's crew finding out." Harper looked around to see if they were being watched.

A little reluctantly, the guys agreed.

"Look, don't get me wrong, I want to help these poor folks. They need someone on their side, and I would like to be part of the team that's on their side. But this is dangerous, and not just for us." Jonathan looked to Logan for help.

Logan nodded his head, and he worried if it wouldn't be worse for those folks if they stayed. "I agree with Jonathan. I think we need the sheriff and his deputies to help. Bart and his crew are dangerous. What happens when we give a gift card to someone who refuses to give it up?"

Elizabeth pursed her lips. "Fiddlesticks. You might be right." She put her hands on her hips and looked around at those with her. "Alright, let's take the gift cards out of the bags. Then they're only getting food that should be eaten today, along with a t-shirt and first-aid kit. If Bart wants those, it's not that big of a deal. Hopefully he won't care about those things. As for the food, let's try to get everyone to eat the sandwiches right away."

Logan, Jonathan, Liam, Noah, and Drake all nodded in agreement.

"I think that's a fine idea, Elizabeth." Drake walked toward an elderly woman who pulled a small cart filled with what looked to be trash and stopped next to her. He was speaking so low, Elizabeth couldn't hear him. By the time he finished and walked away, the woman was scarfing down the sandwich and looking in all directions as she secreted the first-aid kit away and threw the t-shirt under a dirty bag in her cart.

Everyone in the group smiled and went on to do the same.

"Remember, stay close, and if you think you see any of Bart's men, come right back to one of us guys. Don't try to play the hero. I want us all to come back here again, soon." Logan pointedly looked at Elizabeth, who scrunched her face.

Elizabeth had planned on walking a little bit farther away, since there weren't many people on this street. If they all took one homeless person, they would be done. She had to find more, but she also needed to listen to the guys. They were right—this was a dangerous situation, and not just for her and her team, but also for the homeless she was trying to help. As much as it rankled her nerves, she was going to abide by what the guys wanted and stick close to them.

She found a young girl who couldn't be more than eighteen years old and walked over to her. "Hi, my name is Elizabeth. Are you hungry?" She wasn't really sure what to say at this point. But of course the girl was hungry; who wouldn't be if they were living on the street? She doubted anyone here ever had a full stomach.

She held out the bag without the gift card. "Here, it's just a sandwich and couple items we thought you might need." Elizabeth smiled at the girl.

She shrank back and started to walk away.

"Wait, there's nothing in here to draw Bart's attention. No money or gift cards. You should be safe if you eat the sandwich right away." Elizabeth took two steps toward the girl and stopped when she noticed the young lady wince.

Elizabeth looked down and noticed that the girl's left

ankle was wrapped in rags. "Are you alright? Is your ankle sprained or broken?" She wasn't sure if the girl had a broken ankle since she was walking on her left foot, but you couldn't be too careful.

Elizabeth looked around and noticed a bus bench a few feet away. "Come over here and let me look at your foot. I'm only a veterinarian, but I think I can diagnose your ankle. In fact, I have a nurse here as well." She looked up and caught Harper's attention and waved her over.

The rest of the group followed, since they had already given out their bags. There were now eight people standing on the street looking around in fear as they ate their sandwiches.

Elizabeth's heart melted, and she prayed again that God would intervene in the lives of these people. Maybe he would even use her to help them.

"What's going on…" Harper knelt next to Elizabeth and frowned when she looked down at the girl's ankle.

Elizabeth had taken the wrapping off her ankle and it was covered in black and purple bruises. "What happened?" She felt the ankle for any breaks and moved it around slowly as she watched pain cross the girl's face.

Harper tried to take the girl's attention away from what Elizabeth was doing. "How did you hurt yourself? Or did someone else do this?"

The girl's eyes widened, and both Elizabeth and Harper looked at each other. "Big Bart." They nodded in unison.

Elizabeth wanted to take this girl home with them, but she wasn't even sure if the girl was an adult or a minor. Would she get in trouble if she took a minor off the street and to another town? She had no idea what the law said, but she did know that she couldn't let this girl stay on the street.

Almost as though they had communicated telepathically,

Harper said out loud what Elizabeth had been hoping. "We only want to help you. Your ankle is in bad shape, and you shouldn't be walking on it."

The girl continued to stay silent, but she shook her head. The fear in her eyes was evident, and only broke Elizabeth's heart even more.

"I want to take you back with us so you can get the medical care you need. And you would be safe from Bart and his friends. We don't live here in Bozeman, so he won't be able to find you, if that's what you're worried about." Elizabeth stood up and looked for Drake. He was the biggest of the guys in her group, so he should be able to lift the tiny girl without any problem. She couldn't be any taller than five-three, and there was no way the girl weighed more than one hundred pounds. Actually, after further consideration, any of the guys could probably carry her.

Drake walked up and offered to pick her up, but the girl shook her head adamantly. They couldn't exactly take her without her consent—that would be kidnapping.

Drake knelt next to the girl on the bench. "I won't hurt you, I promise. I just want to carry you to the car so you don't have to keep walking on your injured foot." He winced when he looked down at her ankle. "That has to hurt, a lot."

The girl looked between them all and nibbled on her lower lip. When she nodded her agreement, the entire group released a collective sigh. At least one person was going to truly benefit from their trip.

Logan looked around and noticed that two big guys were watching them. "I think it's time we left here. Drake, can you carry the girl all the way back to the cars? We need to get out of here, quickly."

The weather was no longer their biggest concern.

CHAPTER 15

"We really should go see the sheriff," Harper said as she started up her SUV.

"I don't think we have time for that," Logan replied. "We need to get away before Bart can follow us."

Elizabeth's brow furrowed. "What? You really think he would?"

Logan nodded. "Yes, I do. We can talk to our sheriff when we get back to town. He can contact the Bozeman authorities and let them handle Bart and his gang." He looked down at the girl sitting between him and Drake. "Besides, this young lady needs medical attention. She's not looking too good."

The girl's face had paled, and she was shaking.

"Logan, trade places with me." Elizabeth stepped back out of the front passenger seat before Harper could back up. She walked around to where Logan had been sitting and got inside with the girl. "Maybe we should have kept Mia with us instead of the guys."

Drake shook his head. "No, you need protection in the car in case we're chased."

The girl sitting between them shrank down, and a tear

escaped from her eye.

"Shh, Drake. You're scaring the poor girl." Elizabeth put a hand on the girl's shoulder. "It's alright. You're safe now. No one is going to follow us." She looked pointedly at Logan, who seemed to know exactly what she was thinking.

All they needed now was for Bart or one of his goons to find them and follow them back to Beacon Creek. Elizabeth was trying to keep up a strong front, but she did fear that might happen. Those two men watching them had to be Bart's. She wasn't sure what they could do to lose anyone once they were on the road back home. It was mostly a straight shot and not a lot of other roads, except to ranches.

Logan looked around them, and when he was confident they weren't being followed, he sighed in relief. Then smiled at the girls in the back seat.

Elizabeth did the only thing she could think of...she prayed. Asking the Lord for protection seemed to be the only thing that could calm her. A feeling of peace and security came over her in a way no person had ever been able to give her. She knew her Heavenly Father was in control. Whatever happened, it would be because He allowed it and not because some criminal got the best of them.

The farther they got from Bozeman, the more the young girl next to Elizabeth relaxed. When they were only about ten minutes from home, she decided to see if the girl would speak to her. "Well, it looks like no one has followed us. You're going to be safe now." She hesitated a moment. "Do you think you could at least give me your name?"

The girl looked up at her, and Elizabeth could see she was thinking. The girl tilted her head a little, and one of her cheeks puffed out like a chipmunk storing an acorn. "My name is Analise, but everyone calls me Ana."

That was the most Elizabeth had heard from her. In fact,

they were the only words the girl had spoken. She had whimpered and made sounds of pain, but no words had come from her mouth. Even though she was only a veterinarian, even Elizabeth knew that was a good sign. Getting the girl to speak to her would go a long way toward establishing trust, as well as being able to help the girl.

"Harper, let's take Ana straight to the clinic. I want to get an x-ray of her ankle just to make sure it's not broken." It was most likely a very bad sprain exacerbated by all the walking the girl had done, but Elizabeth wanted to be safe. "Do you know which doctors and techs are working today?"

Harper nodded as she turned down the street that would take them to the town's little clinic. "Yes, Doc Reynolds is on duty today. She's really great. As long as there isn't a long line of patients, I'll bet she gets our new friend in right away. As for the x-ray tech, I'm not sure who's on duty today."

The town had three x-ray technicians who rotated their schedule since one of them always had to be on call, in case of an emergency. And someone had to always be in the clinic when it was open. They really needed more staff, but with their small town and smaller budget, they could only afford the three. So they took turns working in the clinic and being on call.

Elizabeth prayed Tom wasn't on duty today; he was rude. Good at his job, but rude. That last thing Ana needed was a rude tech taking her images. She would prefer to take care of the girl herself, but she wasn't licensed to practice on humans, and certainly not to use the x-ray equipment in the clinic.

"I guess, if worse comes to worst, we could sneak into my clinic and get the portable x-ray. It works the same on humans as it does animals." Elizabeth chuckled, as did everyone in the car—except Ana.

She looked around confused, and a little bit of concern was beginning to show through in her eyes.

Elizabeth clamped her mouth shut and realized the girl probably had no clue why that statement was funny. "We have one x-ray technician I don't really like."

Ana's eyes widened, and she tried to inch away from Elizabeth only to come up against a brick wall of a man's shoulder and arm. She flinched and moved back to the center of the row. Her head swiveled from Drake back to Elizabeth, and then to Harper, not really sure who to turn to for help.

Elizabeth realized her mistake. "Ana, it's alright. If Tom is on duty, he won't hurt you. He's just a bit rude, that's all. If he ever hurt a patient, he would be fired. Don't worry. Harper and I will be with you the entire way." She patted Ana's knee as though she were only a little kid who was afraid of a lightning storm.

A little squeak of a sound came from next to her, and she looked back at Ana. "Are you sure?"

Sadness and anger both surged through Elizabeth, and her shoulders slumped. The poor girl had been through way too much, she was sure. There was no way this girl would be this afraid, or worried, if she hadn't been abused.

She put her arm around the girl and lightly squeezed her shoulder. "I'm sure. We aren't going to leave you alone for even a minute while you're being examined." She wondered what would happen if the doctor wanted to keep her overnight. And what would happen if they didn't keep her overnight.

Elizabeth hadn't thought this through very well. If the doctor released her today, where would Ana go? They didn't have a shelter in town. There weren't any assisted living places, either. The girl would need to be around people who could help her, since she was confident the doctor would order bed rest for at least a week. Elizabeth knew Ana had to stay off her foot for a while if it was going to heal.

If Elizabeth didn't work so much, she'd have the girl stay with her no problem. But Elizabeth was only home to eat dinner and sleep most days. She worked long hours and was usually at least thirty minutes from her house when she went out on calls, which was what most of her day consisted of.

She probably could bring home her paperwork and do it there, but that was usually only about an hour's worth of work a day, two hours tops when it was a really busy week. No, Ana couldn't stay with her.

When they pulled up to the clinic, Elizabeth was still thinking about where the girl could go once she was released from the clinic.

"Stay here, I'll go in and get a wheelchair to bring Ana in." Harper left them and ran into the clinic and returned just as quickly with the offered chair.

"Here, let me help you." Drake took the girl from the SUV and gently placed her in the wheelchair that seemed to swallow her up, it was so large. Or she was just that small.

Thankfully, Tom wasn't on duty today and the clinic was empty. The exam went fast, as did the x-rays. Elizabeth and Harper were by her side the entire time. Neither one left her alone. They even went into the x-ray room with her. Although they did have to stand behind the wall that blocked any errant radiation, they could still see the girl and she could see them, which seemed to keep Ana calm.

The doctor had put Ana in a room. She said it was for her privacy, but Elizabeth knew what was coming.

While Elizabeth and Harper were sitting in the private room with Ana, they tried to get the girl to open up about who she was and where she came from, but she refused.

"I can't really tell you much. It's safer this way," Ana

whispered.

Elizabeth's eyebrows raised, and when she looked to Harper, she saw her friend had a similar expression. She wondered if the girl had run away from witness protection or something crazy like that. Whatever was going on, it wasn't important at that moment in time. What was important was getting Ana back on her feet.

Doctor Reynolds walked into the room with a smile, and a nurse came in behind her with a covered tray. The doctor took a seat on a chair next to the bed and pulled up Ana's chart on her iPad. "Well, Doctor Manning was correct—there are no broken bones. But you do have a very bad sprain. You'll have to stay off your feet for at least a week, and then if your foot is progressing nicely, you'll need to use crutches for at least another two to three weeks."

Ana's eyes widened, and she looked to Elizabeth. "I can't."

"Yes, you can. We will help you." Elizabeth, who sat in the chair on the opposite side of the bed, took Ana's hand and squeezed it. "We'll find a place for you to stay today. Somewhere you can be comfortable and have no problem with staying in bed for at least the next week."

A few places came to mind, and she wondered if any of her regular clients would be open to taking in a girl from the streets while she recuperated.

"Actually, I'm not ready to release my patient yet." The doctor waved the young nurse over with her tray. "Ana, you are also severely dehydrated and malnourished. I want to keep you here overnight so we can get fluids and some food into your system."

The young nurse pulled off the cloth covering the tray and set it down on the nightstand next to Ana's bed. "Hi, my name is Betsy. I'm going to put in your IV and then we can begin to get you hydrated. You should start to feel much better in a few hours. I'm also going to wrap your ankle in a bandage and begin icing it. Every few hours I'll be back in here with a new ice pack." She opened up the packaging containing the needle and plastic tubing.

Ana flinched and pulled her arm into herself.

"You don't like needles, do you?" Harper asked.

Ana shook her head.

"I don't either. But Betsy is really great at this. You'll hardly feel it. Let her have your hand, and I promise she'll do a great job." Harper switched places with Elizabeth.

The doctor left the room, saying she would be back to check in on Ana.

Both Harper and Elizabeth spoke to the girl in soothing tones and kept her distracted while Betsy did her job. Elizabeth's nose scrunched when she picked up the acrid stench of the antiseptic when Betsy cleaned Ana's arm. Since Ana was so dirty from living on the street, Betsy cleaned her entire arm, not just the area the needle would be going in.

The whole thing took a little longer than usual, as Betsy had trouble getting a good vein, but Ana didn't seem to notice it. Elizabeth and Harper took turns telling her stories about Beacon Creek and what it was like growing up there. Ana seemed very interested in their tales.

"All done," Betsy announced, then said she would bring Ana some food soon. She was just waiting for the diner to bring it over.

They weren't a hospital, and they rarely kept a patient overnight. Usually if someone needed overnight care, they sent them via ambulance to the hospital in Bozeman. But once in a while they kept a patient there, and the nurses would stay overnight with them while one of the doctors would be on call. And the food came from the local diner.

"I don't want to stay here overnight," Ana whimpered. "I need to go back to Bozeman or Bart will get mad."

Elizabeth realized Bart had his claws in the girl, and it was going to take some time to de-program the poor girl. She also wondered how many others felt as Ana did.

"What will happen if you don't get back to Bart?" Harper moved the greasy bangs away from Ana's forehead.

She shrugged. "Most likely he'll come looking for me, and then I'll be in even worse shape."

"Did he do that to your ankle?" Elizabeth had wondered how she'd hurt her ankle so badly but hadn't wanted to ask until she felt Ana would be more open.

This was the most the girl had told them, and she wanted to get as much information as possible before the girl clammed up. It would only be a matter of time before she fell asleep. Elizabeth hoped the girl would keep talking to them until she fell asleep.

She shook her head. "Not really. It was my fault."

Harper narrowed her eyes and looked to Elizabeth. "How was it your fault?" She looked back at Ana with a calm face that belied how she felt inside.

The patient played with a loose string on her blanket before answering. "I was running from Bart and my foot got stuck in a pothole. So you see, it was my fault. If I had just done what Bart wanted, I would never have been injured."

The sharp intakes of breath from both women caused Ana's eyes to widen, and she looked between them both.

Releasing her breath, Elizabeth placed a hand on Ana's arm. "Sweetheart, it wasn't your fault. Bart shouldn't have been chasing you to begin with. It was his fault."

Ana's head shook violently. "No, I'm a very bad girl. It was all my fault. Bart was only doing his job."

Elizabeth knew that was what Bart told her. He'd probably told her repeatedly, and beaten her while he was telling her it was all her fault. She had seen it before, with ranchers and their animals. Evil men took their anger out on the weaker animal—or in this case, person—and blamed it all on their victim.

She felt the prickle of tears stinging her eyes, but she knew she couldn't break down. Not now.

A knock sounded at the door, and all three women looked as it opened. The person walking inside shocked her. Although she really shouldn't be too surprised; everywhere she went lately, he was there.

"Hi, I just came to check in on the patient. Doc Reynolds said you needed to stay off your feet for at least a week." Logan came inside with a bouquet of daisies.

He was always doing nice things like that for others. If she wasn't careful, that pang in Elizabeth's chest was going to cause those tears she was working so hard to keep at bay to spill over. She needed to remember she was mad at him, and that he wasn't really this nice anymore.

But that darned smile of his. It was like the sun, and she was drawn to it every time he flashed it. Even if it wasn't for her anymore.

"Thank you," Ana demurred and looked down at her blanket.

"Do you have a place to stay once you're released from the clinic?" Logan asked from the foot of her bed while he held the bouquet in his hand.

She shook her head.

"I was just thinking about where she could stay," Elizabeth said. "I think a few of the ranches would be open to taking her in and helping her recover. I was going to check today with Mr. and Mrs. Parsons, and then maybe even the Rodriguez family." She had a few more ideas as well.

"What about your parents' place?" Logan suggested.

Elizabeth and Harper both laughed.

"Do you really think she'd get much rest with all my brothers running around?" Elizabeth shook her head. She had thought of her family's ranch, but changed her mind when she remembered how rambunctious her brothers were. The house was never quiet. No way would Ana get any rest with the five of them running around like they were still young boys.

"I don't know. I think they spend most of their time outdoors running the ranch, don't they? Would they really be bugging a young lady who's in need of rest and relaxation?" Logan quirked a brow and looked directly at Elizabeth, who squirmed under the intense look.

"Well, my mom would definitely go into mother-hen mode and take great care of Ana. And if she wanted to spend some time in the living room, any of my brothers would be able to carry her in so that she stays off her feet." She nodded, thinking it might work.

They had an extra room—a few of them, actually. And her mother would love to have another woman in the house. Being surrounded by testosterone had made her mom call her on several occasions asking her to move back in.

Elizabeth turned to Ana. "Would you like to stay with my parents on their ranch? They have plenty of space, and my mom is one of the best cooks around."

Harper stood up and smiled. "She's wrong, her ma is the *best* cook around. Not to mention the steak that comes from their cattle is to *die* for!"

She may have exaggerated how great Mrs. Manning was, but her declaration about the steaks was spot on. The Triple J Ranch was known for its beef, and buyers came from all over the country to get their cattle at market.

Ana squirmed in her hospital bed with all eyes on her. She

bit her lower lip and narrowed her eyes as though she was concentrating, probably thinking about her options and what she wanted to do.

Elizabeth waited patiently, but she really hoped Ana would agree to stay with her family on the ranch. It would be a wonderful place for anyone to live. There was always something Ana could do, once she was healed. Even a city slicker could learn how to work on a ranch. Sure, it was hard work, but anyone could do it if they put their mind—and back —to it.

"I know my mom would love to have another girl in the house. Right now, it's all men." Elizabeth chuckled.

Ana's eyes widened, and she shrank into herself.

Elizabeth's hands went up. "Don't worry. My brothers are really nice. They've been brought up right—to respect women and not harm them in any way. My dad would beat the tar out of them if they ever hurt a woman. Or mistreated one in any way, shape, or form."

Even though they were allowed to wrestle with their sisters, the Manning brothers never hurt a woman. Period. Not after Matthew had hit one of Elizabeth's friends when he was thirteen. He didn't hit her hard, but she was taunting him, and he couldn't take it anymore, so he slapped her face.

Her father was so mad at Matthew. He was grounded with no TV, and he couldn't ride his horse unless it was needed for ranch business for the next month. Not to mention he was taken out behind the woodshed. When he came back in, Matthew wasn't able to sit for a while.

Not one of her brothers ever hurt another girl again after that. At least, not intentionally. Just about every day, Elizabeth could remember her father telling the boys how to be cowboy gentlemen. There was a code, and it was ingrained in the boys.

The twins were taught by their mother how to be ladies, but also how to take care of themselves. They did have an independent streak a mile long, which was probably why neither of them had settled down yet.

Growing up on the Manning ranch, everyone learned to treat others as they would want to be treated. They all grew up going to church and volunteering for the various events at church and in town. They knew how to give back to their community because their parents taught them the importance of giving.

The situation with the homeless in Bozeman was exactly what her parents would be involved in and expect their children to help with as well. Elizabeth knew her parents would love to have Ana come and stay at the ranch for as long as she wanted. However, she would need to call her mom and ask permission if Ana decided she was interested.

"I tell you what, why don't you think about it overnight? Tomorrow, when you're released, I'll take you out to my family ranch and you can meet my parents and brothers and see what you think. You don't have to make a decision right now. Just think on it, okay?" The more Elizabeth thought on it, the more she realized this was the best solution for Ana.

No way could Ana go back to Bozeman, because she would only end up back on the street again. Plus, Bart would hurt her again. Elizabeth would do anything to keep Ana from getting hurt by Bart or his cronies ever again. If that meant adopting her as one of their own, then so be it.

The young woman lying in the bed nodded, but she didn't smile. It was obvious to Elizabeth that Ana wasn't sure about this plan.

But Elizabeth was.

CHAPTER 16

Elizabeth's mother was more than excited about the plan. When she called her mom that night after Ana went to sleep, her mother went into planning mode and while they were still on the phone, she went into the guest room closest to the living room and began to get it ready for a guest.

Her mother said the girl was welcome to stay forever, if she wanted.

Elizabeth knew that her mom was excited to have another female in the house, but it was more than that. Having a young woman who needed help made her mother feel useful. Not only to the person who needed help, but also for God. Nothing made Mrs. Manning happier than when she was serving her Lord and Savior.

It was time for Ana to leave the clinic, but she seemed apprehensive.

"Ana, you don't have to stay with my family if you don't like. But please, give it a chance. You might like having a bunch of brothers around. Not to mention the food you'll get." Elizabeth chuckled and looked at the tiny frame of the girl in front of her.

Ana needed to get some meat on her bones. The girl looked like she hadn't eaten anything in weeks. Bart was probably keeping food from all the homeless as his way of controlling them. She wouldn't let thoughts of the mean bully get her down. Today was a good day, and she was going to stay positive. Getting at least one person off the street and out of Bart's hands was a great accomplishment. If this worked out, she would see about bringing more people back to the ranch.

The girl nodded. Elizabeth hoped she would start talking more. Non-verbal communication was going to make it tough to understand what Ana really wanted, or needed. If she didn't start to feel comfortable enough to talk, then Elizabeth didn't know if the situation would work out or not.

"Alright, let's get you checked out and head to the ranch." Harper came into the room with paperwork and went over it with both Ana and Elizabeth.

The clinic was usually closed on Sundays, but since they had a patient, a nurse had to be on duty. Once Ana was gone and everything was cleaned up, Harper would get herself ready and head to church.

"Will I see you in church today, Elizabeth?" Harper asked.

She shook her head. "Not today. I'm going to stay with Ana and help her get settled in at the ranch while my parents head to church. We can't leave Ana alone since she has to stay off her feet, and it's also a new place to her. She won't know where anything is."

Elizabeth knew she would get the CD for the sermon on Monday. She wasn't too happy about missing the service, but she also knew God would understand, since she couldn't exactly take Ana to church. Not yet. She did hope that Ana would be able to go the next week, and then every Sunday going forward.

As they drove down the dirt road leading to her family's ranch, Ana stared wide-eyed out the front window and occasionally turned her head to look at a horse here and there. Elizabeth doubted Ana was looking at the riders. It seemed to her that the girl was mesmerized by the animals.

"Have you ever ridden a horse?"

"No, never. I've never even seen one close up before." The awe coming from Ana's voice told Elizabeth this was going to work.

"Wait until you see the cattle, and all the other animals we keep on the ranch. Do you like dogs?" Elizabeth hadn't thought about it before, but the family had four dogs. They were all working dogs, but they did come and go through the house as though they were more like pets than part of the staff.

Although, the staff came and went through the house as well. Considering most of the year-round staff was family who lived in the ranch house, it made sense. They did have a few hands who lived in the bunkhouse year-round. And then a second bunkhouse would be opened up during certain seasons when they needed more temporary workers.

"I love dogs." Ana's voice was stronger than it had been.

Elizabeth knew that the fluids and decent meals she had eaten at the clinic were helping, but she also knew that being on the ranch was exactly what Ana needed.

"Did you ever have one growing up?" She didn't want to pry, but Elizabeth wondered what Ana's childhood was like if she was on the streets so young.

Ana started to nod, then stopped. "No. Not really."

The cryptic reply had Elizabeth even more curious about

the girl's upbringing and her story. She knew better than to push or pry, but man did she want to know what had happened to this girl. *Maybe, just maybe some time on the ranch with my family will help her feel comfortable enough to open up to someone.*

Even if Ana never told Elizabeth her tale, she hoped the girl would tell someone. Judith Manning was a great listener and had a heart full of wisdom to share with those who wanted it.

When they pulled Elizabeth's truck up to the front, Judith came out wearing her usual jeans, boots, button-up shirt, and an apron over the front. Her smile covered her entire face, and Elizabeth couldn't help but smile in return.

"Hi, Ma." Elizabeth gave her mom a hug and turned to the door where Ana was waiting for help getting out.

"Ma, I'd like to introduce you to Ana." She turned to the girl. "Ana, this is my mom, Judith Manning."

Ana smiled and responded, "It's nice to meet you, Mrs. Manning."

"Oh, please, call me Judith. I just know we're going to be the best of friends. I'm so excited you're here." Judith looked around and noticed one of her sons coming near. "John, can you come and help Ana inside?"

Elizabeth's second-to-youngest brother came up to them and touched the brim of his hat. "Nice to meet you, Ana." He put his hand out for her to shake. "I'm John, the strongest and most handsome of the Manning brothers. Do you mind if I carry you in?" He smiled at the girl, who wasn't much younger than he was.

Elizabeth hoped her young brother would behave and not flirt with Ana. Once Ana got cleaned up and put on a few much-needed pounds, she would probably be very cute. She didn't doubt the young cowboys in town would be falling at her feet.

Demurely, Ana nodded.

Elizabeth sighed. The girl was back to not speaking. Just when she got her to open her mouth, the girl went and closed it again. But this time, Ana looked different. She had a bit of color to her cheeks. *Is she blushing?*

Would being around her brothers help Ana to come out of her shell, or make her even more introverted? Elizabeth wasn't sure, but she thought Ana might think her brother was cute. The girl kept peeking up through her eyelashes at John and then looking back down quickly.

Judith walked next to Elizabeth as they followed a little behind John and Ana. "This might be interesting." She raised her eyebrows and looked pointedly at John.

John smiled down at the girl in his arms and chuckled. Ana must have said something, but Elizabeth couldn't hear her.

"Did you hear what she said?"

Judith slowed her pace even more. "No, but I imagine she and John have already hit it off."

Elizabeth frowned and worried for Ana.

Her mother put a hand on her forearm. "Don't worry. I'll have a talk with John, and all the boys, to make sure they understand to be nice and perfect gentlemen with Ana. You know they would never do anything untoward to the girl, right?"

"Of course, Ma. But I don't think they should be flirting with Ana until she's healed and feels more comfortable here with us. I think the girl might have a lot of demons she needs to slay before she's in a position to date." The last thing Elizabeth wanted was for Ana to fall for one of her brothers only to get her heart smashed. Her brothers weren't exactly boyfriend material. Especially the younger ones.

They were all good boys, but not one of them had said anything about wanting to settle down. They didn't date much; they all believed that dating around wasn't smart. They were more into courting a woman than just dating. But that didn't stop them from flirting with all the pretty girls in town.

"Don't worry, dear. I'll have a talk with the boys. They'll be on their best behavior, or their pa will have something to say to them." Judith nodded with a glint in her eye.

No one went against her mother. Well, no one who was smart, anyway. All the Manning kids had tried as children to best their mom, but she was too smart and stubborn for them. If they went too far, their dad stepped in and they were punished. Every one of them learned the line pretty early on and did everything they could to *not* cross it.

Elizabeth hoped that her brothers would listen to their mom.

CHAPTER 17

Two days passed so quickly that Elizabeth didn't have time to go out to the ranch and check on Ana. But her mother did call her each day and give a status update. The girl was shy, but who could blame her? And the boys were behaving, which was a huge relief to Elizabeth.

On Wednesday her schedule was light, and one of the ranches she had to go out to was just past the Triple J, so she stopped in to see her family and Ana.

Judith greeted her daughter with a hug and a smile. "Just in time for lunch. Care to join us?"

"Thanks, Ma. Don't mind if I do." Elizabeth's eyes scanned the living room for Ana but didn't see her. She furrowed her brow. "Where's Ana?"

Her mother smiled. "Follow me."

The two of them walked into the large kitchen, where an overstuffed recliner sat in the corner with the patient lying back in the comfy seat.

"Hi, Ana. How are you feeling?" Elizabeth noticed that the girl was already looking better; she had bathed and was wearing fresh clothes. Plus, her hair was no longer greasy, and she had a smile on her face.

"Much better, thanks to your ma. She's an angel." The girl looked at Mrs. Manning as though she were truly an angel sent down from heaven to look after her.

Chuckling, Elizabeth nodded. "Yes, she really is. I see you have a nice set up here in the kitchen. Do you stay here all day long?"

Ana shook her head. "No, just when Mama Judith is cooking. If she's not in here, then I'm either napping in my room, or in the living room watching TV."

Elizabeth's raiser her brows and looked to her mom before she mouthed, *Mama Judith?*

"Yes. Now that Ana is going to be living with us, I told her she could call me Mama Judith." She bristled a bit at the accusation on Elizabeth's face, but stood her ground.

"I think it's a great idea. I was hoping Ana would become part of our family." Elizabeth was happy that everything was working out for Ana. If Ana felt like she was part of the family, then she would stay, and once she was healed she could help with the ranch. It really was a good situation for Ana, as well as Elizabeth's family.

Without giving it another thought, Elizabeth walked to Ana and looked at her ankle. "How's the ankle? Any more pain? Are you keeping off your foot?"

Ana nodded. "The boys take turns carrying me around. Honestly, I feel a little like royalty with how they're all treating me." A little bit of pink stained her cheeks, and she looked down at her foot.

This was the most Ana had spoken to Elizabeth so far, and she realized how good her family was for Ana. She hoped that Ana felt comfortable opening up to her mother and would get the guidance she needed, as well as feel like staying here forever, if going home wasn't possible.

Elizabeth wanted the girl to stay, but she also thought Ana must have a family somewhere who were worrying about her. They would want to know she was alright and most likely would want her to come home to them. She knew her mother was already forming a strong attachment to Ana, and she would have to talk to her about that.

Until they knew for sure what Ana was going to do, keeping some sort of emotional distance from the girl would be the safest way to go for them all. It was how Elizabeth had gotten through these past ten years.

Now she wondered if letting herself like Max was the right thing or not. He'd not called her since she came back from Bozeman. Even when she called him, he didn't answer, or return her messages. She knew he was in town; she had heard as much. And his big race was in just a few days. She still planned to attend and support him even though they were having trouble. It was something she wanted to do for him.

Lunch was uneventful, but it did show Elizabeth how much Ana had changed in the short time since she'd arrived at the Triple J Ranch. Which was a good thing. The girl fit in with her family, and she was very happy to see it. She was going to have to let Chloe know. Although, Chloe had probably already been out here to see the girl.

Come to think of it, Elizabeth wondered why she hadn't heard from her sister since Sunday. They rarely went a day without at least a text message exchange. It wasn't like her sister to be so quiet. She'd have to call her later after she finished her paperwork for the day. Thankfully, she only had two more ranches to stop by, and then she could go back to her office and finish up on time for a change.

This was a busy season for the cattle ranchers. Most of them sold their cattle at market in the third and fourth quarters, as that was usually the time when they sold for a higher price. This year was no different. So she had a lot of cattle to check on and make sure they were healthy and ready for slaughter. She wanted all her clients' cows or steers to be ready for human consumption.

The rest of the week passed by quickly, and it was already time to head out for the demolition derby race. When Elizabeth had spoken to Chloe a few days before, the two decided to get a large group from town to head out for the races and support Max. She hoped that by doing something nice for her boyfriend, he would be in a better mood.

Logan had been one of the group of twenty people from Beacon Creek who went to support Max.

"Chloe, why did you invite Logan?" It wasn't that Elizabeth felt so mad at the guy anymore—it was that she felt awkward. She was still mad at him, but her anger was beginning to give way to something else. She wasn't sure yet what that something else was, but she still felt strange around her old boyfriend.

Chloe blinked and shook her head. "Not everything is about you, sis. Please remember that Max is the local John Deere rep, and he sells a lot of equipment out of the general store. Logan and Max work together."

Elizabeth winced and knew her sister was right. She was just being selfish not wanting Logan around. She was going to have to get used to him being a part of town life again.

Thankfully, Logan drove his own truck with Leah and a few of his friends.

Elizabeth, Chloe, Harper, Jonathan, and Drake all rode the thirty minutes together to the demolition derby semi-finals. If Max could earn enough points tonight, he would qualify for the finals. It was something he'd never been able to do before, and she knew he wanted this more than anything else right now.

"Drake, have you ever been to the demolition derby races?" Elizabeth walked next to her old high school friend.

"Of course, I even participated a few times. But the last race completely destroyed my engine, so I haven't raced in a few years." Drake shrugged and kept his eyes on the crowd.

"Wait, you've raced before? How come I never knew this?" Elizabeth thought she knew Drake. While they had never dated, they were friends most of their lives, and she saw him regularly.

"Huh?" He looked back at her. "Oh, it was while you were away in college. I went to school in Wyoming, where I didn't know anyone. My roommate was really into it, so I thought it would be fun to join him. I got into it and eventually got my own car from the junkyard and fixed it up. I never did very well. The engine kept sputtering during the events and usually gave out on me. Then the final race it went kaput, as did my aspirations of a drag racing trophy."

The group with them laughed and peppered Drake with questions about what it was like to constantly crash a car. Some even teased Drake, but he took it all in stride and had fun.

Drake spotted a hand in the air. "Look, it's Logan. Let's join him and the rest of the town."

Elizabeth and Chloe both nodded, and they all headed to where Logan was standing. She knew she needed to get along with him, but her stomach was all tied in knots and she wasn't sure she'd be able to keep up a good conversation if he was anywhere near her. So she pulled Chloe to the side. "Let's sit on the other side of group. I haven't had a chance to speak with the Diner Divas in a while."

Chloe chuckled and nodded.

It wasn't five minutes before Elizabeth regretted sitting with the divas. All they did was gossip. The women were sweet, but they just couldn't seem to stop their gossip.

Cindy Macon and her bobbing pink pouf of hair kept peppering Elizabeth with questions about Logan and Max. "Are you and Max doing alright, dear? I heard you two were fighting and that you've spent a lot of time with Logan lately." Her brows raised in anticipation of something juicy she could share.

"Now, Miss Cindy. You know better than to listen to gossip. What does the pastor say about gossip?" Elizabeth wasn't usually so direct, but she was so tired of the gossiping group.

They weren't always this bad, it was just lately. She thought they needed a project to keep them busy. Idle hands and all that was probably what had caused this group of women to be worse than the Presbyterians when it came to gossip.

Cindy sighed and took Elizabeth's hand. "You're right. I don't need to know what's going on with you and Max. But if you ever want to talk to someone, you know you can come to me, right?"

Elizabeth bit back the retort on her tongue. She didn't want to be disrespectful, but Cindy was the last person she would confide in.

"Miss Cindy, I thank you for your concern. I do have something I could use your help with. How about we meet up Monday for lunch to discuss it?" Elizabeth realized in that moment, Cindy and her divas had the most contacts in the area. They would be fantastic help with her latest problem, and it would keep them busy.

Elizabeth wondered how four women who had been retired for so long spent their days. She thought maybe it was boredom that brought them to their gossiping ways. Giving them something to do just might help them, as well as the rest of the town.

Cindy's eyes brightened, and she sat up taller. "Of course. I love to help you in any way I can. Even though my Stanley passed away years ago, I still remember what it was like to be married to a headstrong man. I'm sure I can help you with your Max and Logan issues." She nodded.

Elizabeth groaned inwardly and wanted to tell her what the topic was, but just then the announcer came on and everyone's attention turned to him.

"Ladies and gentlemen! Welcome to the semi-finals of the North American Demolition Derby Competition!" The announcer's deep voice came over the loudspeakers, and everyone began to clap.

Elizabeth heard the engines rev and watched as the first group of banged-up cars with different numbers on their doors made their way to the starting line. She looked at each number, hoping to see Max's number: 66. She knew there would be three sets of races tonight, and the top ten would be moving on to the finals. It wasn't so much about who lasted longer; it was all based on points. She didn't totally understand the point system, but knew enough to know that a good crash was worth a lot of points for both involved, as long as they were both still running. So was the person who had the best time overall for the race. It was a combination of racing and crashing that earned each driver points.

The crashing was what drew the crowds, but the overall competition was what drew the drivers. None of them would ever be professional race car drivers, but all of them had a chance at being champions on the demolition derby circuit.

The first race was exciting. Within the first five minutes, half the cars were down. The other half had crazy dents or missing parts of the body. The crashing was exciting, and the entire crowd went wild whenever someone hit another car.

Elizabeth was just as excited by the action as the crowd was. She was so into the race that she forgot all about her troubles and the gossiping ladies next to her. The Diner Divas had even stopped their gossiping long enough to watch the competition. She knew that come tomorrow, this race would be all the divas would talk about. In fact, they would probably talk about it for a few days.

All of a sudden, Elizabeth was very grateful these ladies came along for the ride. They really did need to get out more. Their boredom was probably what spurred their worst gossip. No one minded a little bit of talking, but the way the divas had been hounding everyone lately was getting on her nerves.

A project was exactly what they needed, and Elizabeth had just the thing for them.

CHAPTER 18

When the final racers made it to the track, Elizabeth was biting her nails—something she never did. Max was finally in the race, and after the carnage of the first two, she was a bit worried for him. Each race was timed, and only stopped when there was just one car left or the timer ran out.

In the first race, only one car remained, and it almost ran the clock out. Which made for an exciting race, but all those cars that were destroyed made her a bit nervous for Max.

In the second race, the clock ran out with three cars still running. She didn't know how the number thirty-two car was still running. Both front fenders were missing, the hood was bent like an aluminum can, and the rear of the car where the engine had been moved didn't have anything but the frame protecting the engine. And even that was bent. Not to mention the side doors. The guy would have to crawl out the open window. She was very grateful that no one was allowed to have glass in their windows. It made sense, since the object was to destroy the cars. Making sure the glass was all gone would help keep the drivers safer.

Now it was the final race, and Max was in it. Somehow

he was in the back of the pack. She wasn't sure if that was a good thing or bad. No one would come up from behind for a little while, and he could easily rear-end others, but was that better?

She watched while nibbling on her nails, and without realizing it, both her feet were bouncing up and down.

"Stop that." Chloe took Elizabeth's hand out of her mouth and put another hand on her knees to stop the bouncing. "He's going to be just fine. Keep in mind that he's been doing this for years."

"I know, but did you see those other cars? I swear, this is the most brutal of all the races I've seen all year. Two guys were taken away in an ambulance already. I hadn't seen that before." Elizabeth knew the contest was dangerous, but she didn't realize how dangerous it could be.

Her sister rubbed her back. "Don't worry, he's going to be fine. Max is a big, strong guy who's had plenty of experience."

Cindy joined in and agreed with Chloe. "Don't worry, dear. I've seen Max race before, and he's going to win. In case you haven't noticed, the winners of each match walked away. It was only the early losers who needed medical attention." She patted Elizabeth's knee like she was a little girl who needed reassurance.

Elizabeth *felt* like a little girl who needed reassurance that her favorite toy was going to be alright after one her brothers got their hands on it. Her head told her all would be fine. They had pretty strict safety protocols in place. The drivers all wore helmets and even fire-retardant safety vests that helped to protect their bodies from the brutality of the crashes.

But she still worried.

Her heart hadn't received the memo about the safety

protocols or about how well Max drove and how experienced he was. Instead, her heart kept watching the other car that rolled over several times and then caught on fire. That was one of the guys who was rushed away in an ambulance.

Logan watched Elizabeth as she worried over the race. During the previous heats when he looked at her, she appeared to be enjoying herself. Now, she was a mess. He knew when she was upset, and she was most definitely worried about her boyfriend. It was understandable, but it still grated on his nerves that she was sitting so close and there was nothing he could do to help her.

Jonathan nudged his arm. "Dude, just go over there and tell her it's all good. She'll probably be happy you said something to her."

He shook his head. "No, man. She has all of those women telling her all will be well. She doesn't want to hear from me."

"You won't know until you try. I thought you weren't going to give up on her?"

Logan shrugged. "I wasn't, until just now. Seeing how much she cares for Max tells me the gossip around town isn't exactly reliable."

"I saw them arguing the other day around the corner from the diner. All's not well with them. They may still be together, but something has gotten between them lately." Jonathan smirked and gave his friend a knowing look.

Logan sat up straight and looked to Jonathan. "What do you mean? What's gotten between them?"

"Like you have to ask. Please, they didn't start to have any problems until you came to town."

"That's not exactly what I heard. Rumor has it they began arguing after her first trip to Bozeman." Logan raised a brow.

Before they could continue their conversation, the crowd went wild, and everyone jumped up on their feet.

Logan and Jonathan did the same, and looked out into the mess that was the race track.

Demolition derbies were always done on a dirt track. It kept the cars from going too fast, but it also made everything so dirty and muddy when water made its way onto the track, as it always did.

Currently, eight out of the ten cars in this heat were smashed into each other. Logan didn't see how it happened, but when he looked up at the screen, a reply was showing.

The number sixty-two car seemed to have started it. He ran up into the rear of the nineteen car and hit it so hard from the rear-left side that it slid sideways and ran into the twenty-nine, and then that car rammed into the seventy-one which did a one-eighty and crashed straight into the ninety car. From there, the other cars behind them had no way to stop in time, and the other three cars rammed hard into the mess of crashed vehicles.

Logan looked for number eighty-eight and saw that he had stopped just before the throng of crashed cars. Max hadn't been involved in the crash; he actually looked like his car hadn't hit much. Logan wondered if that would be good or bad for his points that night.

Max backed up a bit and went slowly around the group of mangled cars. He took the lead in the race, and Logan knew he would have to crash into the remaining car for more points. Unless some of those in the pile could make it out. Then maybe he could crash into one of them.

The other car that was still running came upon Max's backside and tapped his rear. They didn't have bumpers, since those fell off so easily. The bump caused Max to slide a little, but the muddy track kept him going forward.

Elizabeth was chewing on her nails again, or what was left of them. She was worried. Of course she was. But she was also excited. Max had a real shot at winning his heat. If he could get enough points, he would move forward to the finals.

No matter what was going on with their relationship, she still wanted him to succeed. He really was a nice guy, but lately... No, she wouldn't think about that. She needed to keep her eyes on the track and on Max.

Tonight was about his victory, not their issues.

"Dearie, please don't worry so. You're going to start eating off the tips of your fingers if you don't relax just a bit. And then how will you help all those poor animals?" The pink pouf of hair that was next to her had stepped in front of her and made it difficult to see the track. Cindy looked worried for Elizabeth.

She pulled her hand away from her mouth.

"Do I need to put tobasco sauce on your fingers?" Cindy put her hands on her hips and stared Elizabeth down.

Her brows furrowed and she cocked her head to the side. "Tobasco sauce?"

"Of course, dear. I did that to my little Charlie when he continued to suck his thumb after the age of three. It's really not good for your mouth. But after a few times with tobasco sauce, he stopped." Cindy beamed at her method.

"Um, I don't think that's really a good idea, Cindy. Experts are now saying that it's fine until their permanent teeth begin to come in. Plus, tobasco sauce could hurt a child's stomach." While Elizabeth enjoyed the spicy concoction on her omelets, she didn't think it would taste very good to a three-year-old.

Cindy waved her hand in front of her face. "Pish, Charlie's just fine, and he had perfect teeth. He never even needed braces."

Elizabeth knew better than to argue with Cindy, so she let it go and then realized what the woman had done. She lightly chuckled and nodded her head. Cindy had helped her to get her mind off her worries and even helped her to relax her shoulders just a bit.

She looked out onto the track and saw that the mess that was the crash was much smaller than before. Half the cars had moved away and were back in the race. The other half were still there, stuck.

As the audience began to take their seats once again, so did Elizabeth and Cindy.

"See, everything is just fine." The pink pouf nodded, and for some strange reason it stayed in place, even after all the excitement and moving around.

Elizabeth had no clue how Cindy kept her pouf in place at all times. The thing must have been a foot tall. It was dense as a forest, and she had never seen a single hair out of place, not even once. Cindy must have used a can of Aqua Net every day to keep it in place so well.

With her attention once again back on the race, Elizabeth looked for Max. On the other side of the track, she saw him hitting a car. Max's car came up from behind and hit the other car's rear quarter panel. The car veered to the side and did a forty-five-degree turn. Max got out in front again and was leading the pack.

Those who had been in the accident were three laps behind Max, but it wasn't so much about the laps and time as it was the crashing and the points they had accumulated.

"Hey there. Mind if I sit?" Logan was standing next to Elizabeth, and she wondered how he'd gotten there without her even noticing he had moved.

"Uh, sure. Be my guest." She wasn't too happy about him sitting with her, but she couldn't exactly tell him no. Especially not with everyone around them. If Cindy heard her being rude, the entire town would know about it.

"How are you doing with this race? Even my heart skipped a few beats when that crash happened. Thankfully Max wasn't in it, but he lost out on a lot of points by *not* being in it." He emphasized the *not*, knowing it was the points that mattered.

She sighed and gave him a small smile. "Yeah, part of me is glad he wasn't in that crash, but another wishes he could have been at the back of the pack and at least got some points." She shrugged.

"Well, he's most likely going to come in first for time, and with the few hits he's taken, along with those he's dished out, he should place nicely." Logan kept his hands in his lap and looked between the track and Elizabeth.

"Fingers crossed." Elizabeth crossed her fingers on both hands and put them out in front of her for everyone to see. She also sent up a prayer for Max and for her to be courteous to Logan.

He was trying.

She knew that.

But something inside her knew she had to protect herself from Logan. If she didn't, he would be in a place to hurt her again. She was finally healing enough to go out with someone again and didn't want to ruin the progress she had made.

They sat there in silence watching the last of the race. There were only five laps left to go, and with half of the contestants out, Elizabeth figured it should go fairly quickly and easily.

"How's Ana doing?" Logan took his eyes off the track and settled them on Elizabeth.

She saw out of the corner of her that Chloe and Cindy were both watching them. Most likely everyone was. "She's doing great. I think she's going to fit in at the ranch just fine once she heals up."

"That's great to hear. I was worried about her and wanted to stop by and check in on her. So did Drake. Do you think your mom would mind if we came out one afternoon?"

Elizabeth shook her head. "I think she'd like to see you both. And I know Ana would appreciate some company. She's still stuck on the couch and only moves when one of the boys carries her somewhere. My mom is being a stickler about her staying off her feet until the doctor says otherwise."

Logan chuckled. "I can imagine that's going over real well."

His dry humor was always something Elizabeth appreciated about him. She chuckled.

"Yup. She wasn't too happy at first. But when Mom gave her a fairy wand and said she was a princess and princesses never go anywhere without their servants, Ana laughed and took the wand. They've been making a game out of it, and my brothers are even playing along." She laughed.

"Really? Your brothers, allowing a princess to order them about?"

She nodded. "They get points for being the one to carry her around. Pa said the one with the most points gets an entire weekend off. Zero chores, no feeding any animals, no dishes, they don't even have to take out the trash."

Logan laughed out loud, and everyone looked their way, even those they didn't know. "I'll bet Mark is jumping at the chance to win that contest. Does he still hate to muck the stalls just as much as he did when we were in high school?"

She chuckled and felt a bit lighter. It was almost as though the past ten years hadn't happened at all. Almost.

"Yes. He's always jumping at the chance to help Ana. At first, I was worried he might be trying to flirt with her, but when Ma told me about the contest, I knew exactly what he was up to. It's also a chance for him to skip out on chores during the day. He finds ways to come in and check on her and see if she needs anything or if she wants to be moved anywhere."

"I can totally see him doing that. Your mom was smart to make it a contest, and your dad was genius to give the winner a full weekend off. I'd enjoy that too. I'd forgotten how much work went into a ranch and running the general store these past ten years." He shook his head.

"When I was gone, I worked hard," he went on. "But it was a different kind of work. Sitting in an office all day is very different from even running the store. I didn't move anything heavier than a book, and even that was rare."

Elizabeth looked him over and noticed he was in very good shape. Better than she remembered. "But you're in great shape. How'd you do that?"

"Proper diet and lots of hours at the gym each week." His eyes sparkled when he smiled at her.

Elizabeth felt the heat moving through her cheeks and turned her face back to the track.

Max was still in first place for time and laps according to the leader board. The points for the crashing wouldn't be displayed until the final lap.

"Look, there's only two laps left, and Max is currently in first place." She put her entire focus back on the race and Max. If she didn't, she'd start thinking and feeling things she ought not to about the handsome man next to her.

Her heart didn't seem to get the memo, because it was still fluttering at Logan's nearness. She attempted to think harder about Max, but it wasn't working.

When the breeze blew her way, she picked up Logan's unique scent and her heart began to flutter anew. The creamy and slightly sweet aroma of sandalwood mixed with pine and Logan's pure scent always calmed her. It was the smell of home. He was the scent of home.

She needed to get away from him to help clear her head. So she stood up and began clapping and calling out Max's name. If she focused on Max, she felt that she would be able to clear her head of Logan, and maybe even her heart, too. She was still dating Max, technically. Wasn't she?

Although, they hadn't spent any time together in a few weeks. They had barely spoken, and when they did it was short and not sweet. She was beginning to wonder if they really were still a couple. Maybe the gossip hounds had it right after all, and she just didn't realize it.

The thought of not really being Max's girlfriend didn't hurt like it once would have. Did her heart know the truth?

If so, her head needed to get the memo…and soon.

CHAPTER 19

"Yes!" Elizabeth practically jumped with joy and excitement as she watched Max cross the finish line.

He didn't have the most points, but when his points were combined with finishing first and his time, he ended up in first place.

Only two of the eight vehicles that crashed earlier had finished. The rest either didn't make it out of the dog pile, or they petered along the way. Elizabeth knew that had some of them made it to finish line, even if in last place, Max wouldn't have been able to finish in first. He only needed to be top three, but she knew he wanted a first-place finish in his heat to give him a better starting position for the finals that were only two weeks away.

"Wow, that was exciting. It went down to the end to decide the second-place winner. I see what you mean about how much crashing counts. Even though car number nineteen finished last, he was in second place thanks to his crash points." Chloe's smile was a mile wide.

"Does this mean you're now a fan of the sport?" Elizabeth nudged her sister.

"I think so."

It was only two days later when Elizabeth and Max found time to meet up and talk.

She wanted to ask him outright of they were still a couple, but that was rude, and she wasn't sure how he would take it. However, she wasn't good at beating around the bush, either.

"Congratulations, Max, on your win. That was a very exciting race," Elizabeth gushed, not knowing how to start their conversation. It was her idea to meet up after all. If she had left it to him, they might never had spoken again.

"Thanks." His smile was warm, but nothing compared to what he normally gave her.

She could tell he wasn't really into this conversation. He wasn't really looking at her. He only glanced at her and then turned either his head to look around or moved his eyes to look over her shoulder, or next to her. If he did look directly at her, it was only a passing moment.

"Is something on your mind?" She hoped they wouldn't argue, but they did need to clear the air. Whatever had happened over the past weeks needed to come out and be dealt with. She was tired of not knowing what was going on with him.

He nodded, then sat there mute.

Max only looked down at his hands, he refused to look even her way.

She scratched the tip of her nose and wondered what was going on in his head. Then she fidgeted where she stood next to the wood fence separating the path they were on and the river that ran through town. Well, it was on the outskirts of town, really.

The town had built a beautiful park with a softball field, soccer field, and a kiddie playground. Trees were every-where, and picnic benches had been placed far enough away from the others that multiple families could enjoy the park without disturbing other families enjoying their outing. But they could also still hold the town annual picnic, and it was small enough that when everyone was there, it felt like one giant event instead of a bunch of smaller, more intimate picnics.

"Let's take a seat." He directed her to a nearby bench overlooking the slow-moving river.

Once they were both seated, he shifted himself to look at her and he took her hand in his, still not looking her in the eyes.

She squeezed his hand in response, hoping to tell him that whatever it was, she was there for him. Elizabeth didn't want to disturb the peace between them, but she did need to know what was going on. For a moment she considered asking him, but then thought better of it and waited for him.

He probably needed a chance to gather his wits or figure out what he wanted to say to her. She could give him the time. It wasn't like she had anywhere else to be that night. Milton was the one on call, so she doubted she would be getting any emergency calls for the business.

After a few tense moments, he began. "Elizabeth, you know I care a great deal for you, right?"

Even though he wasn't looking at her, she nodded. She didn't want to disturb the peace or open her mouth. If she began speaking, she wasn't sure she wouldn't stop. There was so much on her mind about what had been going on between them lately. She wanted answers, and believed that she deserved some.

He sighed and finally he looked her in the eye. The pain and anguish she saw there gripped her heart. She had to clamp her mouth shut before she said something. He needed to speak, and she understood that.

Elizabeth gave him an understanding smile and hoped that she was conveying how much she cared about him through her eyes, and that he could see it and understand.

He sighed again. "I'm sorry, but I don't know if this is going to work."

She blinked, not understanding where that came from. Then she sighed and realized he was probably right.

"Is it because I want to help the homeless?" She had wondered if that would be what broke them up.

He nodded, then shook his head. "Not really. It might have been the catalyst, but I'm not really mad about that. I'm sad and worried for your safety. Eventually you'll come to realize that I was right."

"I had hoped you would change your mind. Or at least tell me why you're so adamant about your position. What happened, Max, to make you hate the homeless so much?" She let go of his hand and put hers back in her lap.

"It doesn't really matter anymore. It's all in the past. What does matter is that you be careful. I don't want to see you get hurt. That Bart guy is dangerous."

She nodded. "I know. We brought back a girl who had been abused by Bart. She hasn't said much, but what she did say told us enough."

"What? I hadn't heard this. Where is she? Please tell me she's not staying at your house?" His voice was sharp, but not angry. It sounded more worried than anything else.

She put her hand on his arm. "Don't worry. She's staying at the ranch with my entire family looking after her. She's pretty injured and can't even walk right now, let alone do anything to hurt anyone else."

"Well, that's good." His eyes widened when he realized how that sounded. "Not that she's injured. Just that, well, that your family is taking care of her. I know she'll be looked after and get a chance to heal up there."

"Yeah, my entire family has really taken to her. She's sweet, and should never have been living on the streets. I'm hoping Mom will get her story from her and maybe we can help her get home and reunite with her family." Elizabeth knew that even if that wasn't possible, her family would adopt her. They had all already fallen in love with the girl.

"Did your last experience show you that you shouldn't be helping them?" he asked, sounding a bit hopeful she would agree with him.

She shook her head. "No. In fact, quite the opposite. They really need help."

"I know you well enough to know that you aren't going to listen to me without proof on this subject. I just hope that you stay safe and Bart doesn't hurt you." He ran his hand down the outside of her upper arm.

"Thank you, Max. I know you're just trying to look out for my safety, but we brought along a bunch of guys and were safe the entire time. In fact, we left when it looked like it might become dangerous. Logan even called the Bozeman sheriff to tell him about what happened."

Since their last trip to Bozeman, she hoped that the sheriff was getting rid of Bart and helping those poor souls find homes…or make it back to their families, where possible.

"I heard that Logan went with you. Are you two getting along again?"

She couldn't be sure, but she thought she detected a little bit of jealousy in the way his eyes narrowed and his voice deepened when he said Logan's name.

She couldn't help but smile. Not because of spending time with Logan, or at least she didn't think it was because of him. No, she smiled because Max did care after all.

"I'm trying to work through my issues. Everyone keeps telling me I have to forgive him, but I still don't even know why he broke up with me. It just came out of nowhere. Everything was great and on track for me going to college with him, and then BAM! He just broke up with me and left. He didn't even give me a chance to ask questions or try to talk him out of it." She shrugged. She didn't want Max to know how much it still hurt her, but she was starting to realize that forgiveness was what would help to heal her heart.

After the pastor's sermon on forgiveness a few weeks back, she had some more study on the topic and a lot of praying. At first, she had no idea she needed to forgive Logan in order for her own heart to heal. She had thought forgiveness was something the transgressor needed, not the one who was injured.

She was slowly coming to the conclusion that forgiveness was something her own heart needed to do before it could let go of the pain and move on. The act of forgiving had nothing to do with the person who hurt her—in this case, Logan—but everything to do with her and God.

Because she hadn't forgiven Logan, she hadn't been able to receive the peace that only God can give a person's soul.

In her studies, she had learned that God commands us to forgive those who hurt us. And since she hadn't, she'd been sinning these past ten years, which can drive a wedge between her and God. It was no wonder she couldn't get past the pain and find love again.

"Did you ever listen to the pastor's sermon on forgiveness? The one I told you about?" She looked at him and watched, waiting to see if he understood what she was saying.

He shook his head. "No, I have the CD and keep meaning

to listen to it when I'm on the road, but just haven't done it yet."

Taking a deep breath, Elizabeth knew this was the time to speak to him about his past. "I think it would do you a lot of good. I've heard others in the congregation speak about that sermon. I think we all needed to hear it. Whatever happened in your past isn't going to go away. You're going to continue to feel the hurt and anguish until you can forgive."

She paused and looked at him, wondering if he was listening and taking her words to heart. "Do you know what I mean?" she asked.

He nodded. "Yeah, I think I do. I have a road trip again this week. I'll probably listen to the CD when I head out of town."

She nodded. "You've been traveling a lot lately. What's up with that?"

He turned fully and looked her in the eye. His small smile was a nice change from the pain she had seen on his face for most of their conversation.

"The other rep covering the counties next to mine is getting ready to retire and has cut back his hours. Until the company replaces him, I've been tasked with helping to cover his accounts. Actually, that's what I wanted to discuss with you." He rubbed the back of his neck.

"Go on." Elizabeth figured she knew what he was going to say. Something inside her had prepared her for this.

It seemed as though their time together was coming to an end, no matter what the catalyst was.

CHAPTER 20

Elizabeth sat there patiently waiting for him to say what he needed to say. She had an idea of what it was going to be, but he needed to say it.

Max ran a hand through his thick head of hair and sighed. "I guess there really isn't an easy way of doing this. I've thought it about long and hard for the past two weeks, and I think it's for the best. We haven't been getting along very well lately, and we seem to be going in two different directions."

She nodded. Part of her was ready for this, but another part of her wasn't. He was the first man she thought she could trust since Logan broke heart ten years ago. Saying goodbye wasn't going to be easy.

"My company is relocating me to be more central to all the accounts I'm helping to cover. It's supposed to only be temporary, but even when we bring on a new guy, I'll be the one who trains him. So I will most likely be away for at least six months." He still couldn't look at her.

His shoulders slumped, and she knew he felt horrible. The last thing she wanted was for him to feel bad.

"What does this mean for your current clients? Will you still handle their accounts?"

He smiled and replied, "Yes. My schedule is going to be very crazy for a while. I won't have any extra time for myself."

"Or for dating." She knew what he was trying to say.

"I'm sorry, Elizabeth. I truly am. But with the way things have gone for us these past weeks, don't you agree some time apart would be good for us?" Finally, he looked her in the eye. Sadness filled his eyes.

She could tell he was sad about their situation. They had been together for a while, and until she started working with the homeless, it seemed as though they were a good team. Was this God's way of showing them they weren't really meant for each other? She couldn't understand why He even let them get together in the first place. But she wasn't going to be upset about their relationship. They never crossed a line, or even got close.

She trusted him.

Maybe that was what this was for her—a chance to learn how to trust a man again. If so, then she would be grateful for the time she had with Max and all their fun times together.

It was time she told him how she felt. "I understand and I agree, Max. I do think we need some time apart. These past few weeks, everything between us has been so strange. But I will be forever grateful for the time we had together."

She put her hand on his and continued, "You're a great guy, Max. You are going to make some woman very happy one day. I just hope you can find forgiveness for whatever has caused you to hate the homeless so much."

He started to say something, but she put her hand up to stop him.

"I know, there are bad people in the homeless groups, but

you know what? There are bad people everywhere. Just because someone is homeless doesn't necessarily make them bad. But I know we disagree on this, and I don't want to argue over it anymore."

He took her hand in his. "Thank you. I don't want to argue, either. I know that there is something in my past I need to deal with. Maybe this time on the road will help me figure it all out."

"Can we part as friends? It's not like something horrible caused us to break up. I think our time together has come to a natural end." She shrugged, not knowing how to describe exactly what she felt about the breakup. The only thing she wanted now was to know they could see each on the streets of town next time he came here, and everything would be alright. She didn't want anything to be weird between them. He really was a nice guy, someone she could see herself being friends with.

For the first time in weeks, his smile touched his eyes and caused her to smile in return. He really did have a nice smile. The kind that could melt a woman's heart.

"Yes, I would like that very much. I'll be back in town on occasion checking on my accounts, including the general store." He gave her a quizzical look. There was something in his eyes, but she couldn't quite understand what was going through his head.

"Then maybe we can have lunch or something when you come to town next. I would like to know you're doing well once you move away. You're going to be so busy, I worry that you won't get enough rest." Her eyes widened. "Wait! What about the derby finals? Will you get to compete?"

When he chuckled, she relaxed just a bit. She really did like his deep laugh. But it didn't send tingles up her spine like it once did. Was she really over Max already? They'd just broken up like two minutes ago.

"Yes. I told my district manager that I had the finals, and since they sponsor my car, they were adamant that I take the time I needed to get ready for the event and win." The light sparkled off his white teeth when he gave her a toothy grin.

"Am I still invited to watch you compete?" She wasn't sure if he wanted her there, but she did want to go. It was important to her to show she still supported him, even if they weren't together anymore. That's what friends did, right?

"Of course you are. I'd be hurt if you didn't go. In fact, I hope a large group from town joins us. It's less than a thirty-minute drive. It's just on the other side of Bozeman." He rubbed his hands together and looked toward the north, toward Bozeman, where he would be competing in the demolition derby finals in less than two weeks.

Elizabeth stood up. "Wonderful. I can't wait to watch you win. Just…be safe. Alright?"

He nodded. "Of course. I'm always safe."

He gave her a cheeky grin, and she lightly punched him on his shoulder.

"Alright Mr. Crash Test Dummy, I wish you luck and I'll see you soon."

He stood up and hugged her. "Thank you for understanding."

She didn't respond, just hugged him tighter and then let go. Without looking at him, she walked away and toward her car.

CHAPTER 21

The next day, Elizabeth was called out to the Bar One Ranch. It seemed word had gotten out about Mr. William's issue with shipping fever. Now all the ranchers in the county who had purchased any cattle whatsoever were calling and asking to have theirs checked out. Chances were really slim anyone else would have contaminated cattle.

It wasn't like any cattle would need to be put down, if they did have it. Most could be treated with medication and then be fine. The medication would also leave their system well before any of them would go up on the butcher's block. There wasn't a need to panic, but whenever some gossip about cattle and disease spread, panic usually followed.

She and Milton were going to be very busy the rest of the week, at least.

That wasn't even accounting for any of their regular appointments or the horses that were ready to foal. Or even any other emergency situation.

With her schedule, Elizabeth really didn't have time to think about breaking up with Max, or what that could mean for Logan.

So when Logan approached her Friday afternoon, less than a week after she and Max were officially no longer a couple, she wasn't ready to see him.

Elizabeth was coming out of the diner after a quick lunch and was looking down at her phone. She should have been paying attention to where she was going, she knew that. Her sister was the one famous for not watching where she was going. Elizabeth was the one who hated it when people messed around on their phones while walking or driving. It wasn't safe.

"Whoa, be careful little lady." The smooth sound of a familiar voice called out to Elizabeth, and she froze.

Logan chuckled, and Elizabeth slowly raised her head. "Logan, what are you doing here?" She knew it was a stupid response; he worked just a few doors down and across the street from the diner.

His dazzling smile sent chills down her spine, like it always did. But what surprised her the most was that she didn't feel any more anger toward him. She had been praying about forgiving him lately. Maybe it really did help.

"I was heading into the diner to pick up lunch for Leah and me. We're doing a bit of inventory checking and decided to skip lunch." He took his Stetson off his head and ran his hand through his dark brown hair.

Visions of her doing just that to him when they were in high school flashed through her head, and she felt her cheeks begin to heat up. She knew a blush was imminent, and she did *not* want him to see her cheeks turning red while talking to him. She looked back over her should and bit her lip.

Then thought about work.

The idea of putting her arm inside a foaling mare did the trick. All of a sudden, her face felt cool and she turned back around.

He was looking over her shoulder and frowned. "I was sorry to hear about you and Max."

Her forehead furrowed, and she wondered where that had come from. She turned to look back over her shoulder again since he was still looking that way, and she realized he had seen Max coming out of the barber shop. Logan must have thought she was looking at Max the first time she turned her head.

Well, she guessed it was better than him thinking she was blushing over thoughts of running her hands through Logan's hair. Which was not something that she planned to ever do again.

"Thanks." She really never knew what to say when people said they were sorry for a breakup. She wasn't sorry, and she certainly didn't want to talk to Logan about it.

"Soooo." She put her hands in her back pockets. "Inventory? Now?"

He chuckled. "Yes. I know, it's not normal inventory time, but when I got back I noticed we had a lot of big equipment in the store taking up too much floor space. I wanted to see if we could discount some of it and get it out in time to begin bringing in Christmas decorations."

Elizabeth's eyes lit up. "Oh, I remember when we were kids helping your parents bring in the decorations and setting up on Saturday nights after you closed. That was a lot of fun. Those nights were always the beginning of the Christmas season for me."

He looked down at his boots, trying to hide his longing for those simpler times. "Yes, they were always the best times for me as well." He shuffled his boots on the sidewalk. "You know, Leah and I are going to do the setup ourselves. Mom doesn't want to leave Dad alone so late at night. If you want, you could join us. Mom said she'd make her usual deserts and hot apple cider for us to take to the store that night. Maybe even ask Chloe if she wants to join us?"

Her heart pounded in her chest, and had to bite back a yes. She loved those nights, but that was when she and Logan were a couple. Now she didn't even know if they were friends. "I don't know. We're swamped right now, and Chloe's getting ready to leave for her new job. Or at least I think she is. She refuses to tell me when she's leaving, or even if she got a job. I know she did, but she won't tell me anything."

He tilted his head and furrowed his brow. "But I thought the two of you always told each other everything?"

"So did I." Elizabeth had noticed a few packed boxes in Chloe's place the last time she went by unannounced. Her twin had said that she was just getting rid of some things she no longer needed, but Elizabeth knew what was going on.

It frustrated her that her only sister wouldn't confide in her. The entire family knew that she was looking to leave town. They all knew she'd gone on interviews a few weeks back. Elizabeth was convinced they had all offered Chloe a job. Maybe her sister was just trying to figure out which job to take and didn't want to say anything until she had made her choice?

Elizabeth wasn't sure what was going through her sister's head, since she refused to talk about it.

However, one of these days Chloe would have to say something. Surely she wouldn't just up and leave without even a "by your leave," would she?

"I think you two need to sit down and have a heart to heart. Maybe take her to the tree?"

Logan and her brothers had made a tree fort when they were really young. The twins were only allowed in because Logan always brought them. And since he had helped to create the fort, the Manning brothers couldn't say no. Especially since it was on Logan's family's land.

As time went on, it became more and more Logan and Elizabeth's place. The Manning brothers had more responsibilities on the Triple J Ranch, and they also participated in high school sports, and then dating. There just wasn't time or interest in a childhood fort.

Elizabeth smiled. "You know, I haven't been there since junior year." She shook her head. "I don't even remember the last time I thought of it. Is it still standing?"

"Yup. The last time I was in town I went out there and fixed it up. A few boards needed replacing and a few spots needed reinforcing, but it's sturdy and just waiting for someone to use it again." Logan's eyes had that distant look, as though he was thinking back to their time in the tree fort, just like she was.

"Did your sister ever use it?" Once they broke up, Elizabeth never went to the Hayes house, or to the fort. She didn't even ask about it when she saw Leah or her parents in town.

He shook his head. "No, I don't think so. When she was young and used to follow me around, she would always try to get in, but we never let her. So, I think she was conditioned to not want to go in after so many years." Logan had been a bit mean to his kid sister when they were younger, but what big brother wasn't?

If Elizabeth and Logan hadn't been so close, her brothers would have made sure she didn't get to go in either.

Her phone rang, and she looked at the caller ID. "I've got to take this. It was nice seeing you, Logan. Have a great day." And she meant it, too.

He smiled and waved goodbye. "Think about what I said. Leah and I would love to have you and Chloe help us set up. I'll let you know what night we plan to do it, in case you want

~~to join us.~~ Oh, and ~~we'll be playing all the old Christmas~~ songs you used to love so much."

She smiled and answered her phone. It was another ranch calling about their cattle. They had a few of their own heifers who seemed to have caught something. They were worried about the disease that was supposedly running rampart through all the ranches.

Elizabeth knew they were going to have to issue some sort of statement to the county ranches, letting them know that the local gossip was wrong.

She stopped walking when she hung up with Mr. Mendez.

The Diner Divas. She knew how the gossip had spread, and how to fix it. She turned around and began to walk back to the diner to get those nosy women to fix this mess.

After looking at cows and steer from seven different ranches this week, she and Milton knew there weren't any other cases of shipping fever. The gossip had caused so much ruckus for nothing.

Sure, her practice was going to make a lot of money this month from all the exams she and Milton had to conduct, but that wasn't nearly as important as calming down the ranch owners. She would much rather have a slow month than a month of upset and worried cattle owners.

When she walked back into the diner, the divas looked at her and smiled in unison.

Uh-oh. They were up to something, and Elizabeth knew it had to do with her.

CHAPTER 22

"Finally! It's about time the gossip died down, and my schedule as well." Elizabeth sat having lunch with her twin sister almost a week after she had a nice heart to heart with the Diner Divas about the latest round of gossip and asked them to fix it.

She knew their hearts were in the right place, but they did need something to keep them busy. The small town of Beacon Creek was just too small for a group of elderly, retired, single ladies to sit around with nothing but time on their hands.

"Does this mean you're going to help Logan and Leah?" Chloe had heard from Leah about Logan's offer to join them for the Christmas prep at the store. Since then, she hadn't stopped bugging Elizabeth about it.

"Are you going to finally tell me about your new job?" Elizabeth raised her eyebrows. She felt it was time her sister come clean about her future. If Chloe was going to leave town, her family deserved to know about it beforehand.

Ignoring her sister's question, Chloe asked, "So are you going to help them out? I know how much you love

Christmas and doing the reset at the store. I think it's time you help them again."

"Chloe." Elizabeth's voice took a deep tone, and she narrowed her eyes. "I don't want to hear about you moving out from the divas. I think I have a right to know if you accepted an offer and will be moving away. Why won't you tell me about this?"

It was starting to really grate on Elizabeth's nerves. She wondered if Chloe didn't trust her enough to tell her about the offer, but that didn't make any sense. They had always told each other everything, and if something needed to stay quiet, then Elizabeth kept her mouth shut.

Chloe sighed and twirled the spoon in her coffee mug. Then she picked up a few fries and dunked them in ketchup before eating them slowly.

Elizabeth sat there waiting. If Chloe wasn't going to tell her anything, then she wasn't going to talk, either.

"Fine." Chloe's shoulders slumped. "I did get an offer, but before I could tell you about it, they rescinded the offer."

"What? Why didn't you tell me? That had to hurt. I would have been here for you. You know that, right?" Elizabeth's hand moved across the table to take her sister's.

Chloe nodded. "I know, but I was just so embarrassed. I had told one person, and then that night I got the call about them reneging on their offer." She waved her hand over her plate. "I don't know, I guess I thought I had jinxed it by saying something to even one person. So I kept my mouth shut and waited to hear back from the other offices."

"Well, did you?"

A small smile crept across Chloe's face. "Yes, actually, I did. Just last week."

"And?"

"And I accepted. I start October 1." Chloe squeezed her sister's hand.

Elizabeth pulled her hand back and started to clap and squeal in her seat. "Oh, this is fantastic! Tell me about the job. Where is it? How far away will you be?"

Elizabeth didn't want her twin and best friend leaving town, but she knew her sister wanted to live in a larger city. She always had. Even though her sister was going to move away and they wouldn't be able to see each other every day if they wished, she was very happy for her. It wasn't easy leaving home or going after your dream. Chloe had done just that, and she was proud of her.

"Shhh." Chloe looked around the diner and slumped in her seat when she saw the Diner Divas looking at her and whispering amongst themselves. "The gossipmongers are watching."

"Oh, don't pay them no mind. Everyone is going to find out anyway when you move. Actually, the moment you quit your current job everyone will know." She waved her hand in front of her face, not the least bit worried about this gossip getting around.

Chloe sat up straight. "Okay, I guess you're right. It's been a week and they haven't rescinded their offer, so it must still be good, right?" She sounded as though she was worried about losing out on this job as well.

"Hey, don't worry about it. Remember, God is in control. He obviously didn't want you to have the other job. He must have known this one was going to come through, and this is the one He wanted for you. Just remember that."

Chloe shook her head. "You're right. And I should have been up front with you from the beginning."

"So, tell me. What's the job and where is it?" Elizabeth hoped it was close by and would be an easy drive for a weekend trip on a regular basis. She knew her entire family would want to see Chloe as much as possible.

Chloe cleared her throat. "You're looking at the new administrator for the Lolo Regional Medical Clinic in Frenchtown, Montana." She kept her voice low so as not to be overheard by anyone.

Elizabeth guessed Chloe didn't want her parents to hear the news secondhand before she had a chance to tell them. Something she wholeheartedly supported. Her parents would have a fit if they heard from the gossip mill and not from their own daughter that she was moving so far away.

She leaned in and whispered back to her sister, "Congratulations. We'll have to have a party to celebrate on Sunday after church." She smiled and knew she really was happy for her sister. Elizabeth bit her lip, calculating about how long it would take to get to Frenchtown, and realized it wasn't too bad. It would be about four hours each way, depending on weather.

Since there really wasn't much in the way of traffic in Montana, she really only had to worry about snow. However, the majority of the trip would be along the I-90, so it shouldn't be too bad. That freeway was maintained enough during the winter to keep traffic flowing. Well, as long there wasn't a blizzard.

The next day, Elizabeth headed to the general store. She knew it was high time she had a long talk with Logan. If she could just find out why he left her the way he did, she might be able to move past it and be friends with him again. Everyone knew he was home to stay. And since she wasn't going anywhere, ever, she needed to be able to see him and not have her heart ache so much.

It wasn't that she wanted to rekindle their flame—far from it. She needed closure. That was something she'd never gotten. Of course, it was her fault. He had tried in the first few years to apologize to her when she saw him in town during his few visits, but she always managed to avoid him, or ignore him. Now she realized that was a mistake that only hurt her more.

She had listened to the sermon on forgiveness multiple times, and spent time in the Word and prayer. God had convinced her she needed to forgive and move on. God didn't want us to hold grudges against anyone. In fact, His scripture commands us to mend fences before we even give our tithes and gifts—something Elizabeth hadn't heeded all these years. She had tithed even though she still felt anger and resentment toward Logan.

The one thing that stood out the most for her through all

her studies was a book on forgiveness. The reading was a bit dry, but the one thing that hit her the most was the concept of forgiveness being about the person who was wronged—her. The book stated that forgiving someone wasn't about letting them off the hook, or even saying what they did was alright. It was actually an act needed for the person who was wronged to put it all behind them and move forward with healing.

She didn't need to tell him she forgave him—she just needed to do it in her heart. However, the book did say it was rather cathartic to tell the person you forgave them. The psychological impact it had on the forgiver was much more powerful than just forgiving someone in your heart.

The book, combined with her Bible readings in Mark 11:25, Matthew 18:21-22 and so many more, convinced her it was time.

And if she was honest with herself, she did want to help with the Christmas set-up at the general store. That one event always signaled the beginning of the season for her. Christmas was the best time of year; people were always so much happier and more giving. Not that she wanted to receive—just the opposite. She loved to give of her time and talents. Christmas gave her the opportunity to help others who normally wouldn't accept help. Giving, rather than receiving, always filled her spirit with joy.

When Elizabeth walked into the general store, her heart skipped a beat, just as it always did when she saw Logan. He really was a handsome man. Even more so now that he was all grown up. Whenever she allowed herself to remember him, it was always the teenaged version of him with a sly smile or a glint in his eyes that was only for her.

He turned his head, and that special smile that she knew was always for her spread across his face. Even the glint had returned to his eyes. *Oh boy*. She knew she was in trouble.

"Elizabeth." Logan turned from Leah and walked toward her. "It's good to see you. How can I help you?"

She took a deep breath. This was going to be harder than she'd thought. "Do you have a few minutes to talk?" She bit the inside of her cheek, hoping he didn't see how nervous she really was.

Her voice had sounded a little bit ragged, and she knew her pulse was running ragged. If she wasn't careful, her cheeks would heat up soon and he'd know exactly what she was feeling. He always did know what she was thinking and feeling. Once, he told her she wore her emotions on her sleeve, and in her eyes.

At the last moment, she diverted her eyes and looked around the store. They had moved a few pieces of the large equipment out—either that or they sold it—and there were a couple empty shelves along the front where they would most likely put up the Christmas decorations.

Once she got her breathing back in line and her pulse slowed down enough that she no longer felt queasy, she turned her gaze back to him and smiled.

"Sure," he said. "Let me grab my hat and let Leah know we're going for a walk." He turned to leave, but she put a hand to his shoulder.

"Wait, can we go in the back and talk? I'd rather not have the entire town gossiping about us." She raised one brow and knew that he'd get what she was saying.

He chuckled. "Of course, come on back and we can talk in the office. I'd rather not be the topic of discussion for the divas, either."

Once they were in the back office, he shut the door and motioned for her to sit down before taking his seat on the other side of the desk. "What can I do for you?"

She cleared her throat. "Well, I've been doing a lot of

praying and thinking." She put a finger in her collar and pulled it loose a bit. For some reason, she felt like it was choking her.

He nodded, not wanting to interrupt her.

She looked down at her hands in her lap. "When our sisters locked us in the storage closet, you wanted to tell me why you had left me the way you did. I wasn't ready to hear it then, but I am now."

When she looked up at him, his smile had vanished, and sadness filled his eyes. Her heart began pounding so hard, all she could hear was the blood rushing through her veins.

A heavy sigh escaped his lips and he sat back in his chair. "I'm so sorry for that day."

"Which one? When were locked in the room together? Or the day you broke my heart?" She winced, not intending to sound so gruff or accusatory.

"That's fair." He nodded. "And I meant both. My sister never should have done that to you. I hope you know I had nothing to do with it."

"I know." She knew it was her sister and Leah who had concocted the stupid plan. It was strange how she had forgiven them both so easily, but still held such animosity for Logan.

Animosity was probably too harsh a word. But she was definitely hurt by his actions, and angered. She was still hurt by his actions and words from ten years ago, but her heart was ready to hear the truth. Finally, she wanted to get this all behind her and move forward. They had been such great friends her entire childhood. His friendship was something she'd mourned for the past ten years.

Of course, she also missed the romantic part of their relationship and all the plans they'd both had. Those plans would never come to fruition, but maybe, just maybe they could get their friendship back. She wasn't sure if they could ever be as close as they once were, but she wanted to try. It would probably take years for her to trust him again, but she could work on it.

Well, at least until he married. Her heart skipped a beat at the thought of him marrying someone else. She knew it would happen one day, and she didn't want to think about it. *First thing's first,* she told herself, *get our friendship back on track.* Let God worry about his wife.

If she was lucky, she'd get married first.

"But you want to know about the breakup, don't you?" he quietly asked.

Words couldn't form, so she only nodded. Then tried to clear her throat.

"Well, looking back on it now, I was a stupid kid who thought he knew everything." He shook his head. "When I got to the university, my roommate had left a girlfriend behind."

She looked at him with confusion in her eyes and she wrinkled her forehead.

"I know it sounds weird, but Tom—that's my old roommate—he and Sheila had a similar story to ours. They were childhood friends who turned into high school sweethearts. He went away to college and she stayed back on her family farm." He stood up and turned back to look at the wall behind his desk.

Logan knew he was stupid. Tom and Sheila had a different relationship than he and Lizzie had. Besides, they would have been at the same college, together.

"I'm sorry, Logan, but I'm confused. No offense, but what does your college roommate have to do with you breaking up with me?" She ran a hand over her face to move the stray hairs from her eyes.

He stood up and began to pace along the small area behind his desk with his hands behind his back. When he stopped and looked up, he saw the confusion painted on her face and knew he was doing this all wrong, just like last time.

"Let me start over." He turned to face her straight on. "I saw a lot of couples break up during their first year of college. Most of them broke up because they wouldn't let go of their past. Some of the guys I knew wanted to date other girls but didn't want to break up with their girls back home."

Elizabeth interrupted. "Wait, are you saying you wanted to date other girls? Is that why you dumped me?"

He could see the anger in her eyes and knew he was still doing it all wrong.

"No!" He held his hands up in front of her. "Geesh, I'm messing this is all up again." He ran a hand through his hair and sighed. "I thought you might want to date others when you got to college. I didn't want to hold you back. I had no desire at all to date anyone else."

"But Logan, we would have been at the same school. Our story was different than the other kids'." She shook her head and confusion made its way back to her face. Her forehead crinkled, and her eyes narrowed.

The way she slowly shook her head made him want to hold her and tell her how sorry he was for what he had done, but he knew she wouldn't want him to touch her.

Without even thinking about it, he walked to her side and picked up one of her hands. "I was so stupid, Lizzie. I thought I was putting your best interests first."

"How is breaking my heart putting me first?" She pulled her hand out of his and sat back in her chair.

Logan leaned against the desk and licked his lips. "I also spoke to a few professors about your goals." He stopped and winced.

She turned her head slightly to the right and pursed her lips. But she stayed quiet, waiting to hear what he'd say next.

He stood up straight again and moved back behind the desk. "They didn't have a pre-vet program. Sure, there were a lot of classes you could have taken, but in the end, it wasn't the best program for you. I knew trying to get you to go to a different school would have been pointless, but it was what was best for your career."

There, he'd said it. He hoped she would understand and that he hadn't made a complete mess of things. His heart was pounding, and he could feel sweat beginning to form on his brow.

When he rubbed his hand over his jaw, he realized he needed a shave. The stubble rubbed against the new calluses forming on his hands from the manual labor he had done lately. Back in California he never did manual labor, and his hands had lost their calluses over the years.

Elizabeth sat there staring at him. He wondered what she was thinking and hoped she would forgive him.

She stood up, and he thought she was going to leave. Instead she walked toward him, her eyes piercing him to core. Her hand came up and slapped him upside the head. Not so hard that it hurt, just enough to catch his attention.

"You are so stupid, Logan Hayes!" She threw her hands in the air and walked back to the door. She put her hands on it as though she was going to open it, then turned around.

"I had a plan for my classes. I had already worked out with the biology department how I was going to get the classes I needed. There were only three that weren't part of their regular curriculum, and one of the professors was going to offer those to me on a one-on-one basis. I had it all covered. If you would have spoken to me about your concerns, you would have known this." She threw her hands in the air and blew out a huge breath.

"Wait, what?" He shook his head. "You were going to graduate with the degree you needed? What about vet school? The one near my graduate program didn't specialize in large animals." He knew because he had looked into it himself once he had decided on which colleges to attend for undergraduate and graduate school.

"Again, I had a plan."

"Why didn't you tell me any of these plans?" He thought back to their many phone calls and knew she hadn't said anything detailed about her university plans. They just talked about attending the same undergraduate college, and then he chose a graduate program close enough to a veterinarian school that she could attend.

He came to realize while he was away that the choices he made were for his best interests, and not hers. Had he truly thought about it, he would have gone somewhere else. All he could think of back then was getting to California. Since he was a kid, he had wanted to live in California, near the beach. Which was why he chose the schools he did, and why he'd stayed in LA after he graduated.

"Because you never really seemed interested in my plans. You only wanted to talk about the university and how awesome it was." She threw her hands up in the air again before taking a seat. She put her head in her hands. "I realize now that I should have tried harder to talk to you, but you should have never made such a huge decision for us without talking it over with me first."

Logan knew he had screwed up. It was something he'd regretted every day for the past ten years.

"Lizzie, I'm so sorry. I was a stupid, punk kid. You're right, my communication skills were horrible." He strode to her side and knelt. "I regretted it the second I walked away from you."

She looked into his eyes, and the pain he saw there stabbed him in the heart. He could tell she was working hard to keep from crying. Her eyes were moist, and if he wasn't mistaken, there was a tear in the corner trying to make its way down her cheek.

He put a hand on her arm and whispered, "Ah, babe. Please don't cry. I'm so sorry. I never meant to hurt you. I truly thought I was doing the best thing for you and your career. I never wanted to let you go. In fact, my hope that first year was that once we were all done with school, we would get back together again."

"Why didn't you call me, or come back when you realized you had made a mistake?"

He shook his head. "Honestly, I just didn't know what to say at first. We had never fought or broken up, and I had no experience with this kind of thing. Then, when I saw you again, you ignored me. I did try to talk to you that summer, but you wouldn't let me within ten feet of you."

"You didn't try very hard." The accusation in her tone sent another stab to his heart.

His heart was breaking all over again. A hand went to his chest and massaged the phantom pain he felt. It didn't do anything to help. "I saw your mother one day in town and I spoke with her."

Her head shot up. 'What? You spoke to my mom about me? She never told me."

"I'm not surprised. She said that you needed time to heal. That I should wait until next summer, or maybe Christmas break. I listened to her. Each time we were both back in town and I tried to talk to you, you ignored me or ran away from me." He stood back up and leaned against his desk again.

"My mom did try to get me to talk to you that first Christmas break, and then in the summer. But after that, she stopped trying. I told her that I was really happy in my new college and that it was a much better fit for me than California would have been." The wry smile that crossed Elizabeth's face told him that she didn't think it was all that great.

"Were you really happy? I mean, in your new choice of college?" He did want to know. After all, one of the main reasons he broke up with her was so that she could attend a better university for her choice of training.

It was her turn to get up and pace. She walked around the small area between the door and his desk before she stopped behind the chair she had been sitting in and looked at him. She still had pain in her eyes, but no more tears threatened to spill.

She nodded. "On paper it was the right choice. But knowing what I know now, had you spoken to me about your concerns ten years ago, I would have chosen to stay with you. I would have married you and been very happy with living in California. There were several stables I could have worked at after graduating."

He scratched his chin, thinking about what she'd said. "You really did your homework, didn't you? And I never once asked you details about your plans." He looked at the floor and put his thumbs through the belt loops of his jeans. "I was a stupid and selfish kid. I really do regret it all."

He looked up at her and prayed she could see the sincerity in his eyes. "I loved you with everything I had, but I was stupid and thought I knew best. I know better now. If I had it to do all over again, I would never have broken up with you. I would have proposed instead."

"And I would have said yes." Her whispered words sent a chill through his body.

He'd really screwed up. But he wasn't going to let this end. He would do everything he could to get her to forgive him and at the very least be his friend again.

He stepped toward her and took her hands in his. "Can you ever forgive me?"

When he looked at her eyes again, he noticed tears clinging to her lashes. He couldn't help himself; he pulled her in and wrapped his arms tight around her and kissed the top of her head. "I'm so sorry, Lizzie."

She wrapped her arms around him and held on tight. Her face was buried in his chest and she let the tears flow. She couldn't stop them even if she wanted to.

He ran his hand down her back and let her cry. Logan wasn't sure if she had cried over him, but he did know that women needed to cry once in a while to let their emotions out and release the stress of holding them in. Or at least, that's what his mother had said when his sister cried a lot as a teenager.

Seeing her cry into his shirt caused mixed feelings. On the one hand, it felt wonderful to have her in his arms again, even if she was crying. But on the other, it hurt him to know he had made her so sad. He never wanted to cause her pain. Not then, and certainly not now.

"What can I do to show you my sincerity?" He paused. "Is there any way you can ever forgive me?"

She nodded.

CHAPTER 23

E lizabeth couldn't help but cry. It felt so good to finally hear him tell her why he had broken her heart all those years ago. It still made no sense, but one thing she had learned growing up with five brothers was that men never made any sense.

She was so stupid. If only she had let him talk to her that first summer, or even at Christmas, or any of the other times he'd tried. Looking back, she finally realized he did try. She was just too angry and hurt to give him a chance to explain. If only she had listened to God's word and forgiven him sooner. They would have been married and probably had a couple kids by now.

At the very least, they would have had one.

She was stupid. They both were. Why didn't she realize what needed to happen earlier? Even when she took a communications class in college, she should have known that they needed to talk.

It was her sin of not forgiving him that had kept them apart all this time.

Forgiveness was a choice a person made. There were all of these stages, like with grief, but all she had to do was *choose* to forgive him. She knew they couldn't pick up where they'd left off, but maybe, just maybe they could be friends again. Over time, she knew she'd learn to trust him again.

She tried to stop her sobbing and began to hiccup.

Her embarrassment only made her hiccup more, and she held on even tighter.

"Shh, it's alright. Just let it all out. Do you want some water for those hiccups?" he whispered in her ear while he rubbed her back.

She relaxed into his body even more and eventually her tears dried up, but her hiccups didn't.

Once she was ready to pull away, she looked into his eyes and almost began crying again. The tenderness and love she saw and felt coming from him was almost enough to break her heart, again. She tried to take a few deep breaths, but they were interrupted by her hiccups.

He pulled back. "I've got a mini-fridge with cold water." Then he moved back to his desk and leaned down. When he stood up, he had a small bottle of water in his hand.

The condensation on the bottle dripped onto the papers covering his desk.

He walked back to her and opened the cap before handing it to her.

She reached out to take it. "Thank"—she was interrupted by more hiccups—"you." Elizabeth sighed and took a deep breath, then held it as she drank the water.

After a few minutes of alternating between deep breathing and holding her breath, the hiccups finally abated.

"Thank you." She gave him the empty water bottle and smiled tentatively at him.

He returned her smile. "Do you think... Is it too soon?"

She nodded. "Wait. You should know that I forgive you." Elizabeth took a step back and clasped her hands in front of her. "Can you ever forgive me?"

He furrowed his brow. "For what? I'm the one who hurt you and was a complete dolt."

She shook her head. "I should have listened to you when you tried talking to me all those times. And I should have forgiven you way back then. If I had, my anger wouldn't have kept us apart all these years." Her voice cracked.

If Elizabeth didn't get ahold of her emotions, she was going to turn into a water works and flood his office.

"Hey." He took her in his arms again. "It was all my fault. There's nothing for me to forgive."

When he rubbed her back, she sighed deeply and so many emotions flooded her that she began to cry again. Not like before, but tears still ran down her cheeks onto his shirt.

Logan put his hand on her head and ran his fingers down her hair lightly. It sent chills down Elizabeth's spine, just like when they were younger.

She hoped it meant they were going to be friends again. It was too soon for her to think about anything other than friendship, even though her heart pounded so hard her eardrums beat the same tune.

"So, you really do forgive me?" he whispered hesitantly in her ear.

"Yes," she squeaked. Elizabeth couldn't get anything else out. Her voice just wouldn't work. When she tried to clear it, she attempted to say more, but the door opened.

Leah walked in and her eyes bulged. "Oh! Please forgive me. I'm sorry to interrupt, but Chloe's out front and she said it was important." Leah winced and walked back out of the office, closing the door behind her.

Elizabeth pulled away from Logan and missed his warmth

the moment she did so. "I better see what she wants." She looked at the front of his shirt, then up into his eyes and winced. "And you might need to change your shirt." She pointed at the wetness covering most of his chest.

He looked down and smiled. "Guess it's a good think Leah stocked the store with decent shirts."

A small smile crossed Elizabeth's face as she turned and headed toward the front of the store.

The moment Elizabeth saw her sister, she knew something was wrong.

Chloe looked as though she had been crying. Her makeup was smeared, and she was pacing the length of the store.

Elizabeth ran to her. "What? Are Mom and Dad alright?"

Chloe nodded.

"What about the boys? Did one of them get injured? Please don't tell me it was Roman." Elizabeth put a hand to her mouth and worried that Roman had either fallen off his horse, or something worse.

Chloe shook her head. "No, the family's fine. It's Ana. She's taken off."

"What?" Elizabeth practically yelled. "When?"

"Sometime this morning. She left a note for Mom saying she needed to get back to Bart before he found her and hurt her."

"It's been several weeks. I would think he's forgotten all about her by now, wouldn't you?" Elizabeth joined her sister in pacing.

"Has anyone gone looking for her?" Logan asked when he stepped into view of the girls.

The twins turned their heads in unison and looked at Logan. Then Elizabeth looked to her sister for answers.

"Yes, my brothers have all gone out looking for her. But

so far, no one has found her." Chloe looked to Elizabeth. "Why haven't you answered your phone? We've been trying to call you forever."

Elizabeth felt her back pocket and realized she didn't have it. "I'm sorry, Chloe. I think it's in my office."

"No matter. We need to go out and start looking. I don't think she could have gotten far on foot, but I wouldn't be surprised if someone from town picked her up and took her back to Bozeman. We need to head there, now."

"Right, I'll drive. My truck is parked behind the office. Let's go." Elizabeth didn't bother to say goodbye to Logan or Leah; she opened the door expecting Chloe to follow her.

When she got outside, she felt her sister at her back along with someone else. She knew that second presence.

After she stopped, Elizabeth turned around and faced Logan. "What are you doing?"

"I'm coming with you. If you're heading back to Bozeman and Bart, I'm not letting you go alone." He pulled his keys out of his front pocket. "I can drive, and you two can look along the road for her."

"Thank you." Elizabeth smiled and followed Logan to his truck with Chloe on their tail. At first she'd wanted to object, but then she thought better of it. It would be helpful to have Logan along. And as he'd said, he could drive while they looked, just in case Ana didn't hitch a ride to Bozeman. Or if she was let out early.

For some strange reason, she was beginning to enjoy his company. She was grateful the anger had left and she could be around him without feeling so horrible. Maybe this was going to be the start of a new friendship.

No one spoke during the thirty-minute ride to Bozeman, except to ask Logan to slow down whenever they spotted what looked to be a person on the side of the road. Most of the lumps they saw from a distance turned out to be animals hanging out next to the fence along the highway.

One was a tree stump. Elizabeth wondered how her sister could have thought that was a person, but she didn't voice her question. Instead, she kept her eyes on her side of the road and looked for Ana, praying as they went along that the girl would be safe.

When they didn't find her along the way to Bozeman, all of them felt dejected and worried for Ana's safety.

"I wish we would have found her along the side of the road. It would have made this so much easier," Chloe said as she exited the car.

Elizabeth nodded and looked around. They had parked near the area where they'd picked up Ana originally, hoping she would have gone back to the same place.

"Do you think Bart's found her yet?" Logan asked with a scowl on his face.

"Sadly, I do." Elizabeth continued to scan the area, looking for anyone who might be familiar. There were still plenty of homeless on the street surrounding them.

Chloe frowned and put her hands on her hips. "Why hasn't the sheriff done anything about all the people living here? Surely there's something they can do to help them get home, or at least find shelter so they don't have to stay on the streets."

Elizabeth had wondered the same exact thing. Both she and Logan shook their heads. Neither seemed to know what to think. It broke her heart to think that the local sheriff wasn't doing anything to help these people. She knew she was going to have to do something. Her heart wouldn't let her leave this alone.

But first she had to find Ana. She was worried about what Bart would do to the girl. Why Ana would want to willingly go back to him, she had no idea. It was the craziest thing ever. Ana had gotten out. She could have done anything she wanted if she'd only stayed away from Bart.

"Come on, let's go this way." Elizabeth took the lead and decided she was going to stick close to her sister and Logan.

After everything that had happened so far, she knew better than to walk these streets alone. Even though she was confident in her ability to take care of herself, she wasn't stupid. If Bart and his gang wanted to hurt her, she wouldn't be able to protect herself against all of them. If she were seriously hurt, or worse, she wouldn't be able to help those living on the street. It was much more important to swallow her pride and realize she needed help than it was to act tough.

Elizabeth was no wilting flower, but she would play it smart.

A small crowd caught her attention.

"Look, over there." She pointed across the street and down one block. There were at least a dozen people standing in a makeshift circle all looking down at the ground.

Logan picked up his pace and took the lead. "Stay close to me, but watch out."

Elizabeth and Chloe both quickened their pace to stay close on his heels.

When the crowd parted, tears pricked her eyes and she couldn't help but let out a cry of pain. She covered her mouth and willed her tears to not fall. Now was not the time to break down. She needed to be strong for them all.

"Who did this?" Logan's commanding voice rang out over the small crowd.

A few of them turned their backs and walked away as

quickly as they could, carrying or pulling their meager belongings with them. Only two stayed close by.

Elizabeth recognized one of them as part of Bart's gang. She pointed an accusatory finger at him. "You did this, didn't you?"

She kept her eyes on his smirking face until she heard a moan on the ground next to his boots.

Chloe crouched down next to Ana's limp form. She examined the girl for broken bones, and when she was sure there weren't any, she examined Ana's face. There were already signs of bruising all along the left side of her face. Her left eye looked to be swollen.

She looked up at Logan. "Can you carry her to the truck? I don't want to leave her here while we go back for it." She eyed the man standing over Ana's body, who only chuckled.

The guy hadn't said a word; he just laughed and smirked as though this was all fun and games to him. It probably was…for him. But Elizabeth doubted he'd be laughing for long.

Logan bent over Ana, and she stirred as he picked her up.

"What?" Her left eye stayed shut, but her right eye fluttered open and she looked to Logan. "Oh, thank the good Lord." She leaned her head against his chest and closed her one eye again.

Elizabeth's nostrils flared. "This isn't over. The sheriff will hear about this."

Both Elizabeth and Chloe backed up a few paces before they turned and followed Logan back to their car.

Logan drove them straight to the Beacon Creek Clinic. Before they arrived, Ana woke and told them what had happened.

"I hitched a ride earlier this morning into Bozeman with

one of the ranch hands from the Bar One Ranch." Ana wasn't holding back this time.

Last time, it was like pulling teeth to get any information from her. Something had changed, and she was now willingly giving them details she had never wanted to share in the past.

Elizabeth hoped this meant that Ana was beginning to trust them, and that the girl wanted to be here in Beacon Creek.

"Not five minutes after I arrived, Bart and his cronies found me. Five of them each took a punch at me right in front of everyone. He said I was to be an example of what happens when we leave him." A lone tear dribbled down her cheek from her good eye.

"I'm so sorry, Ana. I wish we could have gotten there sooner." Elizabeth was turned around in her seat so she could look at Ana, who sat in the back with Chloe.

Ana was laid out on the bench seat with her head in Chloe's lap.

"It's all my fault. I should have stayed with your family." Ana wrapped her arms around her upper body and looked up at the roof of the quad cab Ford truck.

Elizabeth bit the inside of her cheek as she considered her next words very carefully. "Ana, I thought you were happy on the ranch. My mom told me that you two had spoken about your future and how you could live and work there. What made you decide to run away?"

The girl shrugged her shoulders and turned her head away from Elizabeth, but not before a pained look crossed her features.

Elizabeth wondered if the girl had run away from home at a young age and all she knew was life on the streets. She had to have been under Bart's control for a while to make her feel like she had to return to him. There must have been some sort of manipulation or maybe even a little bit of brainwashing.

Could Bart be something like a cult leader for the homeless? Or did he control them with fear and beatings? Whatever made those poor people follow Bart needed to be discovered and stopped.

Elizabeth set her sights on bringing Bart down.

CHAPTER 24

"She's going to be alright. I want to keep her here overnight for observation. She had a big goose egg on her head, and I want to make sure it's nothing too serious. I can see she has a minor concussion, but I want to make sure it's nothing more." The doctor spoke to Logan and Elizabeth in the hall outside Ana's room.

Elizabeth thought it all felt like déjà vu. They had been here before, and she prayed it would be the last time.

"Thank you, Doctor." Logan nodded, and then continued, "Do you think she'll be able to go home tomorrow morning?"

The doctor gripped her clipboard. "Which home?"

"My family's ranch." Elizabeth wasn't about to let Ana go anywhere else. At least not until the girl was healed and could explain what she was thinking when she left the perfectly safe home of Elizabeth's family ranch.

The doctor nodded. "Yes. Unless something develops overnight, I think she'll be ready to discharge into your mother's care come tomorrow morning. But like last time, she'll need to stay down for at least a week until her body recovers from the trauma she sustained."

"Of course. Thank you, Doctor." Elizabeth ran a worried hand down her face. She tried to keep her anxiety off her face, but she knew she wasn't doing a very good job of it when Logan ran his hand down her back in a comforting gesture.

When the doctor walked down the hall, Elizabeth looked into Logan's eyes. "What are we going to do?"

He rubbed his chin and considered his words carefully before answering. "I think we take Ana back to your family and make sure everyone keeps a good eye on her. We have to make her feel safe and wanted." Logan took a few steps away Elizabeth, toward the other patient room that was currently empty.

"I think she must have felt she wasn't wanted, or maybe overhead something that gave her that opinion?" Elizabeth began her own pacing up and down the small corridor.

He nodded. "Possibly. We should ask your family what they think."

Elizabeth stopped in front of Logan. "You're right. She's going to be sleeping for a while—what do you say we head out to the ranch now?"

"I'll follow you out there, unless you want to carpool. I can bring you back to town after we talk with your family."

She considered his offer and decided friends shared rides. There would be nothing wrong or weird about them riding together. The only problem was that his family ranch was closer to her parents' ranch than town. So he would be going out of his way to bring her back to town where her truck was currently located.

"Sounds good. If we hurry, we might even make it in time for supper." She wasn't sure what was on the menu that night, but she did know that there would be plenty for the both of them if they arrived in time.

The ride out to the Triple J Ranch wasn't as quiet as Elizabeth had expected. In fact, it was comfortable. The way they spoke, it felt almost like old times. However, back in high school Logan would hold her hand as he drove her home. This time, they sat in their respective seats and didn't touch each other.

"Have you heard about Chloe's new job offer?" Elizabeth hadn't had much time to talk with Chloe, but she figured Leah or Logan might know more.

Logan looked over at Elizabeth and nodded before turning his head back on the road that took them to the Triple J. "Yeah, she said she's leaving soon. Do you have a date yet?"

"No, she hasn't told me when she's leaving. But I think it's coming up quicker than I'd like." Elizabeth didn't like the idea of her twin leaving town, but it was something her sister had wanted to do for years. She wasn't going to stand in the way of Chloe's happiness, even if it would make her unhappy.

"To be honest, I'm surprised she didn't leave sooner." Logan slowed down to go around the bend in the road.

When the ranch entrance came into view, Elizabeth sighed. "Every time I go through the arches of the Triple J I know I'm home."

Logan chuckled. "Then why do you live in town? I bet your parents would love to have you back on the ranch with them."

She shrugged. "It's just easier for my business to live in town. Especially when I'm on call, which is half the time. Being centrally located cuts down on travel time when there's an emergency."

"So, you wouldn't be interested in living on a ranch?" Logan was fishing. Now that they were on friendly terms, he was going to press his suit of her. And with his father in poor health, it was important for him to stay on the family farm. Should he and Lizzie marry, they would have to live with his family so he could take care of them.

She did love her family ranch, and he thought she'd love his family farm just as much. He knew his family would be thrilled to have them both there. But if she preferred to live in town, that might not work so well for his father.

Although, it would be nice to live close to the store. Maybe if his father's health improved, they could live in town and visit the farm regularly. Especially if Leah continued to live there.

He knew he was getting ahead of himself, but he also knew he had to have a plan before he asked Elizabeth to marry him. She liked plans.

"Well, I guess if it was centrally located it would be fine. But I really do need to be in town when I'm on call. There's only one ranch close enough to town, and that's not going up for sale any time soon." She chuckled and looked out her window. The smile on her face was enough to get Logan to move mountains to ensure she continued smiling like that the rest of their lives.

Her joy was contagious, and the tightness in his chest began to loosen, and hope filled his heart. If he could find a way to get them close to town and close to his family's home, he would do it.

The moment he stopped his truck, Mrs. Manning came outside and ran to Lizzie's side. "Is she alright? When will Ana be coming home?"

Elizabeth put her hands on her mom's shoulders. "Mom, she's going to be fine. And tomorrow morning I'll bring her out here as soon as the doctor releases her."

"I'll come, too." Logan wasn't about to pass up a chance

to talk more with Ana about what happened and why she'd left. He couldn't understand why anyone would want to leave the Triple J.

"Well, come on in. We were just sitting down for supper. You can tell us all about what happened. Do you know why she left?" Mrs. Manning was just as confused as Logan and Elizabeth as to why the young girl would leave the ranch and go back to living on the streets.

During supper, the majority of the time was spent discussing Ana and what had happened. No one had any clue why she would have left. They all thought Ana was happy and wanted to stay on the ranch as part of the family.

Elizabeth bit her lip and decided it was time to ask a tough question. "Is it possible Ana overheard someone talking about her? Maybe someone said they weren't happy about her being here?"

Her entire family looked around the table at each other. Confusion was written all over everyone's face.

Matthew, the oldest of the Manning boys, spoke up first. "I don't see how that would be possible. We all want her here."

Luke, John, and Roman all nodded their agreement.

"Are you sure? Maybe two of you were out in the barn talking about something? Maybe even joking? It's possible she overheard something wrong. And then just left instead of confronting you." Logan still had no idea why Ana would leave, and it was eating him up inside.

He had started to think of her as a little sister and wanted to protect the girl.

John's face hardened. "None of us would say anything negative about Ana. We all love her like she's one of us."

"Okay boys." Mr. Manning put his hand in the air to try and calm everyone down. "I don't think Logan is accusing you of anything wrong. He just wants to try and figure out why Ana would leave like she did. Miscommunication is all too common these days."

He looked back to Logan and Elizabeth. "I don't see how anyone could have said anything that could be construed in a negative manner. If anything, I think it's possible one of the boys might have flirted too strongly with her. But none of them would have done anything to hurt her or upset her."

Logan nodded. "I agree. Even though I haven't been around in a while, I know your boys wouldn't hurt Ana." He directed his comment to the head of the Manning family. "But you might be on to something."

Logan used his napkin to wipe his mouth. "Are any of you attracted to Ana?" He looked between all five Manning boys. They ranged anywhere from eighteen to thirty. If Ana was about nineteen, then any of these men could be interested in her. She was a very nice-looking girl.

Elizabeth laughed and her eyes widened. "Oh, come on. None of my brothers would have asked Ana out or said anything more than how cute she is. A few of them"—she looked to Mark and Luke specifically—"have a reputation of playing the field, but they would never make a play for a young woman living at the ranch. Especially one recuperating from the injuries she sustained last time."

Mr. and Mrs. Manning looked at each other, and then to Elizabeth with grave expressions.

Mr. Manning swallowed hard. "Well, I have noticed a couple of the boys seem…attracted to Ana."

Mrs. Manning nodded.

"Wait." Matthew held up his hand. "Mark and Luke flirted a tiny bit, but nothing more than friendly flirting. I've been paying attention."

Logan narrowed his eyes at the two middle boys. "Have

you said anything at all that might have scared her? Think. She's probably been beaten up a lot and maybe even worse. Think about your words and actions."

Both young men in the hot seat shook their heads.

"I haven't said anything other than how pretty she is," Mark stated.

Luke followed up with, "I've only smiled at her and paid her extra attention. I don't think I've even flirted with her."

Elizabeth shook her head. "Guys, she doesn't need your extra attention or smiles. Don't you know what the girls in town do when you smile at them?"

Both of her brothers had exceptional smiles. When they turned their pearly whites on the girls in town, they practically swooned.

Mark and Luke looked at Elizabeth as though she had lost her head.

"What do you mean?" Mark asked.

With an exasperated sigh, Elizabeth tried to explain how all the girls in town fell hard for them both when they smiled and paid extra attention to them.

Roman, who'd stayed quiet the entire time, spoke up. "Do you mean all it takes is smiling at a girl and she'll go out with you?" He tilted his head and squinted at his big sister.

Elizabeth chuckled. "No, Roman. It takes a little bit more than that, but when a very good-looking young man of a certain age does it, then girls are known to see more into it at times."

"Look, what your sister is trying to say is that you need to treat Ana like you do the twins. If you tease her and act like she's your sister, then she won't feel as though you want anything more. Call her a good buddy or tell her you see her as a sister. Something to make her understand you aren't trying to do anything untoward." Logan took his last bite of steak and moaned.

"Oh, Mrs. Manning. I had forgotten how good your steak is. Thank you for letting me join your supper tonight. This is the best I've had since the church BBQ." Logan had filled up on the Triple J Ranch steak that time as well. He'd even taken some home for his pops, who was very grateful.

Mrs. Manning stood up and began to clear the plates. "I'm glad you enjoyed it, Logan. You're welcome here any time." She looked at her daughter and smiled.

The Mannings had always wanted Elizabeth to marry Logan. Even when they were young, both families expected the two would eventually marry. Both families were heart-broken when Logan broke up with Elizabeth. Although, the parents had stayed friends and hoped one day their kids would wisen up and get back together.

If what Mrs. Manning was seeing was any indication, their prayers would be answered soon enough.

"I'll talk to Ana tomorrow morning and see if it was something the boys said or did. If it was, that should be easy enough to clear up." Elizabeth stood to help her mother clear the table.

When she came back to the dining room, her mother followed her with a homemade apple pie.

All the men smiled and looked longingly at their mother's pie.

Mrs. Manning held the pie in her hands. "What this means, boys, is that no one from this ranch is allowed to date Ana. You can't even want the girl. Do I make myself clear?" She turned back toward the kitchen as though she was going to take the pie away from them.

All of them, even Mr. Manning, agreed.

"Don't worry, Ma. I'll make sure none of the boys see

Ana as anything but a sister," John said as he licked his lips and stared at his mom's famous apple pie.

That apple pie had won awards at local fairs and bake-offs. If anyone thought they wouldn't ever get it again, they would do whatever their mother asked.

Elizabeth was confident that Ana wouldn't have to worry about any of her brothers flirting or giving her extra attention again.

CHAPTER 25

The next morning before the clinic opened, Elizabeth was standing at the front door waiting to get inside.

Logan walked up just as the nurse on duty unlocked the door and opened it up. "Come on inside. Ana and the doctor are waiting for you both."

Elizabeth looked to Logan, who smiled encouragingly at her, and she followed the nurse inside.

Once the doctor had discharged Ana and everyone was in Logan's truck, Elizabeth turned to Ana. "I'm so very glad you're going to be alright. You have no idea how scared I was for you yesterday."

Logan interrupted, "We were all frightened when we learned you had left." He looked back at Ana through the rearview mirror and hoped that he was showing compassion in his eyes and not frustration. Even though he was frustrated, he also felt bad for the girl. If she thought the Manning boys were romantically interested in her, he could understand her need to flee back to what she knew.

It may have been a horribly dangerous situation, but it

was one she knew. Something she had dealt with. Sometimes, the evil you know is better than the scariness you don't know.

"I'm sorry. I didn't mean to upset anyone. Are your parents mad at me?" Ana looked at Elizabeth and winced.

Elizabeth reached back with one hand and lightly squeezed Ana's hand. "They aren't mad—they were just worried. We all want to know what made you leave and go back to Bart. You had to know he'd hurt you for leaving, didn't you?"

Ana squeezed back and nodded. "Yes, but at least I knew what to expect with Bart."

Elizabeth furrowed her brow. "What does that mean? Did something at the ranch scare you?"

"Or someone?" Logan slowed down for the stop sign at the edge of town.

"Yes. No. I don't know." Ana shrugged and looked down at her hands.

No one said anything for a few heartbeats.

Elizabeth contemplated what Ana was trying to say. "Did my brothers say or do anything to frighten you?"

Ana gulped and looked at Elizabeth with her one good eye. The other one was still swollen shut with black and blue bruising all around it. "Not exactly."

"What does that mean?" Elizabeth tried to stay calm. If one of her brothers said or did anything to frighten Ana, she'd skin them alive.

Ana clamped her mouth shut and shook her head.

Logan put his hand on Elizabeth's knee, which caused her to close her mouth before saying anything else. Even though it had been a decade since they'd been together, she still knew his cues, and he still instinctively knew what she was about to do.

He looked at the frightened girl through the rearview

mirror. "Ana, we're on your side. Just because the boys are Elizabeth's brothers doesn't mean she won't kick their butts to kingdom come for you. You can tell us what happened. I promise we will protect you."

He wasn't sure what had happened, but something did. The boys had lied the previous night, and Logan was going to get to the bottom of it.

Instead of answering, Ana looked out the window. Worry lines developed across her forehead, and she stayed silent for the rest of the ride. Just like she had the first time they took her out of Bozeman.

Logan was furious by the time they arrived at the Triple J Ranch. He wasn't even sure it was safe for Ana. The way she had reacted had him believing one of the boys did or said something to seriously scare or injure the poor girl. It was bad enough that she'd thought going back to Bart, who regularly abused those who were supposed to be under his care, was a better choice than staying in Beacon Creek.

He knew he had to get his temper under control, so he did the only thing he could...he prayed. *Lord, please help me to find out what happened here and do what you would have me to do in order to help Ana. She's had such a hard life. Is there anything I can do to help her feel safe again?*

By the time he got out of his truck and made his way around to the side closest to the ranch house door, a sense of peace had overtaken him. He was still upset with the Manning boys, but he also knew God was in control. Logan trusted God to make sure everything worked out the way He ordained it.

"Ana! I'm so happy you're back home. I've got your room all set up and ready for you. Do you need to nap?" Mrs. Manning was in mother-hen mode, and took the girl's arm and led her inside the house.

Mr. Manning and Matthew Manning were the only ones inside waiting.

The situation made Logan think that there must be something more going on than he was led to believe at supper last night.

Elizabeth was sad the rest of her brothers weren't present, but she figured it was a good thing. It just might help Ana to feel more comfortable, as well as help to keep her from feeling overwhelmed with well wishes.

Ana smiled shyly at her hosts and thanked them for letting her come back. "I do think I would like to take a nap before helping with lunch."

Mrs. Manning shook her head. "Sweetie, I've already been informed that you are to go back to lying around for the next week or so. No helping around the house. You need your rest."

"But that's so boring." Ana sighed and hunched her shoulders.

"I know, but it's what needs to happen in order for you to heal. Please follow the doctor's orders. If you like, you can sit at the kitchen table after you nap and we can chat while I prepare the roast for supper." Mrs. Manning smiled indulgently at her young charge and patted her shoulder. "Now, upstairs with you. I'll bring you some tea if you like."

"No thanks. I think I'll just sleep." Ana headed to the stairs leading up to where her room was located.

"Sleep tight, Ana. I'll be back later to check in on you." Elizabeth waved to the girl as she climbed the stairs.

Once Ana was no longer in listening range, the group sat around the kitchen table with coffee.

"Did she tell you anything?" Mr. Manning inquired.

Elizabeth shook her head. "Not really."

Logan lifted his hand. "I think she did. She left because

she didn't feel safe here. One of the boys said or did something to scare her off."

Matthew frowned and put the coffee mug down before he could take a sip. "Did she say that?"

Elizabeth pursed her lips and stared at Logan. "No, she did not say those words."

Logan stood up and began to pace the small area around the dining room table. "She didn't say it in so many words, but she implied that the boys said or did something to scare her off."

Exasperated, Elizabeth put her hands in the air. "No, she didn't. When I asked her if the boys said or did anything to hurt her, she said 'not exactly.' How is that her saying they did something?"

Logan turned to face Elizabeth, and lines creased his forehead. "How is that saying they *didn't* do something to hurt or scare her?"

Mr. Manning stood up. "All right, you two. No arguing. It sounds like Ana got scared by something but doesn't want to say yet what it was. Making assumptions will do no good. I've raised my boys to respect women, but if they do something to hurt Ana, they won't get away with it. I will find out what happened."

Everyone in the room was quiet. Mrs. Manning cleared her throat. "Alright, I think it's time everyone got back to work." She looked to Logan. "We will find out what caused Ana to run away, don't worry."

Logan was fairly confident Mr. and Mrs. Manning would get to the bottom of things, but he still didn't like Ana being there if one of the boys had scared her off. "Should she come home with me instead?"

Everyone shook their heads.

"No, I think it's best she stays here with us. We have

plenty of room, and I'll keep a closer eye on her when the boys are around." Mrs. Manning stood to clear the table of the coffee mugs.

"And I'll have a talk with them when I get back outside. I know my brothers can be pranksters, so maybe it was something as simple as a snake in her bed." Matthew didn't know what happened, but he was beginning to think something went down. Most likely one of his brothers didn't realize he had done something wrong. He was confident they wouldn't do anything to intentionally harm or upset Ana, or any woman for that matter. They had all been brought up to be gentlemen.

"Alright, I'll be back out later for supper. See you all then." Elizabeth walked out, expecting Logan to follow her.

He did, but when he went to open her door for her, she brushed him aside and got in without looking at him.

Once they were on the road, he glanced at Elizabeth. "You're mad at me, aren't you." It was a statement, not a question.

She nodded once.

"Why?" He wasn't exactly sure what he had done to get her so mad at him, again. They had just made up and were starting to get close again. The last thing he wanted was to make Lizzie mad at him.

She turned in her seat to look at him. "You really don't know? Seriously?"

He wanted to shrug, but at the last second changed tack. "I'm sorry, but I don't understand." Logan kept his eyes on the road, but he wanted to desperately to look at the woman sitting next to him. He'd bet his lucky belt buckle steam was coming from her head.

"Pft. Men. You're all alike, you know that?" She shook her head but said nothing more.

He sat there, driving under the speed limit back to town and weighing his options. He wasn't very experienced with women, but he did have a long history with Lizzie. The one thing he did know for sure was that she needed time to cool down. Whatever he'd said, she would eventually let him know and he would apologize.

When they reached her truck, she still wouldn't talk to him. She got out of his truck and slammed the door behind her and trudged over to her truck. Elizabeth needed to get to work, he knew that. But he couldn't let her leave mad.

"Lizzie, please. What did I do to upset you?" he pleaded with her after he'd jumped out of his truck and followed her to her driver's side door.

She spun around with fire in her eyes. "What did you do? I'll tell you what you did."

"Shh, people are watching." Logan pasted on a smile and almost cringed when he saw the Diner Divas watching them.

She looked around and sighed. "Great, just what I need— more gossip."

Logan put a hand on her shoulder and lightly squeezed. "Please, tell me what I did wrong. I don't want you to be upset with me again. I couldn't take losing your friendship again."

She shook her head. "You won't lose my friendship. I'll get over it, but you should know that accusing my brothers of wrongdoing in front of me and my parents isn't going to get you another supper invite."

"Wait, that's what has you mad? Ana basically said they did something. We have to find out." He eyed her closely and rubbed the back of his neck as though he was trying to rub out a kink in his neck. "You do want to find out the truth, don't you? Even if your brothers did something wrong?"

She sighed. "Of course I do. Don't be an idiot. I just don't think it's smart to put words into Ana's mouth." Elizabeth stopped and looked around. With eyes still on them, she shook her head lightly. "I don't want to argue, especially here in front of everyone. Just don't jump to conclusions yet, okay?"

"Of course. I'll try to keep an open mind and wait to see what Ana says." He lifted his hand to touch her again, but thought better of it with everyone watching, and Lizzie most likely still upset with him. "I'll see you later. Please let me know if Ana says anything, alright?"

Elizabeth nodded and got inside her truck and took off to her office.

Logan ran a hand through his hair and wished he had kept his cool earlier. Elizabeth was right: Ana hadn't actually said the boys did anything. He was just so worried about the girl and wanted so badly to know what had happened. He needed to keep his cool and be patient. Sadly, patience wasn't something one prayed for. God usually gave you patience by testing your limits. That was one thing he didn't want.

He was going to have to work on it himself.

CHAPTER 26

When Elizabeth entered her office, she had a message waiting for her. One of the ranches she normally handled had called and wanted to move their regular checkup to that day. The ranch owner, Mike Montgomery, was afraid that two of his heifers might be sick.

She wasn't surprised ranchers were still a little hesitant since word had gotten out about the Williams' ranch having shipping fever. The disease hadn't spread to anyone else, but the local ranchers were still nervous. Milton said he had seen it before and thought that everyone would calm down once the cattle had all been sold at market that year. Until then, they were going to be busy with extra calls out.

Elizabeth was happy to head out to the Montgomery ranch. It would take her mind off what went down that morning with Logan.

They had just begun to be friends again, and he had to go and accuse her brothers of hurting Ana without any proof. For her part, she thought Matthew may have been right. The boys should have seen Ana as a sister. And as one who was a Manning sister, she could attest to their penchant for practical jokes. A snake in the bed was one of their favorites when they were teenagers. The boys never chose a dangerous snake. They didn't need to. The thought of a creepy crawly thing in her bed made Elizabeth shiver. She hated snakes.

Turned out, Elizabeth had to make two more ranch calls. Nothing was wrong with any of the cattle, but it was getting colder, and the cows were more sluggish. Totally normal behavior when the seasons changed.

Instead of heading back to town, she went straight to her family ranch for supper. Elizabeth hoped Ana would be feeling better and be up for telling her, if not her mother, what had happened.

What she saw when she entered the family home stopped her in her tracks. Sitting at the dining room table were all of her brothers and Ana. They were all playing cards and laughing.

It made no sense at all.

If one of her brothers had done something to upset Ana, Elizabeth was confused as to why they were all acting as though nothing had happened.

She looked to her mother and noticed the slight nod directing her to the kitchen. Elizabeth said hi to everyone and gave her dad a hug before heading into the kitchen to see what her mother had to say.

"What happened?" Elizabeth whispered.

Mrs. Manning sighed and shook her head. "Sometimes, I swear boys are just stupid."

Elizabeth chuckled. "I could have told you that."

"Yes, well. It turns out the McHenry girl is also named Ana, and John and Luke were arguing over who was going to get the girl. Our Ana overheard part of the conversation and thought they were arguing over who was going to get her. Like she was some sort of kewpie doll to win at a carnival."

Mrs. Manning wiped down the kitchen counter near the stove and tsked.

Elizabeth leaned back against the pantry door and opened her mouth, but nothing came out. She shook herself and tried again. "Are you saying that Ana overreacted to something that didn't even have to do with her?"

Her mother stopped her nervous cleaning and looked at her daughter. "Yes. Once it came out, the boys profusely apologized to her and to your father. They know better than to talk about girls as though they were prizes to be won."

"I take it Ana doesn't have brothers?" Elizabeth knew not to take what her younger brothers said with any importance when they were trying to up each other. Boys were dumb, and very competitive. Especially her brothers.

"I think it best not to make a fuss. Ana is mortified over her reaction. She promised she would come to me if anything else bothered her. Now, the boys are just trying to treat her like they would you or Chloe."

Elizabeth held up a hand. "Please tell me Pa told them no creepy crawly things in her bed? Or slithering beasts?" She shuddered at the thought of what Ana might find in her bed the next day.

Mrs. Manning laughed. "Oh dear me, no. Your father had a long talk with the boys, and while they might try pulling some jokes, it won't be anything that will scare her. Well, at least until Halloween. Then I think your father and I will have our hands full. You know how they get with Halloween."

Elizabeth laughed, remembering one year when they all dressed up as zombies and came after her and Chloe saying, "Brains, brains, mmmmm." She and her sister had a hard time getting to sleep that night. It didn't help matters that they had just done a *The Walking Dead* marathon earlier that day. Both girls decided never again would they watch a scary TV show or movie with their brothers.

"So, everything is fine now? No one's upset with anyone?" Elizabeth bit her lip, realizing that while Logan wasn't exactly right, he wasn't totally wrong, either. She'd have to go and apologize to him and let him know exactly what happened.

Her mother smiled and wrapped an arm around her shoulder. "All's as it should be. Ana is here for good, and the boys see her as a sister. She's on the mend and promises to never run away again. I think once she's healed up, she's going to make a fine addition to the family."

Elizabeth couldn't help but smile. She and Chloe had always wanted another sister—someone to help even out the testosterone swarming their ranch. With five burly brothers, the twins had always been inundated with maleness.

With Chloe moving soon, it would be wonderful to have another woman around the house.

"Speaking of sisters, has Chloe said anything?" Elizabeth wasn't sure how much her twin had divulged to their parents. She didn't want to be the one to tell her mother that one of her children was moving away; Chloe needed to be the one who did that.

Her mother looked away. "Yes, she told me."

"Do you know when she's leaving?" That was the one thing Chloe hadn't been open about—*when* she was moving away.

"I think she's leaving November 1."

Elizabeth's eyes widened. "But that's only a few weeks away. And right before Thanksgiving and Christmas. Will she be home for Christmas?"

Her mother shook her head. "I'm not sure. She only told me

earlier today. There was some confusion about her start date, and then it seemed like she wasn't going to get the job, so she didn't say anything until she found out for sure today." Her mother dabbed her eye and looked away. "I hope we see her over the Christmas holiday, at least. It's only a four-hour drive to French-town. She could come home for a weekend, at least, right?"

Elizabeth walked to her mother's side and wrapped her in her arms. "I'm sure Chloe will come home as much as she can. But we have to remember that she's moving to a new town. She's going to need to establish friends and find the right church for herself. However, I can't imagine she would want to spend Christmas anywhere else but here on the family ranch."

Her mother held her tight and did her best not to sob. A few errant tears leaked out, but other than that she stayed strong.

"Ma, don't worry. Chloe isn't very far. And even if she can't come back here for a weekend, you could always drive out to see her. The roads do go both ways, you know." Elizabeth would have to keep that in mind. She spent a lot of time on call, but she knew that she could get a weekend here and there to go and visit her sister.

"I know, you're right." Mrs. Manning stood tall and cleared her throat. "Alright, it's time to serve supper. Help me get the plates on the dining room table."

Elizabeth laughed. "You know if they aren't done with their card game, none of them will want to stop."

"Then tell them that they won't get any of my famous pot roast. Or any of the peach cobbler I have for dessert."

"Yes, ma'am." Elizabeth gave her mother a two-finger salute and walked with purpose into the dining room, where everyone was still playing cards and ignoring her.

She cleared her throat, hoping they would pay attention. When they kept ignoring her, she yelled out, "Suppertime!"

Still no response from those at the table.

Her father looked at her and arched a brow. When he shrugged, she knew she'd have to play her mother's trump card.

"If you don't clear the table and get it set for supper, you won't get anything. And that includes Ma's tempting peach cobbler." She knew mentioning the dessert would get everyone moving. Shoot, it had her moving plenty as a kid growing up in this house.

There was nothing more important than dessert. Especially if it was made by their mother.

CHAPTER 27

After dinner and dessert, Elizabeth called Logan to see if he was willing to talk with her. She shouldn't have worried—he had always wanted to see her, no matter the time.

Since the store had been closed for a while, Logan was already home and had finished his supper by the time she arrived at the Hayes house.

Logan came outside before she could get up the porch steps. "Hi, how ya doing?" He had his hands in the front pockets of his jeans. His lips were quirked in such a way that she knew he was just as nervous as she was.

"Hi yourself." She stopped a few paces from him.

The air at night had grown crisp with the fall weather, and Elizabeth regretted not bringing a jacket with her. She wrapped her arms about her body in an attempt to keep her body heat in.

"Are you cold?" Logan took his light jacket off and offered it to Elizabeth.

She smiled up at him. "But now you'll be cold."

He shook his head. "I can always go inside and get

another jacket if I need it. Come on, let's sit on the porch and talk."

When they walked up on the wraparound porch, so many memories of their time sitting outside watching the sun set during the summers, cuddling up with a blanket and hot cider in the fall, and—when they could—cuddling together under a blanket with hot chocolate during the winter came flooding back. She missed those days.

The way Logan looked at her, with longing in his eyes, she figured he felt the same way.

They both sat together on the cushioned wicker loveseat, just like they did most of their childhood. He reached behind him and pulled off the old afghan that his mother kept on the back of the chair just for evenings like this one. He set it over the both of them and smiled at Elizabeth.

Chills went down her spine, and not from the cold.

Butterflies zoomed around his stomach when their legs touched under the blanket.

"I miss this."

His whispered confession went straight to her heart.

She had to be honest with herself, and with Logan. "So do I."

His hand moved under the blanket, and he took hers. "Your hand is so cold. Why didn't you tell me you were this cold?"

He pulled their joined hands out from the blanket and blew his warm breath on her hand for a few seconds. Then he brought his other hand out and began rubbing his hands against hers until he felt the warmth coming back into her hand. Then he took her other hand and did the same thing.

However, before he let her other hand go, he brought it up to his lips and lightly kissed the back of her hand.

She inhaled and blinked. Her hope was that they would

become friends. Never in a million years did she think anything more could happen. Did she want more? She wasn't exactly sure at that moment what she wanted.

"Lizzie." Logan's masculine timbre shook her to her very core.

"Logan…" She wasn't sure what to say.

When she looked into his eyes, she saw the same love she had seen from him most of their lives. She didn't know what he saw in her eyes, but when he moved closer to her, she knew she was going to let him kiss her.

She wanted it with everything she had.

When their lips were only a few inches apart, the screen door slammed shut.

"Oh! I'm so sorry. Keep going, I'll leave you to it."

Leah's nervous chatter killed the mood, and they both quickly moved apart just like they had when they were teens and got caught kissing in that very same chair.

"No, Leah. It's alright. What did you need?" Logan called out.

Leah's hands fidgeted, and she hemmed and hawed. "Well…I… Um…Ma wanted to know who was here. That's all. It's no big deal. I'll tell her that Lizzie's here and the two of you are having a private discussion." A hint of a smile turned her lips up, and she went back into the house without waiting for a response.

Lizzie giggled, and Logan chuckled. Then he pulled her close to him and sighed in contentment. "This is exactly where we belong." He kissed the top of her head.

She leaned into him and put a hand on his chest. "Is this really what you want?"

He could hear the insecurity in her voice, and it cut him.

"This is all I've ever wanted. I made such a mistake of things when we were kids." He pulled back so he could look into her face. "Lizzie, I love you. I have always loved you, and only you."

Tears pricked her eyes. "But, will you leave me again if you think it's the right thing to do?"

"Never," he boldly stated before he claimed her lips.

The euphoria that came over her was nothing like she had felt before. Even when they kissed as teenagers, she didn't feel this strongly.

Their lips moved together in time with their heartbeats. As their kiss deepened, she pulled him even closer. Logan felt things getting too heated, and he slowed down the kiss before anything got too far.

When he pulled back, he looked lovingly into her eyes. "Lizzie. My Lizzie." He kissed the tip of her nose and pulled her against his chest.

She sighed and knew that here was exactly where she belonged. The contentment flooding her body was nothing like anything she had ever felt.

"What does this mean?" She didn't mean to say it out loud, and she stiffened when she felt him take a deep breath.

He let his breath out and said, "I think this means that we need to see where this leads." He gestured between the two of them. "I know what I want. It's what I've wanted since we were in high school."

She knew what she wanted as well. However, she wasn't sure she could trust him, yet. "So, no pressure. You'll go at my pace?" She bit her lip, hoping he wouldn't push.

Until they sat down, she wasn't even sure she wanted more with him. Could she trust her feelings? They were so all over the place, and she feared he would leave her again. There was no way her heart could take him breaking up with her...again. It would destroy her.

But she couldn't deny what she felt. Love—pure, unadulterated love. The strength and depth of what her heart was telling her frightened her, while at the same time she knew it was...right.

Logan leaned forward and kissed her temple. When he pulled her tightly against him, he said, "Yes. As slow or as fast as you want. But know this: you're mine, now and always. I'm not letting you go again. I'll fight tooth and nail to keep you if that Max fellow comes back. Or if you change your mind."

Lizzie chuckled. "Max isn't coming back. Well, he might for business, but not for me. Our time together is over. We were never meant to be forever." She looked up into his face. "I think he was what I needed to get me ready for you, again."

"Then I'll always be grateful to him for your past." He hugged her back to himself again and kissed the top of her head. "This is your future."

EPILOGUE

OCTOBER 30, CHLOE'S MOVE

"Chloe, I love your house. It's so cute." Elizabeth looked around the outside of the small house located only a few blocks from the center of town, and the small hospital where she would start work in only two days.

"Wait until you see inside. The wainscoting has a little shelf across the top at chest height where I can put all my Christmas figurines." Chloe smiled as she looked at the front of her house and just knew she was where God wanted her. A sense of contentment and peace settled over her, even though she had a lot of work to do before her house was ready for Christmas.

Logan walked up with a bag of snacks in one hand and a cooler full of water and sodas in the other. "Where should I put these?"

"Follow me to the kitchen." Chloe let her sister and her boyfriend inside. She had waited a decade to see them get back together, and she couldn't be happier to see them.

Their families both had been ecstatic when they found out that the pair were back together again. While they hadn't set a day, or even bought a ring, Chloe was confident they'd be married by summer. She only hoped Lizzie would ask her to be maid of honor, even though she was four hours away.

Chloe opened the door and let Logan and Lizzie in before her. The rest of her brothers were still outside by the moving truck she had rented. Even though it was cold, the boys seemed content staying outside and making sure the truck was ready for them to unload.

"The kitchen is to the back." Chloe led her sister and soon-to-be brother-in-law to the back of the house to see her farm-style kitchen. "You can set the cooler down on the island and put the bag of snacks on the built-in kitchen table in the corner."

"Nice, sis. You did good." Elizabeth smiled and took the bag of snacks from Logan's hand and set them out on the oak kitchen table set back in the corner of the room.

Matthew walked into the room. "Where should we start unloading?"

"Right. Let's get the boxes unloaded to the spare room, and then I'll direct you to where you should put the furniture." Chloe walked outside to begin the arduous task of getting all her belongings in the right rooms.

Logan stayed back and took Elizabeth's hand. "So, how are you feeling?"

Lizzie sighed and leaned into his strong chest. "I'm sad to see my twin leave, but so happy for her. This is something she's wanted for a very long time, and I can't be selfish."

He ran a hand down the back of her long hair. "You'll still see her all the time. She's only a few hours away. Why don't we plan on coming out here in early December for a weekend?"

She nodded. "I think that'd be a great idea. I doubt she'll

be coming to visit for a while. She's going to be very busy getting her house in order and starting a new job."

He kissed the top of her head. "Alright, let's get going and help the boys unload the truck. I can't believe how many boxes Chloe has. Where did she put all of this in her old house?" Logan shook his head and laughed.

Elizabeth slapped his arm. "Hey, my sister is not a pack rat."

He arched an eyebrow. "Please tell me you don't have this much junk, too."

She turned her back on him and smirked. "It's not junk if you use it." And walked outside to get a load of boxes.

"What have I gotten myself into?" The wry smile that covered his face belied his words. He was truly happy for the first time in his adult life.

Even though Lizzie wanted to take things slowly, he was already planning to get her a ring for New Year's Eve, or possibly even Christmas Day.

When they were almost finished unloading the furniture, Chloe and Elizabeth had the headboard in their hands, and Chloe slipped on the wet ground. "Oh!"

Elizabeth dropped her end of the oak headboard and went to her sister. Before she could get to her, a masculine set of arms was helping her sister up. The arms belonged to a face she had never seen before.

"Are you alright?" the stranger asked.

Chloe stood up and brushed her hands on her jeans. Without looking at the guy, she responded, "Yes, just embarrassed."

Elizabeth cleared her throat. She knew as soon as her sister looked at the gorgeous face in front of her, she'd be even more embarrassed.

When Chloe looked up, Lizzie noted the red beginning to tint her sister's cheeks, and she smiled.

If this was what the men of Frenchtown looked like, Lizzie was confident her sister wouldn't be single much longer.

In fact, some still, small voice told her that they'd both be married soon.

The End

NEWSLETTER SIGN-UP

Did you enjoy Second Chance Ranch? Want to know more about Mimi and Hank? Then check out Finding Love in Montana today!

By signing up for my newsletter, you will get a free copy of the prequel to the Triple J Ranch series, Finding Love in Montana. As well as another free book from J.L. Hendricks.

If you want to make sure you hear about the latest and greatest, sign up for my newsletter at: https://jennahendricks.com. I will only send out a few e-mails a month. I'll do cover reveals, sneak peeks of new books, and giveaways or promos in the newsletter, some of which will only be available to newsletter subscribers.

AUTHOR'S NOTES

So, what did you think? This was my first foray into the Clean & Wholesome Cowboy Romance sub-genre. I love this type of book and hope you think I did a great job representing the characters and genre.

If you could spare just a couple of minutes to write a review, I would be forever grateful! Since this is a brand-new pen name for me, no one knows who I am yet. Reviews will help readers to know if what I wrote is up their alley, or not. All I ask is that you be honest.

The inspiration for this book came a long time ago. I felt the Lord leading me to join the fantastic line-up of Clean Cowboy Romance authors and I took my time researching and writing this first book. Book 2 is already in the works, but first up will be a prequel.

Actually, this was supposed to be the prequel to the entire series. But as I began writing about Elizabeth and her life, she kinda stole the reigns and put her boot down. Her story couldn't be told in only 30K words or less. She ended up needing over 70K words to get her life on paper.

So, I've had to create the story of Mimi and Hank in order

to introduce new readers to Beacon Creek and the wonderful cast of characters who make up the town. It's now available to those who sign up for my Clean and Wholesome Newsletter!

And if you're wondering about the clean eating I wrote about, it's something new for me. As I started writing this book, I had to change up my diet because I have an autoimmune disease. It's crazy how food affects our bodies and health. So as I wrote this, I was dealing with some of the food issues in real life, like being sensitive to gluten.

If you have any health issues, please talk to your doctor about the possibility of food making your issues worse, or the flip-side. Healthy eating clearing up some of your issues. Once I began to eat healthier, I have been doing a modified paleo diet, some of my smaller issues, like IBS, began to go away. Also, brain fog and fatigue are less of an issue than before. And the plus side is that I'm losing weight naturally.

No matter what you do next, I hope you have a healthy and happy year! Don't forget to check back, or even join my newsletter, to find out about the next book in the Triple J Ranch series, already available!

Keep reading for a preview of Book 2, available now!

For those of you who love social media, here are the various ways to follow or contact me:

BookBub:
https://www.bookbub.com/authors/jenna-hendricks

Amazon:
https://www.amazon.com/Jenna-Hendricks/e/B083G6WQR7

Instagram:
https://www.instagram.com/j.l.hendricks/

Twitter:
https://twitter.com/TinkFan25

Facebook:
https://www.facebook.com/profile.php?id=100011419945971

Website:
https://jennahendricks.com

COWBOY RANCH PREVIEW

A detective's daughter. A rugged rancher. Can they track down cattle rustlers and lasso love?

Callie Houston needs a break from misery. But when her car breaks down on her way to a rodeo, she finds herself stranded in small-town Montana. Praying that God has a plan for her misfortune, she's flattered when two handsome brothers offer their ranch for the night.

Luke Manning isn't sure he's ready to settle down. But when he and his brother stumble across a woman down on her luck, neither hesitates to compete for the beauty's affection. But if he wants to win her heart, he must prove he's different from the shallow men of her past.

As she works with Luke to hunt down a band of cattle thieves, Callie realizes she's falling hard for the kind-hearted cowboy. But when Luke discovers the out-of-towner making plans to head home to Minnesota, he scrambles to convince her to stay.

Will the unlikely couple embrace God's design and discover everlasting love?

CHAPTER 1

"No, no, this can't be happening. Not now." Callie Houston hit the top of her steering wheel with the palm of her hand as her 2012 Hyundai Santa Fe sputtered and slowed to a stop along the side of a dusty, desolate road.

Once she stopped, she tried turning the key, but it did nothing. Without much else to try, she turned the key again. Callie had zero car knowledge except to take it in for service every five to six thousand miles. And oh, it was best to change the windshield wipers every fall before the big rains began.

She sat there on the side of the road feeling as though she had the worst luck in the entire world.

Callie was on her way to a tiny town called Beacon Creek. It was supposed to be her treat for the rotten month she'd just had. All Callie wanted was to forget about her troubles and have some real down-home country fun.

The rodeo and summer carnival was something she'd read about, and could swear she'd seen on a Hallmark movie recently. It was exactly what she needed to put her worries behind her as she headed home.

Instead, she now had to deal with a car not working. She didn't even know how far out of town she was. Would her cell phone even get any service there?

Once she was safely on the side of the road, she looked to her left and right. All she could see were barbed wire fences and brown grasses being nibbled on by cows. In the north, south, and west were the jagged peaks of mountains. The east was mostly plains, from what she remembered on her drive to Seattle.

This little stop wasn't originally planned, but after her failure in Seattle, she wasn't ready to go home to her empty apartment. She thought stopping off for a rodeo would recharge her and help her figure out what she would do next. Her savings account wouldn't last forever, and she needed a job, fast.

She stepped out of her car after looking in front and behind to ensure no cars or trucks were coming and walked to the side of the road before she pulled her cell phone out of her pocket. Callie could have leapt for joy when she discovered she had signal. It was faint, but if it connected her to the road-side assistance service she subscribed to, she'd be happy with two bars.

Callie had always wondered what the small stakes on the sides of roads were for. The numbers never made any sense to her. Now she was grateful the highway authority put them out. Since she had no clue where she was, the towing company would find her thanks to those little numbers on the mile markers.

Once she hung up, she went and leaned against the fence post as she waited for a tow truck to arrive.

It wasn't long, which meant she had to be close to town, right? When the blue-and-white truck with a crane in the bed came into view, she released a sigh.

A tall, lanky cowboy with dirty jeans, dust covering his shirt, and an old cowboy hat stepped out of the truck. "Howdy, ma'am. I heard you needed some help?"

She recoiled, and then remembered herself. The roadside assistance company wouldn't have sent someone dangerous to help her. He was only a dirty cowboy who had probably been in the middle of fixing a car when he got the call to rescue her.

"Yes, thank you. I don't know what happened, but it just stuttered and then rolled to a stop." She pointed back to her sky-blue SUV and sighed. That car had gotten her through so many ups and downs. Her father had bought it used for her when she graduated high school, and then it carried the small belongings she had to her new life in St. Paul, Minnesota. Now it had abandoned her out in the wilds of Montana.

"Let me take a look and see if I can't help ya get back on the road. How's your gas?" The look he gave her caused her to bristle at his insinuation. She had gassed up not one hundred miles back.

"There's still over half a tank of gas, sir."

"Beg'n your pardon, ma'am. I'm Nick Sands." He held out a dirty hand for her to shake.

Gulping down her angry retort, she nodded.

He looked at his hand and dropped it. "Of course, I was working when I got the call. I should have washed up, but thought a young lady shouldn't be left on the side of the road. Please forgive the dirt."

Callie smiled and realized she was being rude. "Of course. Thank you for coming so quickly. I really do appreciate it. I'm Callie Houston." She put her hand back out, and he shook it lightly.

Resisting the urge to wipe her hands on her jeans, she turned back around to her car. "There's plenty of gas, so I don't know what else it could be. The check engine light never came on, and I haven't had any issues other than what you'd expect from an eight-year-old car."

Her father had insisted she take very good care of her car, and it would take good care of her in return. She'd had the oil changed every five thousand miles, done all the factory-suggested maintenance, and kept the car in the garage when not driving it. She didn't even have that many miles on it for a car of its age.

Nick walked to the front of the Hyundai. "Can you pop the hood?"

"Sure thing." She went to her car and pulled the lever to open the hood. Not wanting to get in his way, she stayed next to the driver's seat and waited.

The tow truck driver's head went under the hood for a few moments, and when he stood up and lowered the hood, she worried about the grave look on his face.

This wasn't going to be an easy fix.

"I can tow you into the garage and have our mechanic look at it." He went to work moving his tow truck in line with her car while she waited on the side of the road. It didn't take him long to hook her Hyundai up to the tow truck.

When she got into the cab of his truck, she turned and looked at him. "How far is town?"

Once he was safely on the road, he looked at the woman sitting in his front seat. "Beacon Creek is about thirty minutes from here."

She furrowed her brow. "But it only took you about fifteen minutes to get to me once I hung up the phone. How'd you get here so fast?"

He chuckled. "I was on my ranch, just down the road."

"You own a ranch and work at a mechanic's shop?" Callie shook her head, confused by the man next to her.

"Oh no, ma'am. My brother owns the shop. I just help out when he's out of town. I'm a rancher, not a mechanic." His speed picked up until he was driving fifty miles an hour down the road. Then he eased up on the gas and settled in for a slow drive in. Towing the SUV behind his truck meant he couldn't do his normal sixty or seventy on the open road.

"Who's going to fix my car?"

"We have someone who can fix your SUV, don't worry. Mikey's just moved here from the city, and he has experience with Hondas." Nick smiled at her.

She shook her head. "No, my car isn't a Honda, it's a Hyundai."

"Honda, Hyundai, foreign jobs are all the same." He shrugged and kept his eyes on the road.

She wiped a hand down her face. "What am I going to do?" She thought for sure her poor car was doomed.

"Don't worry, Mikey can fix anything." He beamed in her direction before turning his eyes back to the road.

They drove the rest of the way in silence while Callie worried about what would happen to her Hyundai if Mikey didn't know what he was doing.

When they arrived, a tall, burly man with messy black hair walked out of the shop, wiping his hands with a rag.

Callie jumped down from the truck and approached him. "Are you Mikey?" she asked without any preamble.

He smiled. "Yes, and I take it you're the little lady who broke down on the road into town?"

She nodded. "Do you have any experience with Hyundais?" If this man didn't know what he was doing, she'd have to call her father and ask him for help. Even though he was all the way down in Louisiana.

"Some. Most of what I've worked on were Hondas, but I've seen my share of Hyundais as well as other makes." He

~~scratched his head and watched Nick lower the SUV to the~~ ground in front of the open bay.

It was late in the afternoon, and Mikey had been closing up the shop before they arrived.

"Do you have a place to stay for the night? I won't be able to look at your car until tomorrow morning." Mikey put the dirty rag in the back pocked of his dark-blue coveralls.

"I was hoping to find a hotel room here in town. Can you point me in the direction of one?" Callie bit the inside of her lip and prayed that the local hotel wouldn't be too expensive. And she didn't even want to think what the repairs might cost. Not yet, at least.

But she knew that with her luck, it would clean her savings out.

He shook his head and tsk'd. "I'm sorry, ma'am, but the hotels are all booked up for the carnival."

Callie's eyes widened and her body froze. "What? Are you sure?"

"Yup, my wife works for the Beacon Creek Inn, and she told me just last night that everyone is full up." He winced and began to wrack his brain for a solution.

"Why?" Callie looked around and noted that there weren't that many people wandering around. Granted, they weren't in the middle of town, but the place didn't look very big. Maybe they only had one tiny hotel with just a few rooms?

"The rodeo, ma'am. It's a pretty big deal round these parts. Our one hotel and two B&Bs are all full. In fact, most of the cowboys who come to town bring their RVs, and even the RV park is full now." He scratched the side of his head.

Nick walked over to them. "What about the Triple J?"

Mikey considered for a moment and nodded. "I'll give Matthew a call and see if they have any room."

"Triple J? Is that a bed and breakfast?" Callie would be happy with a bed and breakfast. It would probably be nicer than a boisterous hotel full of cowboys.

"It's a ranch that's setting up to house a few ladies," Mikey called back over his shoulder as he walked away.

Callie wondered what that meant, and turned to look at Nick. With a questioning look at the rancher, she waited for him to explain. When it became obvious he wasn't going to say anything, she asked, "Why are they preparing to house ladies?"

Nick took his hat off his head and smiled. "Miss Elizabeth has been working with the homeless population in Bozeman. She's set up a program to help rehabilitate women and get them back on their feet. Her family ranch is being renovated a bit to help house as many young ladies as they can."

Callie blinked. She wasn't opposed to helping the homeless, but living with them was another thing. However, if she was lucky, it would only be for one night. Two at most. Then she'd be back on the road, heading home.

When Mikey came out, he was smiling. "Miss Elizabeth will come by shortly to collect you and your things. They'd be happy to help out."

Callie wasn't sure what to say, or do. "Thank you. I do appreciate the help. But how long will it take you to fix my car?"

"I won't know until tomorrow, when I can look at it. If you'll give me your keys, I'll be sure to check it out first thing in the mornin'. Until then, enjoy the Triple J. You won't find a better meal than what Mrs. Manning cooks up, or the barbecue the brothers make." Mikey licked his lips and looked off into the distance.

Nick chuckled. "The Mannings have the best beef in the

country. You'll see." He smiled and waved as he walked back to his truck.

Callie looked between the two cowboys. "Where should I wait?"

A beefy finger pointed to the front of the mechanic's shop. "There's a waitin' room in there. But first, you should probably get your luggage out and take it with you."

Both of them walked to her Hyundai, and when she opened the back door, Mikey reached in and pulled her suitcase out. "Is this all you got?"

She nodded. "I wasn't planning on a long trip."

He smiled and walked her to the waiting room. When he set her suitcase down, he pointed to a small refrigerator. "There's soda and bottled water in there. Help yourself. Sorry, but I've already cleaned out the coffee pot."

With a heavy sigh, she waved away his apology. "Don't worry, I typically don't drink coffee this late in the day, anyway. Water will be perfect." She grabbed a cold bottle and sat down to wait for this Miss Elizabeth to arrive.

Made in the USA
Las Vegas, NV
02 April 2021